THRESHOLD

THRESHOLD

Patricia J. Anderson

COMMON DEER PRESS
WWW.COMMONDEERPRESS.COM

Published in 2018 by Common Deer Press
3203-1 Scott St.
Toronto, ON
M5V 1A1

This book is a work of fiction. Names, characters, places, and incidents are either the product of the author's imagination or are used fictitiously.

Library of Congress Cataloging-in-Publication Data
Anderson, Patricia J.--First edition.
Threshold / Patricia J. Anderson
ISBN: 978-1-988761-16-9 (paperback)
ISBN: 978-1-988761-17-6 (e-book)

Cover Image: © Carl Weins i2i Art
Design: Ellie Sipila

Printed in Canada

www.commondeerpress.com

COMMON DEER PRESS
WWW.COMMONDEERPRESS.COM

"We cannot devise, within the traditional modern attitude to reality, a system that will eliminate all the disastrous consequences of previous systems. We cannot discover a law or theory whose application will eliminate all the disastrous consequences of the application of earlier laws and technologies. What is needed is something different, something larger. Our attitude to the world must be radically changed."

— *Vaclav Havel*

PART I

PROLOGUE

The day begins like any other: the sky is clear, the sun shines brightly. No one hears the scraping deep below the surface where a sudden shift loosens shale, shivering against granite. Soon a fracture opens, curling along a fault. The rupture gathers speed, the fault widens, pressure builds, pulsing through canyons of stone. Rock screams against rock. Shock waves shatter space. With a sickening shudder, the earth rises up. The precious concordance of the natural world is torn asunder.

What catastrophe is this? Where might such destruction unfold? To whom does it belong?

The monkey knows. He knows...and a great sadness washes over him.

CHAPTER 1

[Six months earlier.]

"Y ou're out of beer."

"Don't bother me. I'm busy."

"Chips too. There are no chips in this house."

It's twilight in Ooolandia, a world like many other worlds but with an extra "O." A world filled with the feathered, the furred, the scaled, the shelled, the shorn, and the nearly naked. Mammals, microbes, reptiles, arachnids, insects, hominids, and the all-too-humanoid bustle about together, occasionally bumping into those who don't fit into any category at all—those who are, essentially, one-offs.

The discussion regarding provisions is taking place between one such one-off, known as Taboook, and his friend, Banshooo, a monkey on a mission.

"I'm working on something important here."

"Chips are important. Beer is very important."

Taboook is rummaging through the cupboards in Banshooo's kitchen. Banshooo is sitting at the desk in his living room, a cozy

2

place filled with overstuffed furniture, overstuffed bookshelves, and several oddly annotated landscapes hanging slightly askew.

"There's something big going on, Taboook, something so big it's hidden from sight." His thick, fluffy coat and furry face look reddish-brown in the lamp's glow as his black eyes scan quickly through the notebooks piled high in front of him. "I'm seeing so many improbable changes. It's all got to be connected somehow."

Taboook saunters into the living room carrying a jar of peanut butter and a spoon.

"You notice too much, Shooo. There's a lot to be said for simply walking by."

"It's my job to notice things."

"Yeah, yeah, big deal phenologist. I hate to break it to you, buddy, but nobody cares. Nobody even knows what 'phenologist' means."

Banshooo sighs. "I've told you what it means. We study natural events, recording what happens and when it happens. It's how we know that something is changing."

"Great. So you notice things. What's the big deal?"

Taboook sticks the spoon into the peanut butter jar and scoops out a generous mouthful. Covered in shaggy black fur, he stands upright on his back feet, his long forearms sporting sizable paws. He's tall and what might be called...unexpected. His face looks a bit bearish but with long floppy ears that often get in the way of his primary interest—eating.

Banshooo frowns. "You don't understand what's at stake here, Boook. The water's drying up, the weather's getting weird, and some kind of puzzling anemone anomaly has taken hold."

"Hey, I know. Strange things are happening, but they'll figure out something before it all goes south. And if they don't, well, we'll wish we'd loaded up on beer and chips while we had the chance."

Banshooo watches his friend eat and considers, not for the first time, how right Taboook might be. Hardly anyone seems to care about the extraordinary developments that he documents every day, or about the fact that the information he has amassed over the years indicates there is a rapidly accelerating shift occurring; a shift that could result in dangerous instabilities. Even in his job at the

Ooolandian Department of Nature, where you'd think they'd care about that sort of thing, no one seemed to want to hear about it.

Taboook plops down on the couch, puts his feet up on the tea table, and balances the peanut butter jar on his belly. It wobbles a bit then steadies. "Hey! Look at that! Abs of steel." He burps, and the jar topples onto the floor. Chuckling gleefully, he picks it up and scoops out another big spoonful as he looks over at Banshooo. "So. Wanna go bowling later?"

In the meadow outside the little house, the wind makes a low whistling sound through the tufted grass, while across the field, hidden deep inside the center of a wood lily, minute abnormalities uncurl themselves.

☾

Night arrives and the Ooolandian sky reveals itself in all its bizarre beneficence, jam-crammed with an extraordinary complement of stars and planets, not to mention a number of other celestial-type objects floating about. Most spectacular of all are its three big moons. Ooolandians are particularly proud of their moons and they have reason to be. One is crimson, one is blue, and one is a kind of apricot color. It's pretty awesome, actually.

Amid all that rich profusion, there is only the one Ooolandian sun. One big, exploding fireball hanging way out there all by itself. It comes up. It goes down. It comes up again. It's the kind of thing everyone gets so totally used to there's no noticing at all. And so it was that it took a long time to see that something was changing. Something was changing in the Ooolandian sky.

Early on, there were a few who thought they noticed something but they didn't know what, and when they tried to talk to the others about it, nobody listened. In Ooolandia, it can be hard to be heard if you question things, especially if you aren't sure what your own questions might reveal.

Then the bees started dying. Today, there are only three bees left in Ooolandia and they're not talking. Having barely survived the enslavement and poisoning of their entire species, the three have gone into hiding. Permanently. In response to this die-off, the Ooolandian authorities are working to create bioengineered insects for mass pollination while promoting processed rations for all. Fortunately, the general population has become quite fond of disodium 5'-ribonucleotides.

Then too, there was the matter of the fireflies. One of the oldest Ooolandian festivals is the annual Dipper Dance celebrated when the Big Dipper bows down toward the ground while vast numbers of blinking fireflies ascend up to the heavens, creating a dazzling spectacle during which everyone dances, makes music, drinks a lot of sparkling wine, and generally goes crazy all night long. It was a grand tradition celebrated since ancient times, so extraordinarily beautiful that it was enough to stop even the most clever of cynical remarks in mid-snark.

However, each year for a while now there have been fewer and fewer fireflies, so the Ooolandians created electric fireflies, which made them very proud of themselves and filled the sky with blinking lights and which, after you had twirled, whirled, and drunk enough, looked pretty much the same as the living lights of the living fireflies. And so the festival continued somewhat as before, even though all the old songs written about the fireflies didn't really make sense anymore. But they were sung anyway, for old times' sake.

Some old-timers didn't think "old time's sake" was enough and they grumbled and griped and worried about where the fireflies had gone. But the old-timers were, after all, old. They didn't appreciate the astounding ingenuity that had created all that electricity, which was, truth be told, astounding.

Most Ooolandians were very proud of these kinds of accomplishments. They built many magnificent things and then they built some more. They moved the earth, re-routed rivers, cut and cleared, dug and drilled, blew and spewed and sprayed stuff everywhere. Lots of different stuff. Stuff they made in their impressive laboratories. Stuff that gave them control.

Then, one night, the blue moon went into eclipse and didn't come out again. At that point everyone noticed. There was a big hole in the sky, surrounded by a ghostly shadow. You couldn't miss it. Now began much discussion and argument. Some said it was no big deal; some said it was a very big deal. Some said it was in the natural order of things; some said it was extremely unnatural. Some said it would work itself out on its own; some said they should be doing something.

Unfortunately, such arguing can go on forever and sometimes there isn't much time to waste. Sometimes, while everyone is arguing, something bad is going on. Something really, really bad.

CHAPTER 2

Tonight is unusually dark. The sky is heavy with clouds, the stars lost altogether. The apricot moon is below the horizon, the crimson moon is new, and the blue moon is in permanent eclipse.

Banshooo can't sleep. He gets out of bed and shuffles about, making tea and peering through the window at the extraordinary depth of the darkness. He opens the door to his front porch and steps outside. Breathing in the cool night air, he listens for a moment then walks out into the meadow. He can hear the scurry and whispers of the night creatures, a cry, then a brief struggle deep in the underbrush as something small is caught and eaten. He hears the empty pause that always comes after Death has finished, and then, when the pause is over, he hears something else.

A sound is coming out of the darkness. It grows louder by the second, moving through the sky above the field, picking up speed and intensity as it spreads wider, an enormous wave making a high-pitched whine like a scream surging directly toward him. He tries to turn away but is held there, paralyzed. It washes over him. He stands trembling, drenched and dripping with sound.

Then, slowly, everything becomes extraordinarily quiet. Now he's floating through an amorphous cloud, waffling and thick, a pulsing, swirling fog. There's something ahead, something deep inside the fog, something … else. He peers into the thickness. He can almost make it out, a gate or opening bubbling in and out of his vision like a refraction of some kind, like a mirage.

Now he hears what seems to be weeping. He stays perfectly still and listens as hard as he can. Smoky shapes resolve themselves into forms, dimly at first then clearer. A being raises its face before him, then another and another. Banshooo stares, transfixed, as different species appear, one after another, forlorn, wraith-like, curling and uncurling before him, beings large and small, frail and fearsome, dying without succor, without regard.

He leans back in horror, his heart racing. He wants to run away but he still can't move. The weeping grows louder, reaching a frightening crescendo of suffering until it bursts all around him, sending droplets of tears falling like a shower of sparks in a fireworks display. As the sparks fade into the night, the echoing cries die away and, finally, he is again surrounded in silence.

Stunned and shivering, Banshooo can barely breathe. What has he seen? What vision is this, filling his heart with a sadness so heavy he drops to his knees with the weight of it?

Now everything is as it was before. The cool night air, the scurries and whispers, the unusually gloomy sky. He stands upright on shaky legs. He looks around. He waits, but nothing more happens.

After a long time, he walks back to his house. There he pores over all his books and records, looking for any reference to anything even remotely like what had just surged across the meadow and slammed into him. There is nothing. Exhausted, he falls asleep for the last few hours left before dawn.

☾

"You're not going to tell them about this, are you?"

Taboook finishes scooping ice cream into a big bowl and turns to Banshooo. "Everyone over there thinks you're a whack job already. This would seal the deal."

Banshooo prepares his phenology reports for the Department of

Nature, a division of Ooolandian Central Services. It is a very small division, made up of Banshooo and one other employee, his friend and colleague, Sukie, a mathlete as devoted to discerning the nature of reality as she is to discerning the reality of nature. They've both become increasingly aware that the administration has been ignoring their work. They've reported strange occurrences, aberrations and abnormalities, mutant frogs, dead birds dropping out of the sky, and a creeping floral fungus that's spreading rapidly. But the more they describe, the more they are ignored. Lately, the ignoring has gotten worse. There was a rumor going around that Central Services was thinking of phasing out the whole idea of nature altogether.

Banshooo speaks in a low voice. "You don't understand, Boook. I saw an explosion of extinctions."

"You had a dream, old buddy. A nightmare with sound effects."

"It wasn't a dream. It was real. I saw the Unseen."

Taboook cocks his head. "That doesn't even work as a sentence."

"What doesn't work?" A blinking chatterdee has hopped up on the window sill, its eyes bright, its little body flashing on and off, eager to join the conversation.

Taboook glances over at the bird. "Banshooo thinks he saw the Unseen."

Instantly the bird flies off as Banshooo drops his head in dismay. "Great. Now you've told everyone."

And he had. When a chatterdee gets hold of anything of a private or sensitive nature, it will be instantly broadcast to all the other chatterdees in the area and they will make it their duty to be sure everyone is included in the conversation. Soon, whatever slim grasp you might have had over your own experience will be lost completely and you'll find yourself answering rude questions about your use of recreational drugs and that unfortunate incident with the cheerleader. Chatterdees may be cute, but they are not nice birds.

Taboook bites his lip. "Sorry. It's the blinking and the flashing. It makes you want to join in." The chirping intensifies and almost immediately you can hear the verberations and reverberations as flocks of chatterdees take up the call. Soon pesky voices all over

Ooolandia are buzzing to each other and a wave of response comes floating back through the window, the gist of which is: "You're clearly delusional. Don't come near our children."

Banshooo shuffles over to the puffy old sofa in the middle of the living room and sits down heavily. He knows most Ooolandians, if they ever thought about it, which they don't, would think what he does is totally useless—watching, listening, taking notes, keeping records. But his journals make up a long-term detailed report of what is happening in the natural world and they prove that the nature of that world has been changing drastically, changing in a completely different way from the ongoing meandering change inherent in the process of time. Banshooo knows the mutant frogs, the missing blue moon, and the disappearing fireflies are just the tip of the tulip. Something is happening underneath all the anomalies. He knows the whole blooming thing is becoming dangerously unhinged.

The monkey sighs deeply and looks up at the portrait over the fireplace. Gazing back at him is the black and white furred face of his mentor, the giant panda, Isaac Algernon Blooo. Kind, calm, and enthralled with the world's mysteries, he was one of the greatest phenologists who ever lived.

Below the portrait hangs the phenologist's motto, written in a graceful script:

What do phenologists do? They observe and record with respectful attention.
What does respectful attention reveal? It reveals the nature of things.
What is the nature of things? Shared experience through time.

Banshooo first met Algernon when the giant panda stumbled across him one morning at the far north end of Blooo Meadow, where a stand of Ooolandian Bamboo grows in rich profusion. The young monkey was gazing enthralled as the sun flickered through the emerald growth. Algernon struck up a conversation and soon realized this wasn't just another monkey wandering through the thicket.

Banshooo had been discovered when he was a baby, alone and motherless, by a band of mercenaries practicing their martial arts deep in a dark wood. He was not only healthy and happy, he was uneaten, a fact no one could explain since, like most mammals in most worlds, monkeys are completely helpless when young. And, as everyone knows, if you leave the baby alone in the woods, there are really only two possible outcomes: 1) death by starvation or 2) becoming the means whereby someone else avoids death by starvation. Instead, this particular baby greeted his rescuers with a big smile and went on to grow into a strong and healthy member of Ooolandian society. He was too young to remember much of anything and could not explain his own survival or robust good humor.

As they talked more, Algernon discovered that this young fellow was something of a natural, phenology-wise. He invited Banshooo to join him for a cup of tea, and they walked together to Algernon's little house where the door opened onto the rest of Banshooo's life. Welcomed into a world filled with books, charts, maps, pictures, and journals, all detailing the extraordinary story of the natural world, he accepted a tasty cup of frothy, hot chai and realized he'd found a home.

Under Algernon's tutelage, Banshooo read about the intelligence of marine creatures and the microbiome, about the extraordinary secrets of the insect world. He learned that bats use magnetic fields emanating from deep within the Ooolandian earth to guide them through the dark; that wombats tease one another mercilessly; that dingbats are really dumb and there's nothing to be done about it.

Algernon explained the inescapable logic of the food chain. "It actually *is* a jungle out there, Banshooo. Whoever was the first to say this should get a medal for such a succinct summary. Every living thing seeks to survive, which, ironically enough, leads to the death of others. Death plays a key role in all things. This must be acknowledged and accepted. As the great Ooolandian poet Giovanni Giorno pointed out, 'Life is a killer,' and no amount of prettifying will cover up that simple reality."

One cloudy day as they were deep in the middle of the meadow, observing the unfurling of a wild *convooolvulaceae* to determine just how much luminous intensity was needed to encourage it to open into full morning glory, an Ooolandian Longear bounded past so fast they both jumped back in unison. Immediately a gray blur of fur followed the zigzagging rabbit like a knife through the grass and pounced, perfectly on target. A brief flurry of crunching bone ended the rabbit's agony and allowed the wolf to catch his breath, his bloody tongue hanging from his open mouth as he stood over his stilled prey.

As they moved quietly away, leaving the carnivore to his meal, Banshooo said, "You know, I've been thinking, since life is a killer, we're all pretty much in the same boat, aren't we?" Algernon stopped, placed a giant paw on Banshooo's shoulder and smiled. "You have realized a great truth, my son. Let's have cake." (The panda never passed up a chance to have cake. And plum wine. He was especially partial to plum wine.)

Algernon taught Banshooo many things, but the single most important skill he imparted to his protégé was the art and practice of paying attention. "When you pay attention you are paying respect, a respectful witness to the world as it is. No attraction, no repulsion. Just respectful observation."

Banshooo found this to be more difficult than he had, at first, assumed. His monkey mind bounced around like a fat gnat on steroids. Sometimes he felt he might not be able to do it. However, in time, with dedicated practice, he became able to retrieve his meandering mind and settle the flurry of his own awareness gently within the core of the moment.

He learned to maintain a steady gaze when a dragonfly ate the face off a moth; to resist the impulse to turn away when confronted with a pool of maggots wriggling in the belly of a dead deer; to look and not to judge. He practiced and practiced and finally he got it. He saw how to see.

Algernon welcomed Banshooo into the small circle of Ooolandian phenologists (just the two of them at that point.) He raised his glass and toasted the initiate.

"You have become skilled in the art. As you observe what happens over time, you will see experience moving through the world like a wave of living energy. Here's to the breath that flows through all existence." They emptied their glasses. "And now for cake."

At the end of his life, Algernon bequeathed to Banshooo his home, the voluminous phenological record he had maintained until the very end, and the guardianship of the bamboo forest and Blooo Meadow—the large, lush field behind the little house, one of the few remaining undisturbed ecosystems in Ooolandia.

As the panda lay dying, he turned his head toward his student and whispered, "Remember, Banshooo. There is something beyond the Seen, something that reveals itself *in* the Seen but is, itself, Unseen." The monkey can still hear that whisper as he sits on the sofa and gazes at the portrait.

"He understood something, Boook, something important."

"Yeah, I know. It's that underworld thing you go on about."

"Not under ... *unseen* world. *Unseen.*"

"Whatever."

"He trusted me. I can't let him down."

"He's dead, man. He's already as down as he's going to get."

"He's not dead to me."

Taboook comes over and sits on the sofa beside Banshooo. After a moment he offers his bowl. "Here. Have some."

Banshooo looks at it. "Is that ice cream?"

"Butter pecan."

"For breakfast?"

"It's nuts. It's protein. What's wrong with that?"

Outside the little house, the sun spreads across Blooo Meadow, rising and shining through the surround of high pines and yellow poplars, the tall grasses, the lace stalks, the occasional Red Rooofus Bush and the Bloooming Blur Tree covered in big orange flowers, its heart on its leaves. Some dew is still sparkling on the tips of the undergrowth tucked around the nests of svelte party animals who sleep late while a wolverine bites the head off a young possum who took just a little too long to get home this particular morning. Another day is underway in the realm.

At that same moment, many miles to the north, in the far reaches of the Great Ooolandian Icefields, a fissure cracks and slivers, moving across the surface of a glacier like a tongue of flame in a hidden fire.

☾

The Great Ooolandian Icefields are generally ignored by the average Ooolandian. No one wants to go there; it's too cold and you can't get chips. As a result, the fields have existed in relative obscurity, remaining comparatively free of the relentless alterations visited upon more inhabitable geography. Until now. Now, the Icefields have become an innocent victim of a growing calamity. Here's how.

Hidden deep within the infinite complexity of the way things work, there exist many vital relationships. As it turns out, one of these is the connection between the Icefields and the Blue Moon—you might even call it a bond, an attachment, a kind of love. For the moon, the ice provides a broad expanse across which its beams paint their shadowy light, a canvas worthy of their unique beauty. In return, these very rays impart nocturnal nourishment, pouring the nectar of the moon down to all who live within the glacial landscape. This crucial lunar influence has maintained the blue-white ice of the fields since time before time. But now, deprived of the sustenance of the moon's rays, the glaciers are breaking apart. This unprecedented development has gone mostly unnoticed in Ooolandia proper, but among those beings who live in the arctic fields and the oceans surrounding them and who count on the glaciers to provide bio-balance for their lives and sustenance, it has been fearfully noted.

One such being, the Ooolandian Blue Blare, has long lived in secure anonymity amongst the snows and the floes. A large and fabulous creature, the blare lumbers along happily in the cold, perfectly at ease with sub-zero wind chill and frozen Jell-O shots. He doesn't need much, just a nice supply of fish and lots of room to roam; both of which have, until recently, been available to him and his kith and kin. But now the ground is melting beneath his huge paws. The complex systems that provide food, shelter, and security through the seasons are unraveling. The etheric network of communication that has always existed between the arctic beasts has become fitful and fraught. They can feel themselves vanishing, each death a premonition of loneliness beyond imagining. Each death the death of all.

CHAPTER 3

Still haunted by the sound of weeping beings, Banshooo shakes himself awake and goes to work, leaving the leafy greenery of his home and heading into the maw of the constructed world. He stops for a moment after climbing the rise on the eastern edge of the bamboo forest. Morning sunlight dapples the lush teal stalks that stand like sentinels, marking the far border of the meadow. Here, at the top of a high ridge, still hidden within the canopy, he looks out across the ravine that divides his sanctuary from the rest of Ooolandia.

Beneath him lies a wide valley filled with buildings of glass and stone. Centered within the valley is the pentagram-shaped complex that houses Ooolandian Central Services (OOOCS), the headquarters for all official Ooolandian activities. The complex is made of enormous stone buildings connected by a series of asphalt roads and walkways, all conveying a formidable authority.

Beyond this fortress lies the teeming urban center known as the Grand Oooland, "The City That Never Waits." In the far distance, Banshooo can see one shining tower after another rising against the sky like stacks of glass chips in a poker game played by giants. Further beyond the bright city, massive industrial sites and pipelines transport fuels to the capital under a low-lying haze that settles perpetually above the entire scene.

Directly below him the ridge drops down a ravine which straightens out to a flat stretch of scrubby brown ground-cover providing several miles of buffer between Blooo Meadow and the turmoil of perpetual construction sites lining the outskirts of the OOOCS compound. The relentless development seems to lap a little closer each day, up toward the shore of his sanctuary. He sees it pressing on, like a determined tide, every time he makes his way from the wilderness of the meadow to the wilderness of urban pursuit, each, in its own way, "red in tooth and claw."

In this area around the outskirts of the Central Services complex, most of the construction activity is dedicated to installing yet more of the already omnipresent viewing screens called OOOCubes, which have been erected along roadways, around the perimeters of buildings, and at every intersection in the capital. Sitting atop poles standing like road-signs, the multi-sided screens look like big square lollipops transmitting official information framed by cheerful images day and night, beaming bright and bouncy pictures of a happy population enjoying the fruits of a bountiful world. Beings of all species often gather around the Cubes for announcements and special broadcasts, little ones on their parent's shoulders, elderly on their own.

As stories began to circulate about drought and pollution in outlying areas, Central Services installed more Cubes. Now they were everywhere, featuring scenes of crystal-clear lakes nestled in gorgeous mountain ranges, pristine waterfalls and blue lagoons, places that Banshooo, for one, doubts still exist. He walks with his head down. The broadcasts depress him, as he knows they prove only that the authorities have become quite good at simulating a virtual reality, a spectral ambiance so compelling and reinforced so constantly that most Ooolandians have come to presume it's the only one there is.

Suddenly a very large dragonfly zooms out of the sky and flits about his head, then settles, hovering, directly in front of his face. She seems almost to flicker in and out of visibility as her iridescent wings flutter neon blue and green through their own transparency. Her huge compound eyes stare at him, Thirty thousand bits of

17

ocular capacity taking in the entire 360-degree space around them. He recognizes her instantly.

"Hey, Durga. How's it going?"

"How's it going, you ask? How's it going? I'll tell you how it's going." She darts left, then right, then back in front of his face. "Things are getting really weird, Shooo."

"Tell me about it."

She zips straight up, then down, then circles his head several times and comes back to hover. "Did you know OOOCS has created a mechanical version of me? Of me?! How dare they!"

Banshooo had heard this; it was about something called a drone, but he hadn't paid much attention. To tell the truth, he didn't want to know. Not waiting for him to respond, Durga zooms around him again, then over to one of the Cubes, then back to Banshooo.

"And did you know the screens on these things work both ways?"

"I did hear something to that effect…"

"There's a guy. He leaked the whole secret. We're all being watched, twenty-four-seven. Every single one of the screens you see transmitting all these pretty pictures is actually a two-way device documenting who, what, and where everyone does everything they do. All the time."

Banshooo had heard this too but he didn't know what to do about it. Most Ooolandians had already accepted the existence of OOOCScams, the ubiquitous surveillance system that recorded their movements throughout most regions of the realm. Now they seemed to accept the idea that the Cubes knew who they were and what they wanted, even as they watched the Cubes.

"You work for them, Banshooo. Can't you do something?"

"Nobody over there listens to me, even when it's about what I'm supposed to be doing. Believe me, I have no influence."

Durga flicks her wings in disgust. "You're such a goody-two-paws."

"I'm not really. It's just that no one pays any …" Durga has gone. He sighs "… attention."

☾

Banshooo continues on toward Central Services where, deep within the formidable edifice, the Department of Nature has an obscure office at the very end of a little-used hallway that houses mostly janitorial supplies. It isn't the lack of status that bothers Banshooo so much as the fact that the tiny space is too small for the mounds of data he and Sukie have amassed. They have to take turns moving about and it's really hard to keep everything properly organized.

The monkey walks through a wrought-iron gate, above which are carved the words:

OUR EYES UPON YOU

This motto was generally perceived as reassuring, promising safety and security, but the recent revelations to which Durga referred had raised some eyebrows and evoked some fears about exactly who those eyes were upon and what those eyes were doing. However, the fuss didn't last long and was, even now, fading in the face of the attention generated by the chatterdee exposé of an adulterous affair between the Grand Oooland's most glamorous superstar and a six-fingered one-off who helped her escape from rehab. Twice.

Banshooo hurries along the cement walkway lined in neon-green grass. It always gives him the creeps to pass this turf which has been biogenetically engineered never to wilt, never turn brown, and hardly ever grow. Secreting poison within its own seeds, it kills worms, grasshoppers, beetles, groundflies, and ants. Nothing disturbs the perfection of this glowing lawn cover. When it was first introduced, he wondered how anything could live without changing in some way but then he realized—the grass wasn't alive so much as it was, simply, existing. Existing in a way that deflected life.

He scoots up the big stone steps in front of the massive complex and enters a humming maze of hallways lined with offices identical in appearance and possibly also in purpose, though no one knows for sure. Periodically, some malcontent questioned what might actually be happening there, but the systems were so impenetrable and the rhetoric so opaque, they usually gave up after awhile and went home.

As he steps into the building, Banshooo is still weighing the pros and cons of including the sound he's heard in his regular report to the Department. Since he is the only piece of evidence that anything had occurred, he decides Taboook was right and he should keep his mouth shut. As anyone will tell you, beings do not consider other beings as reliable evidence of anything. Even with proof, the bureaucracy had a tendency to ignore the subtler aspects of a thing and move directly to a brisk and usually ill-considered conclusion. That's what had happened to his friends at the Department of Unforeseen Consequences, a small group of researchers who had spent many years studying the phenomenon of the unexpected result and producing a number of well-reasoned monographs proving that the unforeseen existed *within* the foreseen. Given this fact, they had respectfully proposed that it might be a good idea to stop doing quite so many things quite so quickly until they could figure out a way to allow for at least some of the unforeseen, which, they had pretty much proved beyond all doubt, was *always* going to be there.

Unfortunately, as soon as this department produced irrefutable evidence of the direct link between the unforeseen, the unseen, and the underside of everything, they lost their funding, their desk chairs, and their pensions. You can imagine their surprise to find that doing their job resulted in the unforeseen consequence of losing it.

To reach the Department of Nature, Banshooo has to walk past rooms filled with bright shiny screens attached to extraordinary machines called mesmers, their sleek chrome monitors framing dazzling blue images dancing in front of Ooolandian eyes. Everyone loved the mesmers. Banshooo did too. They could do wonderful things, things Ooolandians couldn't do on their own. Banshooo wished Central Services would make them available for his research but whenever the Department of Nature requested mesmer time, they were told there were too many projects ahead of them, projects with a higher priority.

Next, he passes the Surveillance Bay, a vast space filled with long tables where technicians sit staring at monitors receiving live feeds from the system of OOOCScams and Cubes placed throughout urban Ooolandia. The bay was generally pretty quiet, emitting a constant low-level digital hum occasionally punctuated by a mammalian voice here and there when an anomaly was noted, or a transmission requested. To Banshooo, the bay seemed like the generator of a kind of ghost world, a world where the effort to see everything that was happening everywhere created a distraction from what was actually happening. Anywhere.

And at this exact moment, far away from the halls and walls of Central Services, a flock of migratories pass over a mountainous valley in the Great Ooolandian Outer Range. For eons, this valley has been filled with a glacial lake providing rest and refreshment for their demanding passage. Now the glacier has receded, leaving a sloping canyon filled with mounds of rocks, soil, sand, and mud. Instead of respite, they fly on. This year, only a few will survive the journey.

☾

Continuing on through the halls of Central Services, the monkey notices a large group of well-groomed creatures heading toward what was known as the Press-Play Room, an oval space with seats surrounding a platform where announcements were made and chatterdees briefed on the latest developments in the march of Ooolandian progress. As the room fills, Banshooo stops to watch, along with several other passersby standing together in the wide doorway.

Arrayed here today is the OOOCS bureaucracy of managers, made up of representatives from some of the more dominant species in the land, primarily those with opposable thumbs and little significant fur.*

Stepping to the podium is the OOOCEO, a dapper, silver-haired humanoid with a perpetual tan and incredibly white teeth that he displays prominently in a grin of excremental proportions. This grin, coupled with a willingness to spout the most colossal garbage with unwavering conviction, has brought him to the top of OOOCS management. He is the face of everything OOOCS stands for, and today he does that standing proudly beneath broad banners proclaiming the OOOCS slogan:

MORE FOR YOU! MORE FOR ME!
MORE FOR EVERYBODY!

Banshooo turns away as he hears the CEO announcing the development of a new implant, a microchip designed to generate a set of standardized thoughts and opinions that will provide a uniform mind-set across the wide range of diverse beings currently living in Ooolandia, thus eliminating misunderstandings and complex, maybe even unsolvable, challenges. The crowd erupts in a chant of the OOOCS motto:

MORE
MORE
MORE
MORE
MORE
MORE

Banshooo continues down the long corridor as the word echoes throughout the complex.

He's filled with a growing sense of foreboding. What do you do? What do you do when the world you live in is going crazy?

He rounds the last corner in the far hallway that houses the Department of Nature and stops short. Sukie, a blond mouse whose silky coat and long eyelashes belie a sharp and agile mind, is sitting on the floor, leaning against the wall next to their office door. The

---

*As you move up the rungs of the Ooolandian hierarchy, you find more hominids and humanoids and fewer furry mammals. It's a long-standing example of EBPB, or Erect Bipedal Primate Bias. Over the years, groups have formed attempting to address this imbalance, but they have made only a small dent in the dominant makeup of the ruling class. Despite efforts by those who argue there are other assets to bring to the table, the number of EBPs in positions of power has remained a decided majority.

door is padlocked with yellow tape crisscrossing the entranceway printed with the declaration: "Premises denied."

As Banshooo well knew, Sukie's ears perked up when she was happy and drooped down when she was sad. Today, her ears are flat against her head.

"What's happened?"

She holds up an envelope.

Banshooo opens it and looks inside. He pulls out two bright pink slices of paper with their names printed at the top.

"We're fired?"

"Yep. We're fired all right. And look at this." Sukie hands Banshooo a memo from Central Services. It reads:

Ooolandian Central Services is in the process of upgrading to meet the new, improved standards recently established by Systems Operations (SYSOP.) This upgrade will involve changes in all departments and, in some cases, will result in immediate elimination. See immediately below for a list of departments to be eliminated. Immediately.

Banshooo's gaze immediately drops to the list immediately below which contains only one department. In bold: **The Department of Nature**.

Standing up, Sukie grumbles, "You know, technically, you can't call something a 'list' if you only put one thing on it." (Lists and pattern recognition are her specialty.)

Banshooo tries the door, twisting the handle back and forth. Sukie looks at him over her glasses. "It's no good, Shooo. We're done here."

For a moment, the two of them stand in the empty hallway, forlorn in front of what now looks like a crime scene. Sukie sighs. "Do you think this is because we're furry?"

Banshooo shrugs. "That may be part of it, but I think it's mostly because they don't want to know about our findings." He turns to the mouse. "What's going to happen to our research?"

"They're going to shred it. They don't think it's worth saving because we gathered it with the naked eye."

"What?"

"They said you have to use the scanners or it doesn't count. They said what we've recorded isn't worth anything because we saw it with the naked eye. The Section Chief made a joke. He called it 'naked information.' The messenger who brought the envelope said everybody laughed."

"But they can't do that! Our data is the only historical timeline showing what's really happening out there, the only way you can see the details in how these changes are progressing, the mutations, the seasonal shifts, the temperature increases, the lost species…"

Sukie sighs. "Not to mention the fact that we're really close to finding the pattern that reveals the connection between etheric quanta and material existence."

"Yeah, that too."

Banshooo squares his shoulders. "Come with me."

The monkey and the mouse march to the SYSOP office where they confront the SYSOP Supervisor, a freakishly large opossum, sitting behind a desk piled high with memos much like the one declaring their own termination. Standing behind and to the side of the desk is his assistant, a guinea pig who purses his lips and shakes his head slowly as Banshooo and Sukie make an impassioned case for the value of their data. The manager sits unmoved.

"Save your breath, Banshooo. We don't need your input. Now we have omni-scanners recording the natural world. In 3-D."

"But the natural world is more than 3-D. It's maximum-D. There are complicated relationships that we don't really understand, relationships between plants and insects, between geology and the celestial bodies, between our paws and the very soil beneath them. We need to study these relationships so we know how to interact with it all."

The opossum stands up, walks around his desk and stares at Banshooo, shaking his head. "You really don't get it, do you?" He makes a broad gesture. "Why should we waste a lot of time trying to '"understand"' and '"interact"' when our technology allows us to override it?"

Sukie squeaks in frustration. "Because overriding kills! Look what happened to the bees!"

The manager mouths his words slowly, as if to a child. "And even as we speak, our labs are developing robotic bees." He turns to his assistant who looks quickly through the pile of paper on the desk, pulls forth a single sheet, and hands it to the manager who reads: "'Their wings can beat one-hundred twenty times a second, their airfoils rotate independently, they weigh eighty milligrams each, and are projected to be used for artificial pollination.'" He glances up at Banshooo and Sukie who stand speechless, then he continues to read. "'Robotic insects offer many potential applications, including search and rescue, high-resolution climate mapping, and covert surveillance.'"

The manager smiles. "It's progress, my friends. Progress. As we tried to explain to those troublemakers over at Unforeseen Consequences, when a problem occurs, we manufacture a solution. If that solution creates another problem, we manufacture another solution. *That's* progress. Problems are not problems. Problems are opportunities. And nature is the biggest opportunity of all. Our greatest accomplishments have come from solving the problems nature presents. More problems, more progress. More for all."

"But..."

The supervisor raises a big pink claw to indicate the meeting is over. His assistant ushers them out of the office, smiling and bowing as he closes the door behind them.

"More for all."

CHAPTER 4

Meanwhile, in the upper reaches of the Central Services complex, another being sits in another office, an office most Ooolandians know nothing about. Not grand or imposing, furnished only with a desk, several chairs, and a bank of mesmers and screens arrayed along a side table. Light from a single window reflects off the dull gray walls, losing its vitality as it spreads through the room like skim milk, creating a kind of shadowy industrial feel that suits its sole occupant, an especially odd one-off known only as Mabooose.

While there are many departments and many managerial layers and many executives who do many things to keep the wheels of progress turning, it is in this office that the crucial decisions are made, the key policies determined, and the actual plans set forth. Here, unbeknownst to most Central Service employees and undreamt of by the general Ooolandian populace, is where the philosophy of MORE is perpetuated.

Most Ooolandians assume the philosophy of MORE has always been … well … just the way things are. They don't think about the fact that this unquestioned way of doing things is only one of many possible ways of doing things and, far from being just the way things are, has, in fact, been conceived, developed, and implemented by a loose coalition of like-minded entrepreneurs who realized early on that everybody wanted more and the more you promised everybody more, the more you could do just about anything, no questions asked. This worked so well it allowed these beings to amass tremendous personal wealth and retire to offshore locations where they never have to see anything they don't want to see or do anything they don't want to do. This has made them stunningly stupid. However, since they associate only with one another, they are unaware of just how painfully dense they are. In fact, they think they're pretty cool. It's sad, really. However, as with most unquestioned "realities," their presumption perpetuates itself with a momentum all its own. As does the philosophy of **MORE**, guided by Mabooose, who oversees the maintaining of desires, the stoking of fears, the marginalization of the unconvinced and whatever else is necessary to preserve the status quo.

Mabooose is seated at his desk holding a folder labeled Central Services Security. Bright red letters spill a warning across the cover:

FOR NO EYES ANYWHERE

He sits back in his leather chair, opens the folder, and thumbs through the contents. It contains Banshooo's last report describing several new anomalies and concluding with the words,

"The disappearance of the blue moon is only the most widely visible of untoward events taking place in all parts of the realm. There is now no doubt that the unusual scope and scale of pathological mutations, unprecedented levels of species extinction, and breakdowns in minute eco-systems, is increasing at a most alarming rate. Water sources are drying up. Temperature increases are creating the potential for ever more severe drought conditions, while changing weather patterns result in rising waters in areas most unsuited to inundation. It is imperative that we address the causes of these changes before they advance to a tipping point, creating wide-spread disruption. My own data, coupled with reports from outlying areas, confirm that the course we are on is wrecking everything everywhere."

Mabooose closes the folder. He raises his large head (a distinctly peculiar head, even for a one-off) and stares into the distance. Born with a unique cardiovascular system that neither flows nor pulsates, he never cries or worries or experiences heartburn, a real advantage when dealing with the many challenges any ambitious being must inevitably face. His singular constitution has allowed him to maneuver through all manner of political intrigue and establish himself at the pinnacle of power without need of antacids, beta blockers, or any of the fine family of benzodiazepines that most Ooolandians rely upon daily.

While some of his colleagues are creeped out by his lack of affect, most under his leadership admire his "composure." (Often as not, if someone points to the fact that Mabooose doesn't feel anything, the response will be: "How great is that!") Over the years, as robotic technology has begun to be integrated into society, Mabooose has come to be seen as an admirable example of mammalian physiology combined with the implacable personality traits of a household appliance.

Mabooose gets up and walks to the far wall where he slides a framed photo of OOOCS headquarters to the side, revealing a steel-grey safe with a big black combination dial in its center. He turns the dial left, right, and left again. The safe opens with a thick click. He puts Banshooo's Central Services Security file inside. Placing a boney appendage flat against the square of cold steel, he slowly pushes it closed.

☾

Later that day, in the little house in Blooo Meadow, Sukie sits on the sofa, leaning against a pillow embroidered with the words: *Plum Wine is Fine*. Her big eyes follow her friend as he paces back and forth in the living room. She's never seen Banshooo so upset.

"We've got to get our data out of there."

Sukie considers this. "Well, technically, it all belongs to OOOCS. We signed an agreement, remember?"

"But they don't want it."

"Doesn't matter. They own it. They can keep it, they can shred it, they can pee on it, anything they want."

Banshooo sets his jaw. "I'm taking it back."

The mouse studies her cohort. "You're aware that this would be a criminal act."

"I am."

"And if they catch us we'll be sued, smeared, and slurred. We'll go to jail. We'll never work in this town again."

"Does that mean you'll join me?"

"Oh I'm in. I just wonder how the heck we're going to do it. We've piled up a lot of data over the years."

Banshooo thinks for a moment.

"We need a mongoose, a meerkat, or a mole. Know anybody?"

Sukie defaults to her specialty. "I'll make a list."

Turns out it's a pretty short list. The meerkats of their acquaintance have very large extended families and never act on their own. Keeping the project secret would not be possible. The only mongoose they know well enough to approach with this clandestine proposal isn't what you'd call reliable and, while fun at parties, does have a tendency to overindulge and brag about anything he can claim for his own. They settle on Ralph, a mole known to Banshooo for his discretion and loyalty. Soon they are serving tea and describing the situation to a velvety-coated mammal with a pointed snout, tiny eyes and ears, and extraordinary front feet.

The mole listens, thinks for a minute, then addresses Banshooo.

"I would never have guessed you'd go rogue."

"I'm not going rogue. I'm going active. You know, acting … actively."

Ralph shrugs. "Call it what you like. It puts you outside the regular rules and regs."

"I tried the regular rules and regs. They're designed to keep things as they are. It's time for something else."

"Yeah, well, I'm just saying…"

Sukie looks at Ralph. "Do we need to swear you to secrecy?"

Ralph wrinkles his pink nose indignantly. "I'm a mole for crying out loud. I'm small, I'm cylindrical, and I can't see a bleeding thing.

If anyone asks, I never saw you guys before in my life. Literally. I never *saw* you."

"He'll be fine," Banshooo assures Sukie.

The door opens and Taboook enters, carrying a super-giant-economy-size bag of chips. He surveys the scene. "What's happening, peeps?"

Six bottles of Belhaven Ale and a lot of chips later, they've sketched out a map which would have them digging from the far edge of Blooo Meadow, tunneling under the construction sites to the Central Services perimeter, continuing beneath the west wing of the main building and directly up under the Department of Nature. They look at one another hesitantly. A long pause ensues. Finally, Banshooo speaks.

"Hey! It's a plan, okay? I really believe there's a slim chance we can pull this off."

They pour more ale and, later that night, with Taboook's help and Ralph in the lead, they all begin to dig. Soon the three non-moles are spitting and blinking and covered in dirt. "Jeez, Ralphie," Taboook wipes bits of earth off his face, "how do you guys deal with this?"

The mole holds up his front feet. "Check it out. Polydactyl forepaws. Pretty cool, huh?" Taboook draws back. "Whoa! Get those ugly appendages outta my face!"

Banshooo pushes Taboook along. "I think what you mean to say is, 'Thanks so much for your help, Ralph. We couldn't do this without you.'"

"Yeah, sure ... that's what I meant to say." He continues to dig, muttering under his breath. "But that's scary ugly."

Ralph sighs. "Such a narrow standard of beauty in a world that abounds with evolutionary inspiration."

After hours of spitting and blinking and general exhaustion, the mole stops and turns back toward Banshooo. "Okay. We're under your office. I'd suggest you slide up along the crawl space and go in through the wall. It'll be easier than trying to break through the floor."

Taboook looks at the mole. "How do you know this stuff?"

"Experience, talent, and some hard-working DNA. Not that you would know about any of that."

"Hey! Is that an anti-one-off remark?"

"Take it as you will, freak."

"Who you callin' freak, monster-mitts?"

A sudden crash interrupts the quarrel. Banshooo has broken through the wall and into the DofN office. "Come on, guys, we're in!"

One by one they crawl into the room. The small space can barely accommodate the dirt-covered bodies of a monkey, a mouse, a mole, and a one-off amidst the bulging shelves, overflowing files and cabinets, tables stacked with reports, journals, monographs, memoranda, records, notebooks, and a massive number of lists.

Sliding sideways past her colleagues, Sukie makes her way to the door, puts her ear up against it, and listens. All is quiet. "I guess it's a good thing they don't care enough about our work to bother to guard it." Banshooo shakes the clomps of dirt off his feet. "Okay guys, let's do this thing."

For the rest of the night, the four of them move in and out of the padlocked office, carrying years' worth of naked information and trundling it all into Banshooo's house. They work quickly, moving load after load along the musty tunnel and out through the woods. On the last trip, as Taboook and Sukie disappear through the hole in the wall, Banshooo takes a long look around the forlorn space. He's spent years trying to work within the rules of their game. Now he knew he'd never do that again.

"Come on, Ralphie, it's done." The mole is nosing around something sticking out from under an empty book shelf. He reaches in and pulls out a heavy sheet of paper rolled up in the shape of a tube. They unroll a brightly colored poster, a picture of gleaming new buildings across which are printed the words:

DIG WE MUST, FOR A GREATER OOOLANDIA.

Ralph tilts his head. "What do you think?"

"Why not?" Banshooo chuckles softly. The two of them attach

the poster to the wall, slide under it into the hole, then pull it down behind them so it covers the evidence of their egress. They join the others, coming up for air in Blooo Meadow.

Ralph shakes the dust from his coat. "Okay, I'm off to eat some worms." Wriggling his rear end as he trundles away, he looks back at Banshooo and adds, "Good luck, my friend, and please, don't let me know how this comes out. I prefer to remember you as a free mammal."

As the first light of dawn sneaks in through the windows, they stack up the last batch of files and lie back on the living room couch, sore, dirty, and exhausted.

"Do you think they'll come looking for us?" Banshooo asks.

"Probably not," Sukie answers in a sad monotone. "They don't see the value." She yawns. She's very tired.

Taboook gets up from the couch and stretches his arms high above his head, making for the kitchen. "Face it, you guys, you're obsolete. You spend all your time looking at what's already there. Nobody's interested in what's already there. Everybody wants to know what's next. Omni-3-D-scanners are what's next. They can see everything. They can see things we can't see, infrared-type things and like that."

"They can't see *everything*," Banshooo says fiercely. "There's a whole other kind of thing they can't see, that they'll never see."

Taboook stops and looks back askance. "And what kind of thing would that be? The kind that makes swooshing and sobbing sounds in the night?"

"As a matter of fact, yes. *Exactly* that kind of thing."

"You can't prove it, Shooo, and no one cares if you can't prove it."

"That doesn't mean it didn't happen."

"It sorta does. I mean, if no one's there, does it make a sobbing sound in the forest?"

As Sukie dozes off to the cadences of the classic debate on perception versus reality, another day dawns, revealing fewer fireflies, more mutant frogs, and no blue moon. While many miles away, new fissures snake through the Ooolandian Icefields.

On a hill some distance behind the Central Services compound stands a great glass building, strikingly modern and quite unlike the stone colonnades of the main complex. Sweeping mirrored glass covers the entire façade reflecting the surroundings while maintaining total privacy within. There is no name, no emblem, no logo, no identifying signage of any kind, yet no one questions what might be happening there. It is clearly very important, very well funded, and undoubtedly highly scientific. It's sleek. It's silvery.

Mabooose walks crisply toward the bold and shining edifice. He passes along a shaped and sculpted landscape with perfectly pruned trees and bushes lining an immense, pristine lawn, all ordered, tamed, and meticulously maintained. He enters the glass structure, considering the reflections in its enormous mirrored windows. The trees and sky surrounding the hillside look as if they were painted on the building, giving it a benign feel and fitting neatly into the concerted "green" campaign that the PR division has been integrating into the popular discourse so successfully.

Mabooose registers a cool satisfaction. It always pleases him to realize, yet again, how easily Ooolandians can be swayed by images. When rumors began to circulate that ancient water sources were drying up or no longer potable, the PR division transmitted images of pristine rivers and sparkling waterfalls on the Cubes everywhere, day and night. The general populace was reassured. It was another instance of how the constant chatter about everything, which has become ubiquitous throughout Ooolandia, essentially diffracted itself into irrelevance. The capacity to discern the difference between rumor and reality had, for all intents and purposes, disappeared. This unforeseen consequence of chatter-overload has served OOOCS and the ideology of MORE very well, having the effect of turning any potential reform movement into just another momentary meme trending in cyberdee space.

Inside, minimalist silver and gray décor imparts a featureless anonymity. Mabooose passes through a series of security checkpoints and is ushered into a large laboratory. He blinks against the glare from bright florescent lights. Rows of tables are covered with tissue processors, protein sequencers, DNA synthesizers, hematology analyzers, and shelves of centrifuges, incubators, and flow cytometers. Banks of mesmers line the walls, running programs scanning millions of bits of genetic code. The place appears to be empty.

Mabooose frowns. "Doootch, are you here?"

A human figure emerges from behind a partition. Impossibly thin with hair hanging down like a bowl over his forehead, he wears an impeccably clean white lab coat that conceals his slight frame. He looks at Mabooose through thick glasses, behind which sit small blue eyes, oddly unfocused, as if under some kind of a spell. He is Dr. D. Doootch, bioengineering genius, and he is clearly impatient at the interruption. "What do *you* want?"

Mabooose reminds himself that genuine innovation is often achieved by beings with little or no respect for authority. A slight annoyance but seemingly unavoidable. He squares his shoulders and meets the cold stare coming from behind the glasses with an equally cold stare of his own, adding to the unusually frigid temperature in the room.

"I want to see how things are progressing." He pauses. "I *expect* to see how things are progressing."

Doootch nods curtly and walks out of the lab. Mabooose follows. A long corridor leads to a thick steel door in the center of which is a small window reinforced with mesh and bracketed with bars. A robo voice asks Doootch to place his hand, palm down, on the screen of a bio-metric security device. As he does this, there is a loud click and the door pops slightly ajar. Doootch pulls it open. Yelps and howls spill into the hallway. They enter and Doootch closes the heavy sound-proofed door behind them. Inside, they stand amidst a cacophony of wails.

Banks of cages line the walls of this large room. Some contain live animals, and some hold the dead bodies of dogs, cats, mice, and white rats. Some are empty. In the center of the room are three large pens. Each one houses a twisting, whimpering creature made up of an ungainly combination of features, pieces of one thing and parts of another, spliced and diced into an unrecognizable entity.

Mabooose walks over to the nearest cage. He looks at the writhing thing inside. It has a smooth head the size and shape of a melon balanced on folds of skin that pool in layers around two tiny claws sticking out of its torso. Its mouth is permanently open, revealing haphazard teeth and an outsized tongue. Its small black eyes look as if they are pleading for help.

"What's the matter with it?"

"There are issues with the nervous system that haven't been completely worked out. Apparently, the transgenic hybridizing process has a tendency to create exceptionally sensitive neuroanatomical functions coupled with an overly active *locus coeruleus.*"

Mabooose stares at Doootch.

Doootch shrugs. "They have a lot of pain, it stresses them out, they get panicky, okay?"

Mabooose frowns. "What happened to the glow-in-the-dark kittens? They were eye-catching."

"After a while their fur falls out and they go blind. They don't look so good at that point."

"You told me you could re-engineer the genome, create hybrid organisms, manipulate biological codes, mix and match DNA, control the entire genetic process."

"And I can. *Basically,* it's working. We just need to smooth out a few wrinkles. What I want to know is, when can I go public with my work?"

"Not yet. In here, science may reign, but out there, all kinds of beliefs hold sway about all kinds of things. Out there, they aren't quite ready to accept spliced beings." He pauses. "Unless they're cute." He gestures toward the creatures writhing in their cages. "This won't do. They have to be cute."

"But the knowledge I'm accumulating will allow us to redesign the living world."

"And I look forward to that day. But for now, you must consider my problem. It takes a lot of time dealing with so many differing points of view. It'll be better when there are fewer voices, fewer contrary opinions."

Doootch nods. "Yes. Natural selection is inefficient and time-consuming, not to mention the fact that it results in a widely diverse spectrum of needless complexity."

"It won't be much longer," Mabooose continues. "Species die-out is progressing and a lot of dissonant voices are losing strength due to a lack of respect." His tone becomes almost thoughtful as he continues. "It's rather amazing what a simple lack of respect can do. With no attention, no acknowledgement, ideas just die off on their own. It's like starving something."

Doootch nods again. "I've always said it. All the principles of biology can be directly applied to the aggregate of society. The basics are the same. It's the wolf you feed."

"What?"

"It's an old folktale."

"Whatever. When we launch the chatterdee campaign promoting the monoculture concept, we'll be able to move your work out into the open. We're phasing in the robos, more and more of them in more capacities. When you provide no alternative, Ooolandians conform to the technology. Soon, they'll accept it completely and their maddening sense of individual identity will fade." He levels a steady gaze at Doootch. "Your time is coming. I just hope you're ready with something…" he pauses then says, "user-friendly."

Mabooose leaves the chamber. Behind him, the heavy steel door clamps shut, drowning out the cries and whimpers. He heads toward the agricultural wing where they're working to create a botanical organism using a completely original genetic code, one never before seen in any life-form. Maybe that approach will yield more progress. Synthetic plants are easier to introduce than synthetic animals. Mammals have such tiresome misgivings about manipulated versions of themselves. Plants can't protest.

PART II

"Then the spirit of the earth rose up crying out to the sky, and the heavens wept for a world bereft of mercy."

—Ancient Puebloan Prophecy

CHAPTER 5

It comes in the night with no warning, a fierce force, unknown to anyone before now. Even the nocturnal beings are caught unaware by the sudden, swift difference. Beneath Banshooo's house in Blooo Meadow, a low, rumbling sound moves along the ground. The windows rattle. Banshooo stands up from his desk, listening. The rumbling grows louder. Everything begins to throb. A lamp crashes to the floor. He hurries to the porch and looks out into the abruptly foreign night.

Stinging bursts of light flash like knives cutting open the sky. Wind charges across the meadow, leaving the field grass flat against the ground. Banshooo holds tight to the porch railing. A slice of the roof flies off, disappearing into the dark. He watches in shock as a whirlwind spawns funnels in the field, each funnel creating a vortex that lifts grass, leaves, and soil into the air then plunges them back down, as if some huge hand is scooping up chunks of ground and smashing them against the earth. He's in the middle of a storm like none he's ever known, beyond memory, beyond ken.

Deafening claps of thunder burst around him like some unholy beast exploding in anger. Rain pours down in frantic sheets as if trying to escape the roiling darkness above. The atmosphere is filled with an electrical charge so strong it makes his teeth ache. Tree limbs crack, nests break open, and burrows flood out. A tree swallow swoops and staggers over the railing, banging into the front door. A blue-tailed shrew scurries, breathless, onto the porch, his eyes full of fear and surprise. Two squirrels and a beaver follow close behind, drenched and shivering. Above their heads, jets of lightning morph into blue flames sending spikes and streamers dripping down from the sky. A sulfurous smell permeates the air. The rain seems to be exploding in on itself, releasing particles of fire.

Banshooo watches an ancient tree break apart, slowly, like a time-lapse explosion. In the next flare of lightning he sees a fawn trembling on stick legs on the far side of the field. He puts his head down and pushes into the wind. The pelting rain stings his body and his fur stands on end as lightning flashes all around him. Breathing hard, he stumbles forward, ducking a flying branch, his shoulders hunched against the flailing debris. He reaches the deer. Her front legs are cut and bleeding. He struggles to pick her up. She leans in to him and closes her eyes tightly. They stand together in the whirlwind. He looks back toward the house, a shadowy outline intermittently visible in the strobed light. It might as well be miles away. He grits his teeth and begins to stagger back toward the porch.

Suddenly a massive tree trunk crashes down directly in front of them. He pulls up sharply, and the deer cries out. The trunk is so close to his face he can see rivulets of water rushing along the thick ridged bark. He feels the fawn's heart beating fast against his chest in concert with his own. Alone he might've made it over the top but it's much too high to climb with this wounded being in his arms.

Girding his strength, he works his way slowly around the fallen tree, fighting the wind, one demanding step and then another. After what seems like hours, the porch is, once again, in sight. He begins to think they might make it when a sudden surge of muddy water knocks him off his feet. The deer falls to her knees, her head dropping under the rushing stream. Banshooo tries to gather her up but he slips in the current. The deer flails wildly. He tries again. He slides sideways. He can't get his footing. He's about to go under when two big paws pull him upright.

"Really? We're rescuing Bambi? This'll make a great chatterdee post."

"Boook! Shut up and help the fawn."

Together they struggle the last twenty yards to shelter. Clambering up the stairs, Taboook releases the deer who stands bleating on the porch. Banshooo follows close behind. They shake themselves in a vain attempt to get dry. Taboook eyes the water swirling around the base of the stairs. "What's with the flood?"

"I don't know." Banshooo shakes his head slowly. "In all the time I've been here, and in all of Algernon's time, this meadow has never flooded. The topography argues against it."

"Oh yeah? Well the topography seems to have lost the debate."

Another explosion of lightning reveals a monkey, a one-off, a shrew, two squirrels, a beaver, and a young deer shivering on Banshooo's porch and peering uncertainly into a whole new kind of storm. Suddenly a free-tailed bat and three different species of migrating birds fall dead out of the sky. The acrid odor of burning feathers and flesh hangs in the rain. "Whoa!" Taboook steps back. "Zapped in midair?"

A tortoise washes up against the stairs and as they reach down to pull the heavy creature onto the porch, another bird is slammed down in front of them. Still alive, writhing in pain, her mottled feathers drenched, she waves her long legs in the air trying to turn herself upright in the swirling water. Banshooo gathers her up and brings her inside. The shrew, the swallow, the squirrels, the beaver, the tortoise, the fawn, and Taboook follow.

Inside the trembling house, the drenched and shaken beings huddle together. Banshooo is passing out blankets and Taboook is trying to get a fire going. The lamps are dead, the darkness leavened only by continual flashes of lightning that leave red-tinged afterimages outlined on the window glass. Loose branches smack against the roof and the rain has turned the entire house into a snare drum. The commotion is so loud it takes a minute before Banshooo realizes someone is pounding on the door. He opens it to find Sukie leaning, soaked and bedraggled, against the doorframe. He helps the mouse inside and Taboook pushes the door closed behind them.

"My nest is washed out. I had to swim to get here. Swim!" Sukie is exhausted, her glasses are twisted sideways across her nose, and her whiskers drip onto the floor. Banshooo wraps a blanket around her shoulders. "Come in, sit by the fire." She allows herself to be led but her face reflects a fierce concern.

"Flood waters? Here? How can that happen?"

"I don't know, my friend. I don't know."

☾

Dawn comes and the wind wanes. The rain slows, softens, then stops, as if sorry for the unprecedented outburst. The water has ebbed away as mysteriously as it appeared leaving a layer of red silt sprinkled across the meadow.

Sukie is sorting through her calculations, trying to work around a damp shrew-shaped imprint left on her stack of mathematical tables. The beaver sits on his big, flat tail in an effort to avoid knocking things over in the early light. The speckled bird who crashed from the sky huddles next to the fireplace. Taboook is talking to anyone who will listen.

"My whole house blew away. Such a shame. It was a model of sustainable architecture, a regular eco-prototype."

The squirrels roll their eyes. "It was a decrepit shack with fungus and mold growing everywhere."

"Hey! It was *green*."

Sukie and Banshooo are poring over their records, looking for answers in the phenological history of the area.

"It rained upwards. How to explain that?"

The tortoise raises his reptilian head out from his shell. "And what's with the big scary lightning?"

Sukie frowns. "Huge electrostatic discharges do take place in the upper atmosphere, but normally it's far beyond what we can see. I don't understand how that could occur down here, so close to us."

Banshooo is reading through flood plain data. "There must have been a major breakdown in the traditional flow patterns."

The swallow looks down from his perch on a tall lamp. "When

we flew over the northern foothills, we saw they'd been clear-cut. All the ground up there is eroded."

Banshooo frowns. "So there was nothing to absorb the massive amounts of rain. It must have rushed over everything. But from that far away?"

"I'm just saying. A lot of things have been cut, cleared, and killed."

The speckled bird blinks her small black eyes. "We fly across the ocean. Sound carries over the water. We hear terrible things, whales, dolphins, porpoises caught in nets, twisting and thrashing; otters, seals, sea lions trapped in plastic garbage." She sighs. "My mother choked to death on a baggie." Her feathers tremble as she shivers all over. Everyone is quiet.

After a moment, Sukie whispers to Banshooo. "Is that a bar-tailed godwit?"

Banshooo nods.

"But where…?"

"Blown in all the way from the Icefields. They were migrating when the storm hit."

"But that means…"

"I know. It means this was global."

Sukie bites her lip. "Uh-oh."

Later that day, after expending a lot of energy cleaning out storm debris and patching up the roof, Banshooo's houseguests are taking a nap. The godwit whimpers in a fitful nightmare. Taboook is snoring on the couch and Sukie, curled up on the sagging ottoman, mumbles animatedly while, even in her sleep, she tries to calculate what kind of vortex could have created so many waterspouts that it rained upward. Banshooo tiptoes around the ladder left leaning against the rafters and heads outside.

The meadow is quiet now but beaten down as if trampled by very large creatures. Banshooo stops at Algernon's grave, a slight rise surrounded by a thick border of snowy white trillium. Trillium usually die after flowering and can take years to reseed, but these have bloomed steadily, mysteriously, since the panda's death, like an eternal flame of ghostly commemoration. Now they are flattened against the modest mound where they once stood guard. Nearby, a tree has fallen, broken at its base, the fan-like pattern of growth rings revealed in its pink flesh. He can almost hear Algernon's voice.

"Ooolandia's memory lives everywhere, Banshooo. It's in the sediment of a riverbed, the strata on a cliff face, the trunks of trees. These are messages from the past telling us how Now was made. We must pay attention. Otherwise, we are blind."

Banshooo moves on, wondering what the splintered tree trunks, torn foliage, and dismembered branches can tell him about the future. He stops under a frayed bower of pandorea and stares out at the meadow. Broken aspens lean against their brethren lying wounded in the aftermath. Wild holly shrubs hang askew, still shivering in shock. A primal wetness clings to the cracked stalks of tall grass. He watches as a drop slips off a ragweed plant and lands on the fern next to him. It trembles as if an invisible finger had gently nudged the frond and then departed, ghost-like, into the ruin.

Since the storm, the sky has been blurry and the morning light has changed, filtered through ripples of opaque atmosphere, yellowed, like old paper, leaving an undulated pattern on the ground. With a sense of foreboding, he records the conditions in his notebook, entering the data as it appears. Then he begins to walk back to the house. That's when he hears it: the same frightening sound that came in the night, surging through the air, picking up speed and heading directly toward him. The high-pitched whine grows louder and louder. Again, it washes over him, and again he's drenched with sound and then stunned into the middle of the most extraordinary quiet.

Now comes the sense that he's floating through layers of swirling fog. He hears the crying and sees a small being raising its face before him, but this time the face is his own. Flashes of memory flicker. His mother lies dead beside him, her body stiff and cold. Alone, shivering, he looks around desperately. He sees a gateway floating in and out of his vision. He squints as it flickers and then evaporates, dissolves and forms again. Slowly, out of the gateway, a shadow appears, a spectral presence that bends down toward his mother and then toward him. He pulls back, frightened, but when it touches him his shivering slows. He is consoled, enfolded in refuge, held in safety.

A humming begins, a kind of purring, growing stronger until it's moving like music all around him, a rich melodious chorus of complex resonance, pulsing and throbbing in the most intricate of harmonies, verging on the edge of being visible. But now the sound is fading and the shadow retreats, melting into the fog. He tries to move toward it, but as soon as he does he loses his breath and his body feels hollow, as if he's about to break apart. He takes another step and again he's made breathless, splintered. Abruptly, everything drains away. The ground shifts. He hears voices. He opens his mouth to cry out but there is no sound. The voices grow louder.

"Banshooo? Hullo? Hullo?"

Sukie is looking at him intently. "Shooo! Wake up!"

Taboook is waving a big paw in front of his face. "What's the matter, man? You're creeping me out."

Banshooo blinks and shakes his head, then stares at his friends. "I saw it. I saw it when I was little."

Taboook frowns. "You're not making any sense."

"I saw the threshold. I remember now; it was the Unseen."

Sukie's eyes narrow. "You had another one of those … visions?"

"It was real, completely real. You've got to believe me."

Taboook frowns some more.

Sukie pauses, then nods. "Okay. Come with me." She nudges him along. "I know a guy."

CHAPTER 6

In the urban opulence of the Grand Oooland, the unparalleled storm has left shock and disbelief. The wind tore through the great city in a rage. High-rises swayed, skyscrapers wobbled, glass shattered across streets and avenues, creating a random destruction from which the population had assumed itself to be immune.

The strange funnels formed here as well, cyclonic microbursts pulling debris into the air and smashing it back onto the streets, shops, and malls. In outlying areas, water from dump sites was sucked up by the wind and blown into the city. Curtains of polluted rain whirled into eddies that the wind drove sideways, leaving a caustic layer of sulfuric acid dripping off of buildings, massive structures everyone had thought to be impregnable. Most disastrous of all, the waste systems flooded, leaving pools of rank-smelling sludge in previously pristine places. Destruction is widespread, and confidence is bruised. A growing sense of anxiety pervades the land. How could this happen to us—the masters of all things?

Over the following weeks, a massive cleanup effort progresses while, at Ooolandian Central Services, the atmosphere is tense. Tremors are occurring in unexpected places. More and stranger aberrations are showing up in the natural world. The chatterdees are chirping at a fever pitch. The status quo is shaky. A popular marmot has written a catchy song with lyrics implying that MORE might not be all it's cracked up to be. The song is climbing the charts. Something needs to be done.

Meetings are held, suggestions are put forth, profit margins are taken into account, and finally, a group of OOOCS nameless, faceless bureaucrats gather together in a large conference room to discuss possible solutions. Seated around a long table are representatives from key departments. These beings are mostly humanoid but do include several one-offs and the few furred beings who have managed to overcome the EBPB pervasive throughout the administration. They all talk amongst themselves but immediately fall silent when Mabooose walks in and takes his place at the head of the table, implacable as ever. He listens as each department reports.

Security describes a new homeland policy wherein anyone questioning the Philosophy of MORE has been brought before The UnOoolandian Committee and labeled an idealist, made to look childishly naïve, or worse, an outright fool. Those who have refused to appear foolish have been arrested as troublemakers endangering the greater good.

Public Promotions emphasizes the need for a major project around which they can design a campaign to rally the average Ooolandian. They need something big, something galvanizing, something with a new slogan.

The Department of Great Big Projects responds, proposing a number of possible undertakings. As the list is recited, Mabooose rises from his chair and walks over to the window. He stands there without moving, his back to the gathering. The head of Great Big Projects hesitates and stops intoning. He swallows nervously. It's never good to bore the leader.

Mabooose turns. His eyes scan this collection of obedient bureaucrats gathered silently before him. He thinks how right it is that he has authority over these lesser beings. He experiences what would be, in someone with a pulse, a warm feeling. He takes a moment and then says, "We will build a new blue moon."

A stunned silence fills the room, quickly followed by a loud eruption of enthusiasm. "Wow! Incredible! What a great idea!" The Public Promotions animals are excited. "A new moon. It's perfect. It's got everything: drama, daring, bigness, jobs. It's unprecedented. It'll be huge. We'll get the chatterdees on it right away!"

The engineers from the Department of Great big Projects eagerly confer. "We'll have to build up, very high up, which means we'll have to dig down, very deep down, and sideways too. We'll go up and down and sideways but most of all up, really high up. We'll need to remove the clouds of course. Clouds get in the way. We'll develop a substance to disperse the clouds, something we can spray on them. We can do that. We'll find a way to do that. This is great! Drilling sideways, blasting deeper, building higher, spraying things. It's what we do! Every problem an opportunity, every loss a gain, every day a chance to make more. More for you, More for me, More for everyone!"

Mabooose clears his throat and the room goes silent. He speaks evenly as the PR animals take notes.

"We will announce the New Blue Moon Project immediately. It will provide jobs and meet our needs. It will be the most ambitious, most daring, most important project Ooolandia has ever undertaken. It will begin today." He nods to indicate the end of the meeting. Everyone files out of the office, talking together excitedly.

Soon the chatterdee networks are abuzz with news of the massive undertaking while the Cubes broadcast sparkling architectural renderings of a gigantic celestial orb shining down on all of Ooolandia. Speeches are made announcing the creation of jobs and prosperity for all, reassuring the population that, in spite of recent events, the Ooolandian authorities know what's going on and are in control. All OOOCS employees are declared to be a vital part of this unparalleled undertaking.

☾

In the Surveillance Bay brightly colored posters appear promoting the new project. "Build a Better Moon." "Make it New and Blue." "Ooolandia Rules."

Below the banners, the hangar-like space is filled with the humming throb and glow of mesmers and monitors, surveilling, recording, compiling, collating, and storing the movements and activities of all the beings in The Grand Oooland. Assistant managers walk slowly up and down amongst the many rows of monitors, looking over the shoulders of the technicians dutifully sitting at their screens.

Seated at one of these monitors is Joe, an average human-type guy, with hands and feet, ears on either side of his head, a bushy thatch of reddish hair on top, and a nose right in the middle of his fleshy face. Joe used to hang around the Department of Nature and eat lunch with Banshooo and Sukie. He liked listening to them talk about the crazy things they saw in their phenological observations. He liked looking at Banshooo's notebooks and all the drawings and strange words and complicated interwoven timelines. He liked the way Banshooo described the interconnectedness of everything, and he was amazed at Sukie's lists. He couldn't believe how many different kinds of one thing there are.

At his job in Surveillance, trees, bushes, and plants were called "stationary data points," and beings were called "mobile data points." Joe couldn't say exactly why, but it didn't seem to him this was a good way to talk about living things. He'd get depressed sometimes, wondering if this was it for him, a dead-end job with no hope of ever scoring courtside seats to anything. Ever.

Joe glances over at the monitor next to his. It's manned by Jonesy, a big grey badger with a long nose and a lot of responsibilities. Jonesy usually works nights, but he'd been pulling double shifts since his cubs moved back to the burrow. He is now responsible for a sizable clan. He is, after all, the dominant male.

"I feel for these kids today." Jonesy sighed. "It's so hard to find a decent job."

Joe notices that Jonesy's screen is scanning the outlying woods far beyond the Ooolandian foothills, an area rarely observed if at all. "What're you looking at?" He nods toward the screen.

"Beats me. I was given these coordinates. I hear they're looking for new sources of ploootonite*, trying to find new places to drill."

Jonesy shrugs. "Hey, they say 'monitor this,' and I monitor it."

Joe frowns. "Banshooo said we're drilling into something we don't really understand."

Jonesy snorts. "Yeah, well, he's fired. He's on the outside now."

The badger leans in and whispers, "And you know what I heard?"

"What?"

"I heard they fired some others."

"What others?"

"Others."

"Why?"

"They were talking about how Banshooo might be right and how it was a bad idea to eliminate the Department of Nature."

"Really?"

"That's what I heard. I tell you, man, I'm keeping my mouth shut."

"But it *was* a bad idea."

Jonesy looks at Joe with some alarm. "I don't want to hear it."

"Even if it's true?"

"You can worry about what's true if you want, but I've got responsibilities. I can't get stuck on the outside with no way to get by."

Joe looks down at the cement floor that helps maintain the temperature-controlled environment required to keep the mesmers operating efficiently. He knows this can happen. Beings get kicked out of the system, and they wind up alone and without anything.

---

*Plootonite serves as the primary power source for Ooolandian industry. However, after many years of digging, drilling, boring, blasting, and piercing the Ooolandian earth, plootonite is becoming harder and harder to find. Some have advocated utilizing other and varied sources of energy, but the power structure, which has become the power structure as a result of controlling the power source ... structurally... has managed to perpetuate the notion that plootonite is the only way to go, energy-wise. It's the old Too-Late-to-Stop-Now ploy, a tried and true power play used by power structures throughout history. It relentlessly emphasizes the fact that change can require difficult choices, is often inconvenient, full of challenges, and may even be really hard. Nobody wants that. Life is tough enough as it is. Thus, ideas for reasonable ways to innovate change are routinely discounted, resulting in an entire population that accepts the notion that everything has to continue the way it is, no matter what the consequences might be. It's a pretty powerful ploy to play.

Jonesy continues. "You heard what the VIOs said. 'Each one of us is a vital part of this unparalleled undertaking.' Aren't you glad to be a vital part of this unparalleled undertaking?"

"I just wonder if it's such a good idea, you know, in the long run?"

"What do you mean—long run?"

"Well, for starters, what happened to the real blue moon? What if it wants to come back? Banshooo always said we need to watch and see what's already happening and work with it, not against it."

"Banshooo, Banschmooo. Everyone knows that monkey is nuts."

"Who says?"

"The chatterdees."

"You can't believe the chatterdees."

"Maybe, but you know the old saying: where there's chatter, somethin's a-matter."

Joe sits slumped at his station. He feels crummy. His stomach hurts. A supervisor comes by and taps him on the shoulder.

"Get back to work, pal."

And so he does.

☾

Sukie, Banshooo, and Taboook make their way from the meadow to the outer edges of a large grove thick with trees of many species. They follow Sukie up into the nether reaches of a great white oak where they find, hidden within the lush leaves, the abode of Ambrose, a very large owl who can look deep into your eyes and see what you have seen. In fact, this owl can see in many ways what other eyes cannot.

Ambrose keeps the truth of this extraordinary ability to himself. (Were his gifts widely known, he would never be invited to join a poker game again, and he does enjoy a high-stakes round of five-card stud no peeky.) But Sukie knows all about the owl's vision because, one dark night long ago, the owl caught her for dinner. Just as Ambrose was about to take a big bite, he looked into Sukie's eyes and saw that this mouse was a student of advanced mathematics who actually understood the various hypotheses currently being put forth regarding pattern recognition and its application to quantum mechanics. The owl decided to spare her, not wanting to be the one who ate the brain that might generate the next big step toward understanding how the universe works.

Ambrose appears. He is quite large with a patrician head and pointed ear tufts. His back and sides are a mottled golden brown and grey, but his head and chest are pure white, and when he spreads his wide wings, the under parts are white as well. His eyes are huge black pools framed in the disc of a finely feathered face. He is, in fact, quite intimidating.

Sukie nods sideways toward Banshooo. Ambrose nods in response and places a wing on Banshooo's shoulder. "Won't you come in?"

As they all begin to troop inside, Ambrose glances at Taboook and Sukie. "Perhaps you two might like to sit out here and talk. It's such a nice afternoon." He guides Banshooo inside and closes the door. Taboook and Sukie find perches for themselves and wait on the big leafy front porch, relaxing in the sweet breeze.

Inside, Ambrose sits Banshooo down in front of him. "So. You saw something ... unusual?"

"Very."

"No one else saw it?"

"No one."

"And you'd like to be believed?"

Banshooo thinks for a moment. "Yes. Exactly. I'd like to be believed."

The owl nods. "Okay. Let's see what we can do."

He draws back a bit, fluffs his chest, then looks directly into Banshooo's eyes. "Hold your head steady and keep looking at me." The owl begins to hum to himself. Banshooo stares, and the humming grows stronger. Within seconds he is enveloped in Ambrose's big owl orbs, limpid through and through.

Now Banshooo hears the fearsome sound. It crashes upon him. Then the silence. He feels the thickness, sees the spectral phantom faces as the weeping explodes into a shower of tears, then he sees his own face, his mother's body, the ghostly portal, and the shadow that bends toward them. Now his shivering is soothed; the sweet sound comes with that warm sense of safety. Then, as everything begins to fade away, he tries to move forward. His body seems to break up. He is breathless. Emptiness fills his perception and expands beyond him, blowing directly into the owl's face.

"Whoa!" Ambrose pulls back quickly. He shakes his head and blinks. After a few minutes he looks at Banshooo as if seeing him for the first time. "Very interesting. Very interesting indeed."

The owl's voice brings Banshooo back to the present moment. He's being offered a cup of tea. "Drink up. It'll revive your nowness." Ambrose sits back, studying Banshooo carefully. A long pause ensues. Finally, Banshooo says, "So. You can see what I saw?"

"I can see the impression the experience left on your mind's eye."

"Like a memory?"

The owl nods. "Experience creates impressions that are stored as memory, stored in every cell in every living thing."

Banshooo smiles. "Yes, my teacher used to say memory is everywhere, in the trees, even in rocks." He looks at the owl. "Did you know Algernon Blooo?"

"I'm afraid I didn't have the pleasure, but it sounds like he knew what he was talking about. Memory *is* everywhere, and in sentient creatures it's carried in all parts of the body: the nervous system, the muscles, even the bones. And of course, the heart. The heart remembers deeply."

"And you can see all the memories?"

"Not all, no. My ability is limited. You have to get to me fairly soon, otherwise it gets fogged up with all the other stuff you've seen, all the other impressions. In fact, most memories are covered in fog, hiding inside the limbic system and visible mostly in our behavior." The owl leans back. "I can see this one because you just did, vibrant and new. It wants to awaken, to move out of the hidden part of you and into your conscious mind." He pauses, then says softly, "It really wants to be remembered."

More minutes pass. Finally, Banshooo speaks in a low voice. "She was there. My mother. She was right next to me."

Ambrose nods.

"She just lay there." He looks down. "She didn't move."

Ambrose waits in silence.

Banshooo whispers, "I never knew her, but I miss her all the same."

The owl opens one wing and holds it just a feather's width away from the monkey's slumping shoulders, gathering the space around him. Quiet moments pass. Outside, gentle laughter floats along a soft breeze as Sukie and Taboook share a joke.

After a while, Banshooo looks up. "The thing is ... I miss something else too. I miss what happened when she died. The sound that surrounded me. That feeling of safety, of being held within some larger thing." His eyes are wet with tears. "It's not just her I miss, it's what happened when she died."

Ambrose nods slowly. "That's understandable."

"It is?"

"Absolutely. In a way, what happened then *is* your mother. Whatever it was, it cared for you and left you with this awareness." Ambrose narrows his big eyes. "This is not a common experience."

Banshooo sighs. "No kidding."

Ambrose pours fresh tea. "So who was that shadowy being?"

"I was hoping maybe you'd know."

Ambrose shakes his head. "What about all that swirling fog?"

"So you saw that! Did you see the opening?"

"I saw something that might have been some kind of ... something."

"It's a doorway, I'm sure of it. But when I try to move toward it, it's like I'm moving through thick layers that hold me back. My whole body feels hollow and I lose my breath. It feels like I could break apart."

Banshooo looks into the eyes of this being who has just seen so deeply into his own. He speaks quietly but with conviction. "I'm supposed to go there. I know it."

Ambrose considers this. "Go where, do you think?"

Banshooo takes a deep breath and starts to talk. "I believe there is a threshold, a threshold to the Unseen World. I think I'm remembering that I saw that world when my mother died; a world that exists in our world but, normally, we don't see it. I'm sure it's there. I'm sure it's real." Now the words are spilling out. "I have to find it again. I *have* to. I know it's important, *really* important. Not just to me, but in some bigger way, in some way that affects everything."

Banshooo stops talking. He's never said all this out loud. Now that he has, he feels a bit self-conscious. He looks at Ambrose hesitantly. "You probably think that's Ooolandish."

Ambrose perks up his ear tufts and smiles. "On the contrary, my friend, on the contrary. Come with me. There's someone I want you to meet."

CHAPTER 7

Banshooo follows Ambrose into a deep forest known locally as Careless Wood. It's called this because it contains no ploootonite nor any of the other substances needed for Ooolandian industry, and thus, no one could care less. As a result, it's been left to itself, producing masses of thick fecundity filled with hidden scurrying things, reminding anyone who might venture into it why early Ooolandians were afraid of the forest.

The two make their way through this old growth to a dilapidated house covered with vines, overgrown and isolated. They push ahead slowly, brushing aside heavy foliage as they go. Reaching the house, they see a dim light seeping through grimy windows. Beside the door, a small, barely legible sign reads: *Morienus, Master of Alchemy.*

Above the sign is a rusting bell. The clapper is covered with spider webs. Banshooo looks at Ambrose, who shrugs. "He doesn't get many visitors." He swipes off the cobwebs and pulls the bell chain. A small, hollow sound echoes around them. They wait but there is no answer. Ambrose pulls the bell again. Still no answer. He pushes on the door and it slides open with a long, slow, creaking sound. Warily, not wanting to be rude, they walk in.

Seemingly unaware of their presence, a figure appears from behind wobbly tables piled high with bottles, tubes, caldrons, and the bubbling flasks of his trade. Ambrose clears his throat and offers a greeting. The figure blinks, bobs his head forward, and squints over a pair of smudged eyeglasses, as if trying to comprehend these unexpected apparitions. His long white hair frames a wrinkled face that suddenly smiles widely.

"Ambrose! Well, long time no see … or hear or anything."

"Morie my man, how are you?"

"Oh you know, same ol', same ol'. Still working on that whole transmutation thing. Can't quite get it down. Can't quite get it … still trying … still might … still …" His voice trails off as he furrows his brow, apparently lost in the intricacies of some possibility known only to him.

Ambrose tries again. "Morie, I'd like you to meet Banshooo. He has an interesting story to tell."

The alchemist comes back to the moment, squinting now at Banshooo. "Ah yes, yes, very nice. Very nice." He removes a pile of books from a threadbare couch, looking about near-sightedly. "I think maybe I've got some sherry around here someplace."

"That's not necessary, really." Ambrose smiles, eyeing a shelf of cob-webby wine glasses sitting next to a bottle marked sulfuric acid. "We just want to talk."

"Talk? With me? How nice. Yes, very nice, very nice."

Ambrose nudges Banshooo. "Go ahead. Morienus knows about these things."

Banshooo looks at this old man whose long white beard appears to have been used for a napkin. He knows alchemy was once a respected field of study, but it's not anymore; something to do with a failure to turn things into gold. This wrinkled dusty old guy appears to be the last of his kind.

Banshooo hesitates but Ambrose nods encouragingly. "Go on, talk to him." And so the monkey tells the alchemist about the sound that washed over him in the meadow. Morie listens intently, his palms together, his fingers against his chin. Now he nods, thoughtfully, then says,

"Ah yes. That could be. A sound wave is a physical force. Vibratory resonance can open up a state of awareness beyond the usual everyday state."

Banshooo nods. "Yes, that's what happened. After the sound came, I was able to see something else, something I can't see just walking around normally."

"And what is that?"

"Well, the first time I saw … dying. So much dying." He lowers his head. "Extinction everywhere."

"And the second time?"

"The second time I saw…" He pauses.

The alchemist raises his bushy eyebrows. "You saw what?"

Banshooo looks at Ambrose, who nods reassuringly. He continues. "I remembered what happened when my mother died."

"Hmmm." Morie speaks slowly, almost to himself. "This could be a case of resonance, of limbic resonance activating a matched filter."

Banshooo frowns. "What does that mean?"

Morie leans back. "Experience creates a vibration that stays within you. That vibration is a kind of tone, reverberating to certain pitches, certain events and beings. It acts almost like an antenna, picking up one kind of transmission but deaf to others. In effect, everyone is an antenna, vibrating with their own individual experiences." He puts his gnarled, veined hands on the arms of the chair and lifts himself up, walking slowly around the room.

"At the same time, sound waves are constantly moving through space—voices, songs, ideas, spoken, preached and whispered—all looking for something that will receive them. When they find a match"—he stops and brings his hands together—"we resonate." He gives a little half-smile. "In effect, beings are like old-fashioned radio receivers, calibrated to pick up one signal and filter out the others, looking for the frequency that will resonate, that will match." He looks at Banshooo. "A sound can remind you of something you know, even if you don't know you know it, enlivening something hidden within you, for good or for ill."

Banshooo's eyes are wide. "It felt like that, like something reverberating in me. Like something alive."

"So what happened in this re—" he pauses, "membering?"

Banshooo looks up at Morie, ready to tell this old man everything.

"My mother was dead. She was cold. I was cold too. Really cold. Then a shadow came, a shadow shaped like her. And it touched her. Then it touched me. And I wasn't cold anymore. I was all right."

The alchemist is squinting at Banshooo, his expression no longer one of patient instructor. "Are you making this up? It wouldn't be nice, you know, to fool with me."

"No. No. I'm not making anything up." He looks at Ambrose, who speaks firmly.

"He's not, Morie. I saw it too. A shadow bent down and touched them both. It was like the deep heart of ... something. I've never seen anything like it before."

Morienus sits back down in his chair with a stunned expression on his face. After several silent moments he speaks quietly. "You saw a *parayama*, the highest essence of a species. The one who comes for the dead." His eyes narrow. "You're not supposed to see that unless..."

"Unless what?"

"Unless you're dead."

"He's not dead," Ambrose says.

"I noticed that. It's very puzzling." The alchemist continues. "The essence of the species appears only to that being who has died. You can't see the *parayama* that comes for another, you can only see the *parayama* that comes for you."

"But I did. I saw it. I was alone, and it protected me. And then there was a soft kind of purring that turned into the most incredible music I've ever heard. No. Not music. Almost music, *like* music, but different ... it was like they were showing me things, *Unseen* things. And I was safe. I was secure and safe."

Ambrose and Morienus look at each other. The owl shrugs a little. "You've got to admit, it's a miracle he survived. Once his mother died, he might as well have had a sign pointed at his head saying Free Lunch."

Morie nods. "Yes, that's true. That's very true."

Ambrose speaks slowly as he considers this improbable possibility. "It must have been your mother's *parayama*. And it stayed to care for you. That's a very rare experience, Banshooo. That doesn't usually happen."

"Never, actually." Morie stares at Banshooo. "It never happens." He shakes his head slowly and says it again. "*Never.*"

There is a long pause as the ramifications of this statement float through the dingy laboratory.

Finally Ambrose speaks. "There's something else." He turns to Banshooo. "Tell him about the fog. Tell him what you saw in the fog."

The monkey sighs a big one. "Okay, I saw an opening in the midst of a swirling foggy haze. I believe it is the gateway to the Unseen World. But when I tried to go toward it, it was like I was moving through layers of something, and then ..."

"Then what?"

"Then I felt like I was about to break apart."

Morie leans back. "Hmmm. That would indicate you might have been approaching another realm."

Ambrose's eyes grow even wider than usual. "Can you do that?"

"I knew a guy who tried."

"Knew?"

"He's no longer with us."

"Oh."

"There's a molecular dispersion problem involved."

"I see."

"Supposedly there are ways to do it without splintering, but it's complicated. It has to do with perception." He looks at Banshooo. "For instance, you saw something that was happening in another space, like space travel but in your mind. If you could access that perception, if you could go into it, so to speak, you might be able to travel there without dematerializing." Morie speaks slowly as he thinks out loud. "Time and space and perception. They're joined, allied in some fundamental way. Exactly how and in what manner ... *that* is the question." He rocks back and forth slowly. "Are light-years a measure of the distance to enlightenment? I wonder ..."

He stares off toward some remote point as the fading afternoon sun flickers through the cobwebs. Banshooo and Ambrose wait for him to continue, but clearly he has lost track of time and space and possibly a number of other things as well.

Suddenly a beaker on the table next to them explodes. Banshooo jumps up. "Whoa! What was that?" Ambrose coughs and ruffles his wings as smoke pours through the room. Morie waves away the billowing puffs and removes the beaker from atop the burner. "Ah. It's my latest experiment." He pours a thick purple liquid from the beaker into a cracked bell jar. It continues to bubble ominously.

"And that would be…?"

Mori's old grey face breaks into a wide grin. "An energy drink! I don't know why I didn't think of it before. It's what everybody wants. More energy!" He stops smiling and looks at his visitors with sudden concern. "That's right, isn't it?"

Ambrose flaps his wings back and forth to clear away the smoke. "Yeah, pretty much." He squints at Morie. "So, what's in it?"

"Guarana, theo-broooma, and several other"—he signs air quotes—"'all-natural' substances." He chuckles, peering through the smoke that continues to pour from the jar. "Plus my secret ingredient."

"Which is?"

"A teeny tiny pinch of crystal meth. That really does the trick." He pours a dollop of the potion into a chipped espresso cup and hands it to Banshooo. "Here, try this. You won't exhale for days."

Banshooo politely declines. Morie turns to Ambrose, who does the same.

"No? Really? Well, you don't know what you're missing." He looks at the cup warily. "Actually, I don't know what you're missing either. I'm a little afraid to try it myself, but it should be quite popular, don't you think?"

Ambrose points his ear tufts and nods in what could be considered an encouraging fashion. Morie puts the cracked jar back down, seemingly unaware that the liquid is slowly oozing out onto the table.

Banshooo stands up and nods toward the old man. "Well, thank you very much for your time. I appreciate your, uh, knowledge and all."

"Wait." Morie looks at him. "You said you think this is about the Unseen, right?"

"I did. I do. I'm sure of it."

The alchemist looks around the laboratory then heads toward a wall of bookshelves on the other side of the room. "I think there's something here that might be ... relevant ..." His voice trails off as he runs a finger across the spines of the many esoteric tomes filling the shelves. He stops and pulls out a very old book, its antique cover bound in leather, the gilt lettering on the spine no longer legible.

"Ah, here it is." He flips through the pages, stops and reads to himself for a few moments. Then he reads aloud.

"... and in the future, it shall come to pass that belief in the Unseen will wane with the tide of time, and those poor unfortunate beings who lose sight of the Unseen will live in ignorance, harming themselves and all those around them until a witness comes to defend that which is beyond the ordinary world, a witness who brings testimony to the Seen, knowledge that holds the hope for redeeming the future and saving the Seen from certain destruction. And he shall be a regular guy."

"Huh." Morie stares at the page. There is a long pause.

Finally, the owl breaks the silence, trying for an upbeat tone. "Well now, that's interesting, isn't it?" Banshooo sits mute, his brow furrowed, his eyes cast down. Ambrose turns to the alchemist. "So. How far into the future are they talking about in that book?"

"Let's see, this was written ..." His eyes narrow as he figures. "Okay, allowing for the shift in the sidereal record and that glitch in the arrow of time ... plus ten, divided by seven, carry the two ..." He counts on his fingers, then he stops and looks up.

"Well I'll be damned. It's right now. The future is right now."

The alchemist comes back across the room and stands in front of Banshooo. He straightens up and squares his shoulders, looking directly into Banshooo's eyes. He suddenly seems to take on an air of authority, as if calling on the strength of alchemy's ancient powers.

"You have been chosen to rekindle the connection with the Unseen world and to save life as we know it. This is your destiny."

The words echo as though they have come from another age, another time. For a moment, the cluttered space of the laboratory seems to vibrate with the prophecy. Ambrose whistles under his breath. Banshooo gulps. Then Morie turns and trips over a pile of discarded Bunsen burners, breaking the spell.

As the clatter dies away, the old man recovers himself, bending down to pick up a piece of the equipment he's just tripped over. He studies it to see if maybe it's still workable.

Ambrose raises his high, feathered brow. "Supposing this is true, how is he to do this exactly?"

Morie comes back to attention. "Ah, yes, well, that's a good question. Heck if I know. These things are very mysterious. You're probably looking at some kind of quest type thing."

"Probably?"

"And another sign. There are usually three signs." He tilts his head. "You've already had two. The first one showed you the future. The second one showed you the past. There'll probably be another."

"Another vision?"

"Not necessarily. The third sign could be anything. It's not spelled out exactly. To tell the truth, the whole three signs thing is more a guideline than a rule." The alchemist shrugs and does that thing with his face that sentient beings do when they're trying to make the best of an iffy proposition. "Divining isn't what you'd call an exact science, Banshooo; it's more an art … an estimate. It's a guess, really. We do the best we can, but there are no guarantees."

Banshooo swallows hard. Morie puts his heavy hand on the monkey's shoulder. "Here's what I know for sure: this is your destiny Banshooo. There is some reason that you have been chosen. We may not know exactly why, but it's not a mistake. At least, I don't think it's a mistake. Of course, if it *is* a mistake, you're in big trouble. But never mind that. You must be brave. Yes, that's the thing. You must be brave. Your destiny will unfold, and you will know what to do when the time comes."

He pats Banshooo's shoulder awkwardly, his bushy eyebrows sticking straight up. "Persevere and follow your heart." He pumps a fist in the air like a coach encouraging a player from the sidelines. "Forward, ever forward!"

Banshooo looks over at the table where the energy drink is still oozing slowly onto the floor. He swipes his paw through the purple goop and brings it up to his mouth. Just as he's about to lick it, Ambrose places a wing on the monkey's arm, shaking his head. He turns to the alchemist. "Thanks for your help, old friend. Great to see you again." He pushes Banshooo forward and steers him toward the door.

"Anytime, Ambrose. Anytime." The alchemist follows them out and stands on the porch, watching the owl guide the frazzled monkey down the overgrown path. Then he goes back inside where he picks up the leather-bound book, thumbing through the pages and stopping near the end. He reads silently to himself, then frowns and flips to the last page. After a moment, he closes the book, slowly shaking his dusty old head.

"Poor kid. He doesn't stand a chance."

CHAPTER 8

"He said it's my destiny."

"Who said?"

"The alchemist."

"And you believe him?" Taboook squints hard at Banshooo, who is trying to pace back and forth in his living room but is having a hard time making a path between the piles of data and the remaining refugees from the storm.

The one-off is sprawled on the couch eating nuts and drinking beer from a bottle, resting up from the unaccustomed exertion required to fix the roof. Sukie perches on the purple ottoman pondering this turn of events. The godwit is nested near the fireplace. Since the tempest she's been a nervous wreck, every bone in her feathered body tensed up and on the alert. Being close to the warm glow of the fire helps her relax. The tree swallow has chosen to stay inside, and the beaver is sleeping between stacks of the Journal of Higher Mathematics. The squirrel and the shrew have headed out to try and rebuild their homes, and the fawn has set off to find others of her kind. The tortoise is making his way to the door. He started six hours ago.

Sukie puffs out a little sigh. "I don't know, Shooo. Molecular deconstruction is pretty dicey. You can wind up inside-out or fragmented beyond recall."

"The alchemist said there are ways to ... hold yourself together."

"What ways?"

"Well, he didn't know exactly, but it has something to do with time and perception and space and ... things like that."

Taboook sniffs loudly. "Jeeez."

Banshooo takes a deep breath. "Look. I don't want to disintegrate any more than the next guy, but something has to be done. What's happening is really not okay."

The swallow pipes up. "You got that right. Try migrating—you see it all. Forests clear cut, mountains sheared off, wetlands drained, toxic holding pools, and towers of flaming methane blow-off all over the place. We saw a flock of mallards get to their usual stopover and the first couple of guys to touch down on the lake croak immediately. Like, *immediately*. The whole lake was poisoned. They had to keep going even though they were exhausted."

Banshooo nods. "The migratories bear witness. There's a catastrophe coming, and Ooolandians aren't doing anything to change that."

Taboook grumbles, "Hey! I recycle."

"This is bigger than recycling, Boook. We need to consider what we're doing in a whole different way. Beings have to change how they think about all of it."

"Beings don't like to change how they think about *any* of it let alone *all* of it, and I don't blame them. You spend a lot of time thinking the way you think. It's hard to change that. It's not comfortable."

Sukie clears her throat. "So. The alchemist said there will be a third sign?"

"He said maybe. *Maybe* there'll be one."

The tortoise has finally reached the door. Banshooo opens it for him, and a sudden whirring zooms in and circles around his head, coming to a stop in front of his face. Every eye in the room is fixed on the dragonfly who's fluttering her terminal appendage so fast it strobes.

"So they gave you the axe, eh?"

Durga's big, all-encompassing eyes always seem to be accusing him of something. "Yes, Durga. Sukie and I have been made irrelevant."

"You and the moon."

"Excuse me?"

"They're building a new blue moon, the next big step in the march of progress. Everyone is very excited about it."

"You're kidding."

"Nope. They're drilling down deep in the Icefields and sideways too."

Sukie frowns. "That's not good. Something like this could create an exponential fractal. It could be a tipping point."

Durga whirrs over to the mouse. "There's more. They're going to erase the clouds."

"*Erase* …?"

"They're going to spray chemicals into the clouds so they disappear. No more storms."

Taboook wrinkles his brow. "Wait, no clouds? That can't be right."

Everyone begins talking at once. Banshooo is thinking. "Synthetic biology, robotic pollinators, an artificial moon." He clears his throat. The group quiets, looking at the monkey who speaks slowly and deliberately. "They're trying to re-engineer the natural world."

The tortoise has turned back into the room. "Who would vote for that?" Everyone looks at the unwieldy reptile, who is the eldest amongst them and is thus deserving of respect, but who has asked a question so painfully clueless no one knows what to say. An awkward silence prevails until Taboook speaks up.

"Sorry to be the one to tell you this, old chap, but Ooolandia isn't a democracy anymore."

"What is it, then?"

"It's a business. Has been for some time now."

The tortoise shakes his wrinkled head and sighs. "I must have missed a memo."

"Or twenty," Taboook whispers under his breath.

"Let's stay on point here, campers." Durga is whirring loudly in the middle of the room. "Banshooo is exactly right. They're trying to re-engineer the whole bleeding thing." She zooms over to the monkey, her eyes glinting like little disco balls of determination. "And they're going to keep doing it, too, unless somebody stops them."

Suddenly a thick piece of the ceiling crashes down onto Banshooo's head, knocking him unconscious. Durga zooms out the door, the godwit flaps and squawks. Taboook jumps off the couch, and Sukie follows. They gather around the monkey who is coming to, blinking and shaking his head.

Taboook lifts Banshooo by the shoulders, and Sukie raises a forepaw in front of his face. "How many digits am I holding up?"

"Uh …"

"Come on, buddy, you can do it. Who am I? Where are we? What's the square root of four-thousand three hundred and seventy-eight?"

Banshooo stands up and looks sideways at Sukie. "You know I'm no good at math."

The mouse smiles. "He's okay."

Taboook looks at the ceiling where several slats are dangling loosely. "Huh. I guess I shoulda used more nails."

Sukie studies the object that bounced off Banshooo's head. "What is this, anyway?" She kneels down and paws through the broken bits of wood. "It must have been hidden up there."

A cedar box the size of a lunch pail lies in pieces on the floor, its hinged lock split open and its lid askew, revealing something wrapped in black velvet. Banshooo picks it up. He unwraps the cloth to find a dark brown leather pouch held together with a strip of knotted string. He unties the string and opens the soft flap. Inside is a thick square of very old vellum, folded upon itself. He lifts it out, unfolding it carefully. As he does, a sound lofts into the room.

They all look up at each other. "Was that a kazooo?"

The square of yellowed paper rests in Banshooo's paws. Black lines scurry across the parchment like ants, finally organizing themselves into a complex network of shapes and forms.

Taboook gulps. "Okay, that's weird."

Sukie gazes at the parchment in wonder. "It's some kind of invisible ink becoming visible as we watch. Some kind of ink that can... move."

The tortoise mumbles, "I'd call that a sign."

They all stare as the fluttering lines settle down and come into focus. A spidery stripe that could be a path or road moves out of a collection of tall shapes—shapes that look almost like trees or tall stalks. It snakes past a pentagram and then through a series of other geometric forms toward what could possibly be something like mountainous terrain. Then the line disappears into a foggy, undefined area that fades off the edge of the parchment—a fog very like the fog in Banshooo's visions.

The monkey lays the document on the tea table and gently straightens the wrinkly surface, studying it closely. He points to the bottom edge. "Look at this. It's Blooo Meadow." He runs his paw along the line that goes up toward the pentagram. "This is Central Services," he continues to trace the route, "and The Grand Oooland, and past that, the foothills leading to the Outermost Range."

Sukie squints hard and purses her lips. "Well, maybe. It *could* be, but ..."

Banshooo interrupts her. "And look, look past that, in the midst of all these foggy smears. There are letters in there." He points to a black mark visible within a swirly area. "Isn't that a T, and here, doesn't that look like an H?"

"Well, kinda ..."

"No, look." He points to what might be an E.

Sukie looks up. "You know, that could spell The Last Gate."

Taboook jumps back. "Whoa. You're not supposed to go to The Last Gate. No one is supposed to go to The Last Gate. It's too far away, it's too dangerous, it's too ... Last."

Sukie eyes Taboook. "That's just an urban legend. There probably isn't any such place."

"I wouldn't be so sure. The edge of everything is somewhere, and we've been well-advised to avoid it."

Banshooo speaks slowly. "The Last Gate could be an entryway. It could be the Threshold to the Unseen."

"Again with the Threshold already."

"The Threshold is the gateway to change, Boook."

"Or it's the gateway to something really bad. Have you ever thought of that? These spooky letters could be spelling 'There Be Dragons.' It could be a warning."

Banshooo looks up at Algernon's portrait. Sukie follows his gaze. "Do you think he hid this map?"

"He must of done."

"Why?"

Taboook rolls his eyes. "Probably because he didn't want anyone to find it and wind up turned inside out and deconstructed."

Banshooo looks at Taboook. "This map came to me because it's my destiny."

"Came to you? *Came* to you? It dropped out of the ceiling and hit you on the head!"

Banshooo doesn't want to argue. "This could be a map to the Unseen World. I'm the one who knows it exists, and I'm the one who believes it will help us understand and change what's happening here. I'm going there."

Sukie steps up. "I'll go with you."

Banshooo shakes his head. "No. You need to stay here and keep working on finding the answer in our data. Just in case I ... don't make it."

Sukie frowns but says nothing. She knows Banshooo is right.

There's a long pause. The godwit widens her eyes. "Don't look at me."

Taboook's shoulders slump as he sighs loudly, staring at Banshooo.

"Okay, let me get this straight. You heard a big wet sound and saw a lot of hidden dying. You heard the sound again, remembered something, tried to go toward it, practically got dissolved, and now you're going to follow a freaky map that draws itself. A map to a place no one ever goes because you don't come back from there."

Banshooo nods. "Yeah."

Taboook strokes his chin thoughtfully. "We'll have to pack plenty of food. No telling how long this will take."

PART III

"The future depends upon the power of our imagination. Conservation requires us to reach beyond what we know to protect that which we can hardly comprehend."

—Andi McDaniel

CHAPTER 9

Spreading across the vast expanse of the Icefields, trucks, plows, trenchers, and gigantic digging machines have created a mass of roads, rigs, platforms, pipelines, drilling sites, and support facilities where armies of Ooolandian workers are executing the New Blue Moon Project. Hundreds of thousands of holes have been drilled. Kerosene and freon have been poured into the holes to prevent them from freezing closed again. Enormous tanks of fuel sit next to massive hangars housing the largest engineering equipment ever built. What was once a pristine landscape is now a colossal industrial enterprise.

On the outskirts of this mammoth undertaking, the last Blue Blare is freezing to death. The disappearance of prey has starved her and without body mass, she has no insulation to shield against the extreme cold and wind. Her coat hangs limply from the ridge of her backbone down across her ribcage, visible through thinning fur. She tries to stand but her legs give way. She rocks her head from side to side, her black eyes desperately scanning the estranged landscape.

She begins to shiver uncontrollably. Soon her entire frame is wracked with convulsions. Her heart pounds. Her head splays back against the ice. Her mouth opens, gasping. After a time, the spasms slow and quiet. She slips sideways and is still.

In the immense space that houses the scanner control site, Joe sits amongst the endless rows, staring at his monitor. He's tired. He didn't sleep much last night. He kept thinking about what happens when you're kicked out of the system, about the whole idea of being alone and without anything. He didn't want to think about that and trying not to think about it had kept him awake all night. He yawns and stretches his arms back. Suddenly, in the corner of his screen, he sees a monkey and a one-off with a giant backpack enter the frame and march determinedly toward the outer woods beyond the Grand Oooland.

"What the …?"

Joe follows the two figures as they make their way through the underbrush, but soon the picture begins to break up into fragments, going fuzzy and finally disappearing altogether. Joe knew there were areas that weren't covered by the cams, places here and there where the sectors didn't overlap coherently, leaving gaps in the surveillance field, gaps that OOOCS didn't want known. There was a big one directly outside the monitor bay where the workers would go to smoke and play Ooono on their break. There was another one along a rear wing in the upper reaches of the main building in the complex. The employees called it the "blind spot." No one was allowed to go there. No one knew why. Was this another such gap? He turns to Jonesy to see if he can recalibrate his monitor to the far sector.

"We don't have access to the far sector. We're not authorized."

Joe mutters, "But Banshooo was heading out there."

Jonesy looks at his colleague with sympathy. "Look, I know you were friends with the guy, but you gotta let it go. It's over for Banshooo and his woo-woo ideas. This is the real world. Get with the program, Joe." He turns back to his monitor and commences recording data on potential drilling sites.

Joe sits staring at the fuzzy screen. He remembers Banshooo telling him how some birds fly along waves of light invisible to everyone else. Were there more things like that? Things the scanners couldn't see? He's beginning to wonder what can be seen and what can't be seen. And who gets to decide which is which.

❈

Banshooo and Taboook have trekked through the Ooolandian foothills. The one-off is carrying a humungous backpack filled with all the things they might need because you never know. The monkey is carrying the leather pouch slung over his shoulder, the map tucked securely inside. They enter a formidable mountain range leading, if the map is to be believed, to The Last Gate. Clambering along pebbly paths winding through rocky outcroppings, they climb and climb and keep on climbing.

Valleys nestle within steep peaks. Snow lies in patches along ancient grey-brown glaciers, and the narrow path is often lost entirely in muddy ponds and puddles fed by ice-cold streams. Taboook and Banshooo slide and grapple their way along, sometimes pushing, sometimes pulling one another upward. The sky is crystal clear, and the sun is hot during the day, but the nights fall into an inky darkness and a shivering cold. Banshooo is glad for the extra socks that Taboook pulls from his backpack.

The only other beings they have seen are a bar-headed goose and an eagle who took one look at them and made a funny sound.

"That guy just snorted at us."

"Eagles don't snort."

"That one did."

Fighting exhaustion, they ascend yet another peak, gingerly creeping along an extremely narrow ledge with barely room to walk single file. They slide ahead, hugging the mountainside, trying to avoid looking down the sheer cliff as bits of gravel and shale scatter from beneath their feet and over the edge to the rocky tors below. Taboook has begun a running monologue on the overrated value of loyalty and friendship, culminating with the observation that, as a one-off, he shouldn't be bound by conventional customs and doesn't know why he ever thought he was.

"The next time we're called upon to save the world, let's not and say we did, okay?"

Banshooo doesn't answer because he's so focused on not falling to his death; he doesn't have enough energy left to form words.

The trail curves along a big granite bulge in the mountainside, and when they've followed it all the way around, they are surprised to see it open onto a wide col, green and grassy and nestled between the flanks of grey and silver rock surrounding them. Grateful to make it to this stretch of inviting ground, they scurry to safety.

A crystalline waterfall cascades down the face of a high escarpment, creating a deep pool in the granite base. Taboook sticks his snout into the pool, slurps a significant portion, then raises up and shakes his head. His long ears flap about, spraying droplets everywhere. He slumps down on the lichen, muttering to himself.

"We need a Plan B. I'm never doing this again without a Plan B. I swear, if it wasn't such a long way back I'd just turn around and go home. Turning around. Going home. That would have been a good Plan B. We've gone too far. Going too far is not good." Leaning against his backpack, he exhales loudly. "Let's stop, okay? Let's just stop now."

Banshooo reaches into the pouch and pulls out the map. He opens it carefully. The sound of the kazooo cuts through the crisp alpine air. He furrows his brow, his tail twitching as he stares at the map. He moves his head back from the parchment then toward it again like he's trying to get a bead on things.

Taboook's eyes narrow. "What?"

Banshooo looks up at him. "It's blinking."

"Let me see."

Banshooo hands him the map. The foothills, the midlands, the peaks and valleys, all these features have been erased. Now, the words THE LAST GATE are written clearly and are, in fact, blinking on and off in stark relief to the cream-colored parchment. A large arrow, also blinking, points toward the foggy swirls that still hover at the periphery.

Taboook eyes widen. "It *is* blinking!"

Banshooo looks around. "It must mean we're there. We've reached The Last Gate."

"What are you talking about?" Taboook stands up and waves his arms in the air. "There's no gate here. No last gate, no first gate, no half-way gate. No gates at all."

A stand of high trees marks the end of the col, tall sentinels with hanging moss drooping from their branches like fuzzy green curtains strung across a stage. Banshooo lifts the nearest flank of moss and tromps into the trees with determination. "It must be in this wood somewhere."

Great northern pines and purple heartwood rise above them. Bramble and groundcover have obliterated any semblance of a trail leaving no obvious way in. Banshooo pushes ahead into a thick undergrowth of scruffy bushes. Taboook follows reluctantly. After a lot of labored shuffling, the monkey finds a slight demarcation in the brush that might once have been a path. He proceeds forthwith. A sad sound spools through the air overhead. Taboook whispers loudly. "Is that somebody crying?"

"It's the wind in the pines."

"Are the pines crying? Cause it sounds like crying."

"Nobody's crying."

As the underbrush gets thicker, Banshooo slows his pace, looking down to negotiate his way through the tangle. Taboook stops altogether, staring past him, pointing toward a clearing just ahead. There, nailed up and down the trunk of what once must have been a spectacular white pine, hangs a parade of signs.

BEWARE!
THIS IS THE LAST GATE!!
TURN AROUND!!!
GO BACK!!!!
DON'T EVEN THINK OF GOING ON!!!!!
YOU WILL DIE HORRIBLY AND BECOME GONE
FOREVER!!!!!!
NOT KIDDING!!!!!!!

Banshooo walks up to the tree, now long dead from the crucifixion perpetrated upon it. He looks closely at the signs. He invites Taboook to come closer.

"Look here, these are silly signs. They've been carelessly made. The paint is peeling off, and they're rotting away. This is some kind of bluff."

"What bluff? Why bluff? Who would bluff?"

"I don't know." Banshooo shakes his head slowly. "But I don't believe this. I don't believe any of it."

Just beyond the signs they see a cord that might once have stretched waist-high across the path but is now so old and torn it droops to the ground and just lies there, like a rotting velvet rope hanging forlornly across the entrance to a club long out of fashion. It creates a kind of line between where they stand and the rest of the wood ahead. Banshooo turns to his friend.

"Come on, Boook. You know what they say: 'Go to the places that scare you.'"

"Who says that?"

"The great teachers say that."

"Why? Why would they say such a thing? The places that scare you scare you because you're *not* supposed to go there. That's the whole idea! Why would *anyone* say that?"

Banshooo looks at the map again. It continues to blink. He folds it up and puts it back in the pouch. He takes a deep breath, grits his teeth, girds his loins, and jumps over the line. Taboook grimaces. They both wait. Nothing happens. Banshooo looks up, then down, then around. He holds his paws in front of his face. He pats his arms, his chest, his head. He's completely, solidly himself.

"I'm all of a piece. No rearrangement of molecules or anything else. And look." He points to the bush next to him. "This is barron groundwillow, totally normal for this terrain. And here," he points to a shrub with dense green leaves and tiny buds, "a nice, healthy *loiseleuria procombens.*" He bends over and scoops up some soil and lets it sift through his paw. He smiles up at Taboook. "*Terra alpinum.* Regular old alpine dirt. I'm telling you, there's nothing unusual here." He walks further on. Taboook follows hesitantly.

"What if there's some kind of monstrous fiend in there?"

"I'd see some evidence—tracks, spoor, rub marks on these tree trunks ..." He goes to the nearest tree and inspects the bark closely.

"Look here. I can count three different species of insects grazing on the yeasts and algae this tree is so generously providing. That's not a sign of danger; that's just normal, healthy food chain activity."

"It's the food chain I'm worried about. Maybe the only thing left are bugs. Maybe everything bigger than a bug has already been eaten."

"I'm telling you, nothing is different on this side of that silly line. It's safe. I can feel it."

"Oh. Well. He can *feel* it." Taboook rolls his eyes yet again. "That changes everything."

"Okay, so I don't know what's going on here, but I can tell you one thing: whatever it is, it's not dangerous."

A sudden shriek pierces the canopy and a gigantic winged creature drops from above. Two fierce, taloned claws spread wide, grabbing Banshooo and Taboook each by the scruff of the neck and dragging them upward. With tremendous strength, the being flaps its wings and flies over the mountaintops, carrying them through the air. They dangle fearfully, like the last little shreds of confidence left in … well, pretty much anything.

☾

In his office, Mabooose scans the bank of monitors lining one entire wall. From this vantage point he can key in to any of the countless OOOCScams surveilling throughout Ooolandia, as well as all OOOCubes transmissions. He has watched, with steely interest, as Banshooo and Taboook climbed through time and the tors, heading toward The Last Gate. Suddenly, to his chagrin, the signal begins to degrade and the image breaks up, flickering in and out of focus until finally fading away altogether. Mabooose pushes a button on his desk, and within seconds, the Colonel, head of OOOCSecurity, is in the room.

"I've lost transmission," Mabooose states coldly.

"It's a problem, sir. We still can't surveil beyond The Last Gate. The Information Domination Command has run into significant challenges on that front. It has something to do with mythology."

"How so?"

"They say there might be other stories there. Maybe even myths."

"But they don't know for sure?"

"They're working on it, sir."

Mabooose leans back and studies this paragon of discipline, a tall, buff member of the sapiens species. An astoundingly clean-shaven control freak in the spotless uniform of a military officer whose substantial energies are dedicated to following orders while seeing to it that others do the same. Mabooose is quite pleased with his decision to make OOOCSecurity the agency that oversees all other functions. He knows that security is best left in the hands of those who are most paranoiacally insecure. He tilts his head back and narrows his eyes. "I hardly need mention last year's disastrous breach."

"No, sir!" The Colonel reddens under this reminder of the worst lapse of his command. A low-level security contractor had secretly copied masses of classified data and released it to the general public, data that revealed the fact that the Information Domination Program gathered all sorts of info on every being in Ooolandia. Whoever they were, wherever they went, they could be tracked, tailed, and targeted. It was the signature achievement of the program, highly classified, top top secret.

The traitor had fled into exile. Heads had rolled. A serious upgrade in employee screening regulations was still underway. Swallowing hard, the Colonel stands even straighter. For him, this had been a terrible humiliation. For Mabooose, the entire event provided an interesting test, measuring just how passive the general population had become. He had been gratified to find that as long as Ooolandians were kept worrying about their jobs and focused on acquiring MORE, they didn't have a lot of time left over to address the issue of personal privacy, mammalian or otherwise.

Mabooose speaks curtly. "Make The Last Gate a higher priority. It must never be revealed that we can't see everything, do you understand? Remember," the one-off intones. "Reality is what we say it is."

The Colonel nods. "Yes, sir. Understood, sir." He hates complexity, and he never ceases to admire how Mabooose can cut to the core of any issue. No hesitation, no ambivalence. He would die for the guy.

After the Colonel leaves, Mabooose gets up from his desk and walks to the window. He sees a shadow fall across the manicured lawn below. He looks up. Flying high above in a perfect V-formation, a band of migratories moves through the sky. Mabooose squints. What are they? Geese? Godwits? God knows what. He turns away in disgust. So much unfathomable difference. Different beliefs, customs, ways of thinking, acting, all uncontrolled, unauthorized, unpredictable. Monoculture will solve that problem. Mono the whole damn culture. One smooth, efficient holding company. It can't come soon enough.

CHAPTER 10

Banshooo and Taboook sail through the air in the grasp of something quite extraordinary. Banshooo is thinking maybe he should listen to Taboook on occasion. Taboook is wishing he'd finished off those last two jelly-filled doughnuts hidden in the backpack while he still had the chance.

Before they can get much deeper in self-reflection, the creature swoops downward and circles over a lush expanse of foliage, finally placing his passengers gently on the ground. They look up to see what had them in its clutches and find themselves face-to-face with a giant hawk-like bird with the head of a dragon and a long reptilian tail. They shrink back in fear. The bird creature cocks its head to one side and blinks. For a moment, the three beings stare at one another, then the creature smiles and says, "Have a nice day." It spreads its magnificent wings and glides effortlessly into the sky.

Banshooo watches in awe. "Did you hear that? He said …"

"Yeah, I heard."

They both stand still for a moment, trying to figure out what just happened. Banshooo wrinkles his brow. Taboook blinks a lot.

"Do you …?"

"I got nothing."

"Huh."

They begin to look about, adjusting themselves to this new cir-
cumstance. They're standing in a meadow sprinkled with an astounding variety of radiant flora, a panorama filled with undulating shafts of sepia-toned sunlight sparkling with narrative promise.
Even the sky seems different, the clouds moving across and around
the sun in spectacular formations, creating extravagant lighting effects morphing into scenes worthy of the landscapes in the olden
art books gathering dust in the few libraries left back in Ooolandia.
Ethereal birdsong wafts about their heads and shimmering silver
and cobalt trees dot the landscape. In front of them, aqua and ivory
and purple blooms blend in a soft watercolor merging. There is so
much dazzling plant life it takes a few moments before they see the
bits of multi-colored light drifting down from a tree overhead, a
tree with leaves that seem to be acting as prisms, breaking the sunlight into shafts of colors, spinning pixels forming and reforming
like thoughts born in the trees and reflected into the world.

Banshooo gathers himself together, pulls the map from the
pouch, and unfolds it eagerly. The kazooo's little notes float out
as if grateful to be released. In the middle of the parchment, a
swirl of bird-shaped ink has appeared, along with an image of lush
vegetation. The words "The Last Gate" have been replaced with
the words "Into The Mythic." The arrow is still aimed toward the
foggy, undefined area falling off the edges.

Banshooo lifts his head and gazes out at the maze of shadowy
colors. He turns around in wonder, his big black eyes shining with
excitement. "We're in The Mythic."

Taboook squints. "Is it supposed to be so bright?" He digs through
the backpack and comes up with a pair of sunglasses. Banshooo
bounces over to a tall, flowering plant, its stems climbing joint by
joint upward into fan-shaped petals of a soft yellow hue, glistening
like gold. He turns to Taboook excitedly. "Do you know what this
is?"

Taboook squints. "A leafy vine with little buds on top?"

"It's *tinospora cordiflora*. In Ooolandian mythology it's called Soma.
Is this great or what?"

"Can you eat it?"

"Well, it is the elixir of the gods, but I don't know how to prepare it. You need to be well-versed. Some of this stuff is dangerous if you don't know what you're doing." He sees Taboook reaching out toward a cluster of purple berries growing at the end of a long grayish-green stalk. "No, wait. Don't touch that. That could kill you. Or give you a rash."

Taboook slumps down, leaning against the prism-leafed tree. Banshooo sits next to his friend, studying the map.

"That whole Last Gate thing must be OOOCS trying to keep anyone from coming into The Mythic. But why? What would be so bad about that?" As he examines the parchment, a big arrow appears pointing straight up with the word "Further" blinking under it.

Taboook sighs. "What's it doing?"

"It's blinking again."

"Is it blinking words?"

"One word."

"What word?"

"*Further.*"

"I don't want to go further. I like it here. It's better than anywhere else we've been so far."

"I think the blinking means that's the next step."

"Maybe it means it's broken."

A shadow falls across the map. "Was that a kazooo?"

They look up to see a bibballooon staring at them curiously. Banshooo hops to his feet. "Wow. They said you guys didn't exist."

The bibballooon* plants his claws in the soil. "Oh we're real. It's Ooolandia that's gone all sur."

"Sur?"

"Sur … real." The animal makes a snorting sound that might be the equivalent of chuckling but how would you know.

---

*The bibballooon is a large four-footed beast with long, thick hair covering most every part of its body. Peeping out of the hair is a wide black nose and two small brown eyes. One of the mythical creatures of ancient Ooolandian tales, the bibballooon bulk, contrary to all appearances, behaves like a big balloon, boosting them aloft. Although they can take a deep breath, curl their long claws down into the sod and stay ground-bound if necessary, they find it easier to just give in and sail upward. They like to float. Up. High.

Banshooo smiles hesitantly. "Ah. Well. Yes. Very funny."

"Not really. We can't breathe there anymore. Used to be the mythic names were uttered in story and song. We were taken seriously." He puffs out his sizable chest. "We were inspiring, encouraging, cautionary. We warned of arrogance, greed, vanity. We were… paid attention to." He drops his huge hairy head. "Now we've been dismythed, turned into cartoons, distractions—distractions from the arrogant, greedy, and vain things that are happening." He raises his head. "And you know what they say."

"What do they say?"

The bibballooon hesitates. "Oh… You don't know?"

"Well, maybe. Could you narrow it down a bit?"

The bibballooon breathes slowly in and out. Moments pass. Then, "Oh, yeah … It's about stories. It's what they say about stories." He takes another deep breath. Taboook and Banshooo wait. Finally, the beast says, "Right. It's how stories create the world we live in."

He pauses again, then continues. "A lady said that. Ursula. Yeah, Ursula. I like her. She's one of Dionysus's daughters. They're a lot of fun." He seems to mull that over. "Haven't seen them around for a while." The beast sighs.

Suddenly a huge white insect swoops over them. Its transparent wings create a draft so strong it ruffles their fur. Taboook and Banshooo duck as the creature flies away, its long antennae wriggling furiously.

"What the heck is that?"

"A moth."

"But it's so big."

"It's a moth of myth. A myth-moth."

Taboook mutters to himself. "Great, a comedian."

The bibballooon makes that snorting sound again. "Don't worry, most of us are pretty easygoing these days. I'd stay away from him though." He nods toward a dense stand of trees. "He can get grumpy."

The ochre light filters through the leaves and onto what appears to be the rear haunches of a large lion until it turns around and they see the mane is framing the head of an eagle and the flank is sporting wings.

Banshooo whispers, "Is that a griffin?"

The bibballooon nods. "Takes all kinds, don't it?" He looks at Taboook for a long time, as if he's about to say something, then decides to change the subject. "So. How'd you guys get here, anyway?"

Taboook grimaces. "We were picked up and dropped here by a gigantic hawkish-dragon thing."

"Ah, that'd be Adar Gwin. He likes to transport beings into The Mythic. He hasn't had much chance lately. Nobody comes anymore." He sighs again.

Banshooo holds the map up in front of the bibballooon and points to the blinking arrow and the word "Further."

"We're following this map to the Threshold, so that's where we need to go. *Further*. Where would that be exactly?"

The bibballooon sticks his hairy head toward the map then leans back. "Well, that would have to be up. There's nowhere further, unless you go up."

Banshooo thinks for a moment. "If I remember the old stories correctly, bibballooons go up, right?"

"We do go up. High."

"Would you take us up?"

"That depends. What's in it for me?"

Banshooo turns to consult with Taboook and sees him heading off along the tree-lined path.

"Where're you going, Boook?"

"I'm just gonna check out this singing."

Banshooo turns to the bibballooon, who shrugs. "It's some kind of siren song. Some hear it, some don't."

Banshooo yells after the disappearing one-off. "But we need to go further."

"I'll be right back."

Taboook follows the song into a lush rose-covered arbor hidden within the entwined tree boughs of this exotic landscape. Delicate pink and white blooms hang on thick vines, their petals bathed in a soft light that seems to emanate from a deep blue pond in the center of the bower. Reclining next to the pond, a languorous female form looks up at Taboook, her long red hair falling across her naked shoulders, and a diaphanous gown draped about her slender body.

"Hello, Taboook." Her voice is hypnotic, and the one-off gazes with rapt adoration as she smiles at him. "Thirsty?" She offers him a bejeweled goblet filled with a nectar so inviting he can almost smell the promise of pleasure wafting up from its golden bowl. Banshooo's warning about poison plants flits across Taboook's mind, but at almost the same moment he realizes that lying with a beautiful nymph in a rose-filled bower while drinking what could be the most wondrous intoxicant in all the many realms was *exactly* how he would choose to die.

He nods his long-eared head. "Yes. Yes, I am."

Meanwhile, Banshooo is negotiating a ride. He rifles through Taboook's backpack. He knows the one-off will have squirreled away some last treat, and he finds it: a bag containing two dough-nuts, supersized and jelly-filled.

"How about these?"

The beast nods his big head. "That'll do it. Hop on board."

"Hold on a sec. Let me get Taboook."

Banshooo hurries down the path and soon finds the bower where, in the midst of a rose-scented array, Taboook lies with his head on the shoulder of the water nymph, his expression one of complete and total contentment.

"Oh, ahem." Banshooo hesitates.

Taboook looks up, his eyes glazed over with contentment. "Hey ole' buddy! Meet Naomi. She's a nymph. She told me about the water." He sticks out his lower lip in a pout and shakes his head sad-ly. "We're really messing it up, Shooo. Naomi had to leave because we were poisoning her."

"I know, Boook."

The nymph rests her jade green eyes on the monkey. "You must be Banshooo."

Banshooo bows awkwardly. "Yes, ma'am, yes I am, and it's nice to meet you, but we must be on our way."

Taboook lifts his head from Naomi's soft shoulder. "Oh no, not 'we,' monkey man. I'm staying right here. You should too." He picks up the goblet. "Try this. It's ambrosia. It's unbelievable! Have some." He looks into the empty vessel. "Oops, all gone." He giggles. "Sorreeee."

The sound of something large clearing its throat causes Banshooo to turn around. The bibballooon is standing at the entrance to the bower.

"So, you coming or not?"

"Hey bib!" Taboook is waving the goblet about, the jewels sparkling in the soft light. "How come you didn't tell us about ambrosia? This stuff is amazing!"

"Yeah, everyone seems to like it." He shrugs. "Myself, I miss Cinnabons."

Banshooo interrupts. "We really need to get going. Come on, Boook. The bibballooon is going to take us further."

"I don't want to go further. You go ahead." Taboook leans back. "I'm staying. You can come get me on the way home."

Banshooo climbs aboard the bibballooon, eager to get started before the beast changes his mind or forgets the arrangement entirely. "Are you sure you want to stay here alone?"

"Who's alone?" Taboook links arms with Naomi, who smiles and ruffles the fur on the top of his head. He chuckles with delight.

The bibballooon is loosening his claws in preparation for takeoff when a fierce, bone-chilling howl rips through the air. They all turn to see a blood-red three-headed dog pawing furiously at the undergrowth. The bibballooon coughs.

"Oh. I forgot to mention Cerberus. He's terminally pissed."

Taboook looks at Naomi, who shrugs her perfectly shaped porcelain shoulders as if to say, *Don't look at me. I just work here.* As the monstrous animal bears down on them, spittle flying from all three fang-filled jaws, Taboook finds a reserve of energy he never knew he had, running furiously and jumping higher than he has in his entire life. With his hind feet pumping through the air and every sinew pulsing forward, he manages to reach Banshooo's outstretched paw. The monkey pulls him on board just as the slathering jaws snap at his big feet. As they fly off, Taboook cries, "Goodbye, Naomi, sweet

Naomi, beautiful Naomi-oh," and they sail up and further upward while the swirling colors of The Mythic grow smaller and smaller and finally disappear altogether. "Goodbyyyyyyyyyyye."

☾

Deep in the bowels of the Central Services complex, the Colonel makes his way through the lifeless corridors of binary displays and microprocessors, past server farms and automated control rooms filled with electrical switches clicking on and off constantly, their changing patterns of charges translating complex data pools into zeros and ones. He has passed through five security checkpoints and eight electronic ID devices to reach the door of Central Services secret Total Information Domination Command. For him, this is a comparatively easy process given that he has recently had encoded subdermal microchips implanted in both of his bulging biceps, bypassing the need to use voice, retinal, or paw print identification. He quite enjoys the sense of superiority he feels as massive steel doors swing open at his approach, and robotic security drones usher him along the corridors of clandestine power. Now he stands inside the nerve center of all OOOCS surveillance operations—the iris of OOOCS's eye.

Unlike the vast observation bay where monitors track and record all movement throughout the realm, this room is comparatively small, discretely lit by the pulsed electromagnetic radiation streaming from the huge screens lining all four walls of the vibrantly humming space. The ghostly light illuminates the faces of the small group of elite technicians and engineers who sit at command desks and maintain ultimate control of the center. Very few of those faces are furry. Here Erect Bipedal Primate Bias reigns.

The supervising technician is explaining to the Colonel.

"Look, we don't know why we lose focus past The Last Gate. At first, we thought it might have something to do with the altitude so we developed customized hardware but that didn't make any difference. Then we tried recalibrating all the recording hardware, thinking it might have something to do with the transmission itself.

Nothing. The fact that the signal breaks up before it goes dead indicates there could be some kind of ground loop interference but none of the standard solutions to that problem made any difference. So we developed what would've been brilliant nonstandard solutions, if they had solved the problem, but they didn't. "We've run through every possible variation on depth of field, aspect ratios, encoders, decoders, and vertical interval switching. We've panned, we've tilted, we've zoomed, we've opened ports on routers and widened bandwidth to the max. We're using the latest remote access software, specialized infrared cameras, hypersensitive motion detectors, and a new state-of-the-art capture program that has to be seen to be believed. Unfortunately, it doesn't appear to be seen or believed past The Last Gate."

One of the engineers whispers to another, "Ya think it could be because it's not real there?" A snickering response draws the Colonel's attention. He looks into the shadowy room. He's never been comfortable with these nerdy types. Their lack of respect for authority makes him furious. His eyes narrow to a squint and he speaks slowly.

"Are you sure of that? Are you *absolutely* sure?" His voice picks up steam. "Because should there *be* something real there, and should it escape our awareness, we would be in danger of losing control of the narrative. And, as even *you* can understand," he pauses and then barks out in clipped syllables, "that would be UNACCEPTABLE."

The room falls silent. He turns to the supervisor.

"Do whatever you have to do but find a way to surveil past The Last Gate. Do you understand?"

The supervisor nods and the Colonel leaves the room. As soon as the door is firmly closed, a collective disdain is expressed.

"Scheez, put a jock in a uniform…"

The supervisor rolls his eyes. "I knew him before he joined up. He was always like that."

CHAPTER 11

The bibballooon sails beyond The Mythic and further still, rising quickly into the upper atmosphere. Astride the beast's broad back, Banshooo and Taboook hold tightly to masses of thick, coarse hair. It's a bumpy ride. Air currents buffet them amongst the clouds and the two hitchhikers slide about nervously, teeth clinched and hearts pounding as the bibballooon dips and dives. Taboook, wondering if it would be better to be eaten by a three-headed dog or splattered all over the bottom of the world, whimpers. "Are we going to die?"

"Chill, dude. We got spheres up here, atmo, tropo, strato. It's a trip. And these days, there's all kinds of crap blowing up from below. Space weather's a lot bumpier than it used to be. Plunging happens."

Taboook gulps so loudly it echoes through the jet stream. The bibballooon snorts his mirthful chuckle. "Relax. I've been sailing around these solar winds since I was a little looonie. You'll be fine."

After a while, the tumult calms down and they rise upward. The beast gathers himself, catches a solar updraft and settles once again into a steady ascent. Taboook's breathing returns to normal. Maybe this won't be so bad. Maybe wherever they wind up next will have ambrosia.

The air is sharp and fresh, and Banshooo's thoughts rise along with this improbable flight. Why has The Last Gate been demonized? Why have the myths been marginalized? What's so taboo about The Mythic?

Suddenly they are thrown forward with a forceful bounce as a solar flare bursts out of the blue and spits a mass of high-energy particles directly in their path. They are caught in a roiling swirl. Banshooo is dizzy. Taboook is about to throw up.

Although mythic, the bibballooon is, like the rest of us, not totally in control of life's myriad ups and downs. Caught in the midst of this geomagnetic storm, he begins to twist wildly. They are tossed about in what may already be outer space. In a wild thrashing, they slam into the side of a totally unexpected mountain.

Some risky moments ensue as Taboook and Banshooo come close to being crushed under a bibballooon bouncing across arctic tundra, spinning and rolling over until finally landing upright in a cloud of lichen dust. The beast steadies himself in the bibballooon way, curling his long claws into the ground. He shakes his thickly maned head and looks around.

"Huh. Must be One More Mountain." He snorts. "I've heard of it." He makes the chuckling sound. "Always one more than you counted on, right?"

Taboook and Banshooo stand up on shaky legs, taking stock of their bruises and their surroundings. They appear to be on a wide granite shelf set in the rock face of an enormous peak. Lichen provides some cushion between huge moss-covered boulders where patches of icy snow collect in shadowy crannies. The entire scene exudes a frosty coldness making everything blue and shivery, adding a kind of miasma, a sheen, like water but not wet. Like mist but not exactly. Like a smoky haze. Sort of.

The bibballooon begins to loosen his claws one by one in preparation for sailing away. "Well, guys, good luck with whatever the heck it is you're trying to do."

"Wait, where are you going?"

"You said 'Further.' This is as further as I go."

Taboook squeaks. "But you can't just leave us here."

The bibballooon turns his head and looks at the one-off. "Show me the doughnuts."

Taboook frowns, then his eyes widen slowly as the implication of this request dawns on him. He dives into his backpack, poking around frantically, tossing aside hats, socks, an alarm clock, and a bottle of aspirin. He comes up empty, glaring at Banshooo who says, "Look. If we hadn't left The Mythic, you'd have been eaten by Cerberus. You have to admit, that would've been bad."

"But I was saving those. They were ..." he stammers, "... for emergencies."

"It *was* an emergency."

The bibballooon retracts his last big claw. "I'll leave you to sort this out." He floats sideways for a moment then catches a down-draft. "Stay crazy, fellas." He is lost from sight as the word "crazy" echoes in the wind blowing around the mountainous crest. The two adventurers stand alone in the cold, spooky landscape.

Taboook groans. "Great. Now what?"

Banshooo tries to sound upbeat. "Don't worry; we'll be okay. The map will tell us what to do next." He pulls the document from its pouch. The kazooo shivers in the frosty air as he carefully un-folds it across his lap. Again, the map has changed. Now all words have faded away completely, and a wispy rendering of an extremely high mountain sits alone in the center of the parchment. The arrow isn't blinking, which disappoints the monkey. The blinking had im-parted a certain confidence, something more than ink on the page, something certain enough to draw attention to itself. But now the arrow just sits there looking a bit sketchy, hesitant even.

Banshooo bites his lip. Taboook, still focused on the loss of the two jelly-filled big ones, gathers up the strewn socks and hats, grum-bling. "You should've asked me first."

"You were in a bower, sampling ambrosia."

Taboook growls and reaches back into his pack. He pulls out two blankets and two pillows. He kicks one of each toward Banshooo and, still grumbling, pulls on the socks, stuffs his long ears into a wool cap, and slides down on the lichen, yawning widely. Muttering something about the altitude, he wraps himself in the blanket, curls up in a ball, and is immediately asleep, snoring loudly, his breath puffing out into the cold air.

Banshooo's energy for pushing ahead is also fairly low at this point. He dons the extra socks and cap and sits on his pillow, staring at the map. After a few minutes, the arrow begins to move, scooting first toward one side of the parchment and then to the other, as if looking for something. It stops in a corner of the map and sits up, its shaft arching back, its triangular head bobbing up and forward in a sniffing motion, like a dog trying to find a lost scent. After a few seconds, it moves to the opposite corner, sniffing some more. Finally the arrow moves to the middle of the parchment and just lies down, as if it too has decided to take a nap.

Banshooo stares ahead. What he sees is not inviting. Shadowy cliffs surround them. Some distance away there is a stand of skeletal trees with black bark and bare limbs hanging down toward the ground like long fingers frozen in place. He doesn't recognize these trees. He's never seen anything like them before, even in Algernon's books. There are no birds, no scrambling chippies. Aside from the low whistling of wind through the crags, it's eerily quiet.

He shivers deep inside himself, feeling his confidence slip away. He'd gone this far because the map had told him to, but it's become clear that what he does makes a difference in what it shows him. Maybe the map is waiting for him now. But to do what? The Last Gate and The Mythic were not The Threshold. They must have been passages to whatever waits within the swirling fog. But instead of getting through the fog, he keeps bumping into more questions. Is he closer to The Threshold, or is he on the wrong track? Is One More Mountain a dead end? What should he do next? What's up with the arrow?

A wave of exhaustion moves through his furry body like the tide pulling sand out to sea. He gathers the blanket close around his shoulders and leans back on the pillow. Maybe he'll take a little nap as well, just for a minute.

☾

Back in Ooolandia, drilling in the Icefields has proceeded on schedule in spite of harsh weather, unpredictable ice floes, and an increasing number of earthquakes, which have become a test of nerves for the workers who joke amongst themselves about hazardous duty pay.

Then, one day, the massive drills bump up against a subglacial layer of huge monocrystals, each one miles in diameter and as hard as diamonds. Equipment breaks down and progress comes to a halt.

Challenged by this unexpected development, the industrial brain trust goes into hyperdrive. Biochem labs are put on overtime, developing ever more corrosive solutions. One after another of these formulas are tested and applied in every conceivable manner in an effort to dissolve the dense crystals. Nothing works.

Secret meetings are held. A sense of emergency pervades the upper echelon of Ooolandian policy makers. The blue moon project has been widely promoted as the ultimate demonstration of Ooolandian power, a testimony to the capacity of the authorities to develop, control, and utilize whatever is needed for the good of MORE. Should the project fail, it would be a public relations nightmare, undermining confidence in Central Services and perhaps even giving rise to a reconsideration of erstwhile marginalized ideas and proposals about other ways to live and work together.

Mabooose sits in his dimly lit office contemplating the problem. He can't let this obstacle create a toehold for malcontents, providing credibility to those who believe that unlimited development might not be the only way forward.

His eyes are narrow slits, his breathing slow, his body eerily still, as if every ounce of energy in his entire being has been routed to his brain. He remains like this for some time, then, abruptly, he stands up and walks over to a large filing cabinet. He pulls out the top drawer and thumbs through the folders until he finds a surveillance dossier marked "Careless Wood." He opens it and reads the security report on the last living alchemist in Ooolandia. The shadow of a smile crosses his colorless face.

Shortly thereafter, a fracturing fluid is shipped to the Icefields. No one knows what's in it; the mixture is classified as a "proprietarial formula," the contents of which cannot be revealed by law, in order to guard trade secrets. These powerful secrets are injected deep beneath the arctic surface. Soon the drilling resumes, expanding the cracks and crevices already snaking under the melting tundra. The mysterious solution oozes everywhere, flowing like time-lapse photography and spreading toward the deepest bulwarks of crystals, speeding the dissolution of the adamantine depths and further undermining the equilibrium of the subglacial ice sheet. The engine of progress resumes its consuming momentum.

❨

Banshooo wakes with a start. How long has he been asleep? He sits up, runs his paws over his face, and looks around. Taboook is still snoring away. The granite outcropping surrounding them looms over the ledge on which they have landed. A wind has come up, clearing the air of the hazy sheen. It's cold. He wraps the blanket around his shoulders and reaches for the map. It's not there. He stands up, moving quickly, intently, poring over the ground, moving in wider and wider circles with a growing apprehension as he comes up empty-handed.

"Taboook! Wake up!"

"What! What's happening?" The one-off sits up in alarm. "Is it that fiendish dog? Are we being chewed apart? What!"

"It's the map. It's gone. Help me find it."

Taboook slumps forward, muttering: "Ah yes, of course, the bloody map. No food, no drink, no clue where we are, so let's find the map that led us here." He unfolds himself and stands up in no great hurry, rubbing his eyes and stretching slowly.

Banshooo bends over, his nose close to the frosty ground. He examines the lichen closely. Paw prints are faint but visible. They lead into the grove of skeletal trees where a gutted path winds through the ropey vegetation. Banshooo steps onto the path with Taboook tagging along behind, being careful to avoid the spidery limbs that reach out to trip them. As they edge their way along, the low growth becomes thicker and higher, making it hard to see ahead. They push on around a sharp bend and are suddenly back in the open, face-to-face with a massive slab of rock rising high above them. Not ten feet from their noses, an arching cavern sits like a dark shadow beckoning them into the core of the mountain itself. Banshooo walks up to the cavern opening and peers in. After a moment, he steps into the inky hole and disappears.

Taboook groans. "Again with the jumping into scary spaces."

He tiptoes forward, peering around nervously. "You realize we're making the same fatal mistake made by every wide-eyed co-ed creeping down the dark, dank basement stairs of every horror movie ever made." Banshooo ignores him.

Surprisingly, as they move deeper into the cave, they are gradually able to see better. A faint, watery light emanates from the stone walls, as if the rock itself was illuminated from within. Shadows flicker as they tiptoe through the winding cavern until, rounding a turn, they come into a large open space and stop dead in their tracks. What had been surprising is now really incredibly surprising.

They are staring at a fully decorated living room with a couch, a love seat, area rugs, throw pillows, and several fashionable accents scattered about stylishly. Leaning up against the cave wall is a gigantic whisk broom casting *Sorcerer's Apprentice* type shadows over the whole scene. Taboook hurries over to the wall. "Wow. Look at this whisk broom. It's a regular work of art."

In the middle of this unexpected space, a nineteenth century Italian Renaissance table holds a collection of *objet d'art* including a ceramic duck, an elegant gold-flecked rococo picture frame holding a paint-by-numbers version of Manet's *Déjeuner sur l'herbe*, and an antique Underwoood typewriter. In the center of the table, the map sits on top of a stack of books. Banshooo picks it up. A loud voice echoes off the cave walls.

"What do you think you're doing?!"

The two trespassers turn in fear to see what must be a very large being to own such a big voice, but are surprised to be looking at a rather ordinary-sized raccoon standing upright on his back feet, holding a bright red megaphone in front of his mouth.

"Oh man, it's just a raccoon."

The raccoon lowers the megaphone and gives Taboook a fierce look.

"I mean, uh…" Taboook's voice trails off.

Banshooo sets his jaw. "You stole my map."

The raccoon looks Banshooo up and down. "Whadaya mean *your* map? It's *my* map."

"No, it's *my* map. It fell on my head and led us here, and now I need it in order to continue my journey to The Threshold. So, if you don't mind, I'll be taking it back and we'll be on our way."

The raccoon narrows his eyes and steps in front of Banshooo. "Yahright. You expect me to believe that story?"

Taboook walks over to the raccoon. "Hey, Rocky, my man." He sticks out his paw, grinning broadly. "I know it sounds crazy, but my friend's telling the truth."

The raccoon ignores the paw. "Don't call me Rocky. My name is Raoul, thank you very much, and I want the map back." He steps closer to Banshooo, blocking his path.

Taboook continues, "Okay, Raoul. I know it *sounds* whacko, but it's the truth. We've followed the map all the way from Ooolandia and it ain't been no vaycay. We don't even want to be here, so if you'll just step aside, we'll be on our way and everyone will be happy."

"I won't be happy. I won't have the map."

Banshooo frowns. "You can't just take something that belongs to someone else. That's stealing."

"I don't steal. I take what's forgotten, discarded, or lost. Stuff no one else wants."

"What, like a dumpster diver?" asks Taboook.

Raoul crinkles his nose. "Such an inelegant phrase, don't you think?"

"Descriptive though, you gotta admit…"

"I hate to interrupt this edifying exchange," Banshooo moves toward the cave opening, "but I'm taking my map back. It wasn't forgotten. I did not discard it, nor did I lose it. It was *appropriated* from me…" he pauses, raising his upper lip to reveal a sharp incisor, "and now I'm taking it back."

The raccoon steps closer. "You can't take it."

"Oh yeah? Who's gonna stop me?"

"I am."

"Oh yeah? Well you may not have noticed, but there are two of us and only one of you."

"Oh yeah? Well you may not have noticed, but I know karate." Raoul hops straight up in the air and lands in a compact crouch, swiping his long, clawed paws through space with a menacing growl. The monkey and the raccoon circle one another threateningly.

Taboook watches this unexpected turn of events. He sees the determination in Banshooo's eyes, a determination born of anger and frustration, the kind of anger and frustration that often leads to bad judgment resulting in bruising, bleeding, and property damage and the like. This is not the moment for Banshooo to unleash his inner kung fu fighter. Everyone knows raccoons are crazy fierce—even vicious—when their territory has been challenged. He assesses the odds. They're not good. Taboook steps between them and smiles a big insincere smile.

"Well lookie here now. Isn't it amazing how quickly a simple little disagreement can turn into a situation where wounding might occur?" He appeals to Raoul. "I'm sure there's some other way to settle this." Raoul looks at Banshooo. Banshooo looks back at Raoul. A long minute passes, and then Raoul lowers his arms, shrugs, and says, "Eh, take the damned thing. It's all fuzzy anyhow." He squints at the monkey. "What's the deal with that, anyway? I mean, what good is a fuzzy map?"

Taboook, relieved to find they're working with a reasonable raccoon, raises his long arms, paws outward, in a gesture of empathy. "What an astute question, my friend." He turns to Banshooo. "Care to answer that, buddy?"

"No." Banshooo begins to stalk out of the cave.

---

*The mushroooms to which Raoul has referred are renowned as a substance guaranteed to produce, in the average mind, the ability to weave a story so insanely unlikely (and yet, to the weaver, apparently true) they have earned the nickname "fantasy fruit." These moldy, fleshy fungi are said to rival the potions that inspired Coleridge's *Kubla Khan and the Rubiyat of Omar Khayyam.* Unfortunately, after the initial euphoria wears off, your legs don't work so well and you find fur on your teeth. It's a mixed trip.

The raccoon calls after him. "What is this Threshold of which you speak?"

Banshooo stops and turns around. "What's it to you?"

"I'm always interested in the possibility of possibility. If it's real, that is. The question here remains: is your story true, or have you two been eating Ooolandian mushroooms?"*

"We haven't been eating *anything*!" whines Taboook. "You didn't happen to steal any food recently by any chance?"

"I told you, I don't *steal* things."

"Okay." Taboook tries again. "Do you have any cookies you found somewhere or were given as a gift or were invited to take home after a party? Peanuts? Walnuts? Doughnuts? Any kind of nuts? Anything at all?"

The raccoon smiles graciously. "As it happens, I was just about to have tea. Care to join me?"

Nodding enthusiastically, Taboook follows this enigmatic being around a curved corner in the cave wall where a small apse holds a lovely table, prepared and waiting. A white linen cloth is arrayed with plates of fruit, cheese, and a variety of sandwiches. A classic leaded-glass lamp provides a warm glow. The one-off sits down eagerly looking over the delicacies with anticipation.

"Dynamite spread. You really know how to set a table."

"Thank you." The raccoon bows graciously.

Banshooo holds back. "What's all this? Who were you expecting?"

"No one really, but it's always good to be prepared. You never know who might drop in." Banshooo hesitates. Raoul puts his arm around the monkey's shoulders and ushers him toward a chair. "Relax, fella. Eat a little something. You'll feel better." He pours the tea and passes around a plate of appetizing finger sandwiches, then slips the cozy over the teapot and smiles.

"So. Who the heck are you guys, and what's the deal with the map?"

Between bites, Taboook regales Raoul with the details of their journey to date, finishing with the fact of finding themselves on One More Mountain, alone and uncertain about the next step.

Raoul nods approvingly. "Well, it takes a lot to go this far further."

Banshooo fixes his gaze on the raccoon. "So how did *you* get here?

"Past The Last Gate and through The Mythic, like you."

"Why?"

"Let's just say, I needed to be away for a while."

"You're hiding out."

"I wouldn't put it that way, exactly. It's more like an extended vacation, a break, a rest from the rigors of choice and requirement… and the expectations of others."

"I totally get that, dude." Taboook reaches for a bowl of nuts.

The raccoon smiles. "Yes. This mountain does provide sanctuary for those who don't exactly…how should I say this? Fit in?" He lifts the flowered translucent pot gently from its porcelain base. "More tea?"

"Don't mind if I do." Raoul refills his cup with a fine Keemooon blend, rich and fruity with just a hint of floral aftertaste. He offers Banshooo a buttered scone. "So, you think you can get to this Threshold?"

Banshooo answers evenly. "It's my destiny."

"Okay. Let's say that's true. What are you going to do when you get there?"

"Bring back proof of the Unseen so Ooolandians can learn to work with it, not against it."

"And how are you going to do that exactly?"

A long pause ensues. Finally Banshooo mumbles, "Some … how."

"Ah-huh. I see I'm looking at one of the last living optimists. Good for you. So, what's your next step?"

"It'll depend on the map." Banshooo takes the folded map in both paws and slowly opens it. It toots forth in the echoing cave.

The raccoon frowns. "Is that a kazooo?"

Banshooo says wearily, "It does that when I open it."

"Huh. Personalized. Nice." He moves the tea pot and a fruit bowl out of the way to make room as Banshooo spreads the map on the table, anchoring one end with a candlestick and the other with a lovely little vase of violets. They peer at the document spread before them. It's fuzzy at first, but soon the fuzziness dissolves and spidery lines begin to run across the surface, quickly coalescing into a picture of the cave, the whisk broom, and the blurred, foggy areas Banshooo has come to realize represent the next step.

Raoul's eyes widen. "Now that's something you don't see every day."

Taboook nods, his mouth full. "Itsh fa shur weurd."

The arrow has awakened and is blinking again, aiming straight into the fog.

Raoul tilts his head toward Banshooo. "Is this how it worked before?"

"Yeah. It would be foggy until I reached a certain point, then it would change, showing where I'd been. Then the arrow would point to the next place to go."

"What would make it change?"

"It seems to depend on me making a decision."

Raoul strokes his whiskers thoughtfully. "You know, this could have something to do with time. I mean, consider: At any given moment there are many possibilities, but once we act, all that could have happened coalesces into what did happen. What if this is as much about time as it is about space?"

"What good is *that*?" Taboook is genuinely puzzled.

Raoul raises what would be eyebrows if he had any. "Well, my friend, they say there's a point where time and space become the same thing. They're very cozy that way."

Banshooo stares at the map with new eyes. He sees a flicker of light flashing across the parchment for just a split second. He shifts his head and it happens again. He slips down to the edge of the table so he's looking across its surface from eye level. Raoul does the same. They both see it—a kind of geometric pattern, like a funnel or a tornado or a very large egg timer. It's almost transparent, like a watermark hidden inside the paper, and it quivers. Then it disappears entirely. Raoul sits back in his chair.

"That could be a wormhole."

Taboook wrinkles his face. "Worms?"

"Worm or rabbit, depends on if you're reading science or *Alice*."

Banshooo is thinking out loud. "I remember Sukie mentioning something called superluminal travel. I wonder…" He ponders.

Raoul assumes a self-satisfied smile. "There you go. The possibility of possibility." He reaches for the tea pot. "Another cuppa?"

Suddenly the lovely little vase of violets shakes violently as a thunderous boom reverberates through the cave.

"What's that?" Taboook cries.

"Could be an earthquake. We've been having some tremblers lately. Or it could be giant footfalls."

Another great boom rattles the table.

"Yeah, it's footfalls."

Taboook's eyes are very wide. "Who has feet that big?"

"It's probably Yomolakhi. His feet are huge."

The booms continue.

"Friend of yours?" Banshooo hurriedly rolls up the map to protect it from the jostling jam pots and sloshing tea.

"Sort of..." Raoul steadies a plate of cheese that threatens to bounce off the table. "We're in the middle of what you might call a...negotiation."

"You stole something from him, didn't you?"

"I didn't steal it. He claims it's his, but he has no proof. And besides, I really need a whisk broom."

"Is he another felon?"

"Hey! Innocent until proven, okay?" Raoul ducks under the table.

"He sounds pretty mad." Taboook joins the raccoon.

"Don't worry. He can't get in here. He's too big."

"Too *big*?"

A plate falls to the cave floor with a loud crash. Taboook frowns. "You mean he just stands out there and stomps around?"

"Yeah."

"How long does he do this?"

Raoul sighs. "He seems to have unlimited foot-stomping reserves. I tried sleeping through it once. You really can't."

"This is a regular thing then?" Banshooo catches the sugar bowl just as it bounces off the edge of the table.

"Pretty much. He comes and stomps around until I go out there and we discuss the matter. He's not the brightest star in the sky, and to date I've been successful in convincing him of my rightful ownership, but after a while the logic of the thing seems to fade in his mind and he comes back again.

"Is he dangerous?"

"Well," Raoul peeks out from under the table, checking for clattering silverware, "anything that big does command respect."

Taboook goes to the heart of the matter. "What does he eat?"

"There's the problem, really. I know he likes monkey meat, and I have heard him refer to the strange delicacies of his childhood. It sounded like he was talking about one-offs..."

Taboook and Banshooo have already grabbed their things.

"Hate to rush, but we've got a date with destiny, and we're pretty late already. It's been very nice and we do appreciate the hospitality." Banshooo shakes the raccoon's paw furiously.

"Yes, absolutely smashing hospitality."

As another piece of fine china crashes to the floor, Taboook says, "Okay, where's the back door?"

"There isn't one."

"No?" Taboook is incredulous. "What kind of burrowing animal doesn't have a back way out?"

"First of all, I'm not a burrower, I'm a borrower. Secondly, I can always talk my way out."

Banshooo holds the map close to his chest. "Well you better start talking before everything in here is smashed to smithereens."

"Right. I'll distract him and you two sneak out while he's not looking. Ready?"

Taboook glances over at the table. "Do you think we could take one or two of these *petit fours* along for the ride?"

As Taboook is stuffing food into his backpack, Raoul whispers to Banshooo.

"Don't assume, my friend. Assumption is presumption."

Banshooo's response is lost as another massive footfall echoes off the walls of the cave, but we can assume from the look on his face he's not presuming. Anything.

CHAPTER 12

An animal covered in bright, brassy, carrot-colored fur stands at the opening of Raoul's cave. He's as big as an elephant, and his thick legs seem to rise out of the ground like tree trunks. The raccoon stands in front of the beast and looks up. Way up.

"Hey, Yomo, how's it going? Stomping like crazy I see. Have you ever thought of going for a world record? I'll bet you could make it into the Many Realms Book of Bests. In fact, I'll bet there isn't anyone anywhere who could even come close."

Yomolakhi, having been raised to be polite, is waiting for Raoul to stop talking. Prattling on continuously, Raoul moves sideways, positioning himself so that the beast has to turn away from the cave entrance in order to relate. Behind them, Banshooo and Taboook slink out, sliding flat along the slippery side of the cave. Yomolakhi is now engaged in trying to explain to Raoul that, although the last time they spoke he did agree to give up the whisk broom, he's had a chance to reconsider the original argument and he'd like to point out that, in fact, the broom was in his possession when the raccoon whisked it away, so to speak, and he's recently learned that possession is nine parts of the law, or nine-tenths of the law, or has nine times more of something he can't really remember what but he wants the broom back.

Underneath the cover of this intense discussion, the two escapees make their way to a little rise above the cave opening. There they hide behind some thick brush until Raoul has Yomolakhi completely occupied with trying to follow the complicated logic behind the case for his own rightful possession of the broom. Seeing the animal shake his head and lean in toward Raoul, they quickly hightail it further up the rise. Safely distanced, they stop on a ledge in the rock face and ponder their situation as they survey the scene.

Below and to their left the arcane argument continues in front of the cave opening. Below and to their right lies flat terrain covered with thick, undulating scrub brush. Above them the rocky ridge crests upward, offering only occasional toe and paw holds in an otherwise sheer face. Nothing looks particularly inviting. Slowly, carefully, Banshooo pulls out the map. In spite of all recent evidence, he is still hoping it will give them some clue as to what to do next. He prepares to unroll the parchment.

Little does he know he is standing within a hollow in the cliff face that is shaped so as to create a perfect parabolic amplifier. This type of rock, and the manner in which it is curved, has produced a rare acoustical anomaly—a configuration that will greatly magnify any sound made while standing in front of it. Many eons of weather, glacial formation, and erosion have colluded to create this extraordinary spot—a spot that has been sitting here waiting for something to amplify for a long, long time. A spot that is, you might even say, *eager* to amplify something, anything, if only it would happen directly in front of it. And sure enough, this is exactly the spot where Banshooo opens the map, and the sound of the kazooo blasts through One More Mountain like the winner of the annual Ooolandian Air Guitar Contest.

Wildly amplified ear-splitting noise crashes down the rise, bouncing off granite and stone, echoing against the cliff face and reverberating all the way to the cave entrance. In shocked surprise, Yomolakhi turns around to see a monkey and a one-off quite unexpectedly within eating distance.

Raoul covers his ears and shakes his head in dismay. Yomolakhi cocks his head to one side as he weighs staying and arguing versus taking advantage of this unusual gastronomic opportunity: monkey meat *and* one of those exotic treats created by an innovative gene pool. No contest really. He lumbers toward the hapless pair in gigantic strides.

Banshooo and Taboook throw themselves down from the ledge and onto firmer ground, turning to run as fast as they can. The beast gives chase, leaping forward with unexpected dexterity. Careening wildly, predator and prey crash across the scruffy terrain.

Banshooo yells, "Serpentine, Taboook. Serpentine!" and the two of them swerve in a zigzag pattern. Yomolakhi zigs and zags right behind them. Laboring under his heavy backpack, Taboook begins to lose ground. Banshooo screams. "Drop the pack! Drop the pack!" Taboook tries to undo the Velcro straps but it's too late. Banshooo watches in horror as Yomolakhi catches Taboook and snatches him up by the pack. Coming to a complete stop, the beast lifts the squealing one-off into the air. Taboook wiggles furiously but the straps of the backpack hold firm. Yomolakhi raises him up to mouth level as if he were chopped liver writhing on a cracker. Taboook twists sideways just as a mouthful of sharp teeth snap shut. Yomolakhi gets half an ear. Taboook screams.

In desperation, Banshooo drops the map and leaps forward, grasping onto an orange leg. He pounds his fist against the hairy appendage as hard as he can. Yomolakhi growls and shakes his leg trying to dislodge the monkey. Banshooo loses his grip, sliding onto Yomolakhi's big flat foot. He opens his mouth wide and sinks his incisors deep into the beast's fat toe. Yomolakhi howls in pain dropping Taboook who falls to the ground, his backpack in shreds all around him. Banshooo jumps free of the foot and grabs up the map. The two of them run blindly ahead, trying to put some distance between themselves and certain death. In their haste they fail to notice they are running directly toward a great crevasse, lurking like a deep blue knife blade hidden in the tundra. Banshooo sees it first and stops suddenly. Taboook bangs into him. Banshooo points to the crevasse. Taboook gasps.

A shadow falls over them. They look up to see a very angry creature as intent on vengeance as he is on meat. The monkey and the one-off quiver. They're about to be eaten or shattered in free fall. Either way, it's the end of their journey.

Suddenly, the map in Banshooo's paw sounds loudly, a kazooo imitating a bugle announcing the arrival of the cavalry. As if coming alive, it pulls on his arm, stretching him ahead like a leashed terrier taking the scent. Banshooo stumbles forward. The map is heading straight for the crevasse, accelerating determinedly. Taboook yells, "Let go!" but Banshooo doesn't let go. The map gathers speed, pulling him to the abyss. Taboook runs after him.

"Stop, Banshooo. Stop!"

"We have to follow the map!"

"I don't want to do that anymore!"

Yomolakhi stares in confusion as the map hovers over the lip of the chasm, suspending Banshooo in thin air. Taboook grabs his friend's feet in a last desperate attempt to stop him going over the edge.

The orange beast stands in stunned silence as both his appetizer and entrée plummet into the crevasse and disappear from sight.

❨

Banshooo and Taboook are falling in a void. There is no ice, no rocks, no ledges, no edges of any kind, nothing to grasp. The sides of the crevasse have disappeared and the two of them careen headlong through empty space. They can't see much, and all they can hear is their own screaming as they twist and turn, flailing away, expecting, at any moment, to smash against the bottom of this terrible abyss, expecting, at any moment, to be crushed to bits as they plunge toward ground so horribly hard and terribly unfriendly to their furry bodies that they will, almost certainly, be completely annihilated in a most grotesque and awful manner, smooshed into something not entirely unlike creamed corn. They are expecting, as we all expect, when falling, to land badly.

But they don't land, badly or any other way. They just keep falling. Soon they're falling slower and slower still and, after a while, they get used to it. They stop flailing about. They find themselves in a sort of swooping situation, sailing through the air as if they were skateboarding. They look at each other and, after they've stopped screaming, they consider the circumstances.

"Well. *This* is kinda weird."

They both think a bit and then Banshooo says, "There's no point in screaming and flailing about, is there? I mean, even if we're going to be smashed to bits against some awful bottom, it's not going to do any good to scream and flail, is it?"

"Not really. No."

"So."

"So."

A long pause ensues while they sail further downward.

Taboook frowns. "Do you think we're going to be smashed to bits against some awful bottom?"

"That would be what would usually happen, but this doesn't seem that usual."

"Ya think?"

Banshooo is considering the possibilities. Taboook is nursing his ear.

"He got a piece of me."

"It's better than being eaten whole."

"Speaking of eating…"

"Don't start."

"But…"

"Don't!"

They try to adjust themselves as conditions warrant. Taboook spreads his big front paws out alongside his body to see if he can affect his rate of descent, experimenting with various glide paths and pitch angles. It doesn't seem to make much difference. Banshooo has decided to let his body just float along and use this moment to try and sort through a multitude of feelings, most of them more meta than physical. What has happened? What does floating through space mean, really, in terms of his destiny? How could he have thought he had a destiny to begin with? Could he be more helpless? He hopes not.

He looks at the map, still secure in his paw. It is now, like the two of them, dirty, bruised and covered with scratches. Bits of torn

parchment fringe out along its frayed edges. He opens it carefully. The kazooo wheezes as if, having given its all, it has little left.
Taboook, who had closed his eyes for a moment just to see what it
felt like, opens them and growls.

"No."

"It saved us, Boook. It pulled us into this, uh, whatever it is, to
show us how to escape."

"To what end, Shooo? We're falling. What's the point?"

Even though he, too, is feeling a great deal of doubt, Banshooo is
defensive, as beings often are when they're unsure. "There must be
some...some reason or...something."

He looks at the map. The foggy bits are gone, and the disappearing ink has disappeared. The only image left is the transparent
watermark that seemed to hide in the parchment when they were
in Raoul's cave. Now that delicate cone shape flickers like a mirror
catching the sun, growing weaker and weaker until, with one last
fluttering blink, it dies.

For a second, Banshooo thinks he hears whispering. But it's not.
It's the swooshing sound like surf, the sound that came that night
he couldn't sleep, the night he first heard the sobbing and saw all
the death. The sound that came again, when he remembered his
mother. It's the same but very faint, an echo of his own memory,
trying to remind him of what he knows.

Taboook is rubbing what's left of his ear which is quite sore.

"I'd like to go on record as being against the whole trick map
concept altogether. It's unreliable. The purpose of a map is to provide reliability. I mean, when do you use a map? You use it when
you're lost. You open it up with the assumption that it's going to
help you get from one place to another place."

Banshooo's ears prick up. "...*the assumption...*" *Assumption is presumption.* That's what Raoul said. And what did he say about the
map? *"Maybe it's as much about time as it is about space."* *Time and space
... And what did the alchemist say? "Time and space and perception."*
Morie's voice mixes with Raoul's ... *The edge of our perception. Time
and space ... a place where they become the same thing. Another kind of space
travel ... in your mind ...*

While Taboook continues to voice his displeasure, Banshooo thinks as hard as he has ever thought—time, space, perception, assumptions—there's something there, something that would help if he could think it through far enough. Think! Think! Think!

But the harder he tries, the more knotted it all gets. He's so tired and bruised and confused. He can't figure it out. His brain crashes. Exhausted, he closes his eyes. He gives up. The faint sound of a dying kazooo floats through his empty, surrendered mind.

Then, in the vast space of no thinking, a new possibility whispers gently, revealing itself like a soft breeze: *Maybe it's not a map to a place. Maybe it's a map to a moment. Maybe The Threshold is the next **moment***.

And with this thought, Banshooo stops falling. Taboook, however, continues to float downward, talking, gesturing, complaining about the map as if they were still falling together. But Banshooo is stopped stock still. He watches as Taboook becomes smaller and smaller and finally disappears from sight.

PART IV

"*We all accept the existence of things that we cannot see but could see if we moved to a different vantage point or merely waited, like watching for ships to come over the horizon. Objects beyond the cosmic horizon have a similar status. The observable universe grows by a light-year every year as light from farther away has time to reach us. An infinity lies out there, waiting to be seen.*"

—Max Tegmark

CHAPTER 13

Banshooo is suspended in space. Everything is quiet and soft, a shimmering transparent surround with no fixed point. Layers of perception unfold before him, slowly opening into a crystalline realm of radiant energy.

He is standing within a vast and glistening network of interconnected threads, incredibly delicate and fine like a spider web covered with dew, and in the places where the threads meet there is a flawless jewel, each jewel shining like dew drops in the morning sun. And every jewel contains the reflection of all the others, and in each of those reflections are the further reflections of all the other reflections and it goes on and on, pulsing within itself, each reflection opening outward, forming and transforming in a never-ending dance of diversity.

Now he hears what sounds like music, a rich melodious chorus of complex resonance, pulsing and throbbing in intricate harmonies, verging on the edge of being visible. It's the sweet sound, the one hidden within his memory, and it is surrounding him.

He looks for Taboook, but he isn't there. Instead, Banshooo begins seeing something else. It appears the sound *is* becoming visible. There are waves, circles, spirals, stars, shapes of all kinds in dazzling colors. These shapes seem to be emitting light, some like mirrors, some like prisms, others dense and deep, velvety rich in texture, all moving about in a purposeful manner, almost as if they are *working*.

A long, rectangular form appears in front of him. It speaks.

"You should close your mouth, Banshooo. Something could fly in there and you never know where it might have been."

Banshooo manages to get his mouth shut, but he still can't put a sentence together. "Who? Where? Whaaa?"

The rectangle speaks again. "Searching for a handle on the moment?"

Banshooo nods. The rectangle continues. "I'll wait until you find your words. Don't worry. No rush."

Banshooo realizes he is being reassured by a rectangle and that this, in and of itself, would not be reassuring in any other situation he's ever been in, but this isn't like any other situation he's ever been in and, oddly enough, he finds himself reassured. He tries his voice.

"Where's Taboook?"

"Not here."

"Where is here?"

"Ah, good. Are you paying attention?"

Banshooo takes a deep breath, straightens his shoulders, and tries to be especially alert in spite of his profound confusion. He begins to see something he hadn't seen at first. The rectangle has eyes, big brown eyes, and they are looking at him with a kind of kindness.

"You, Banshooo, have crossed The Threshold of Perception and entered into the Unseen World, the realm in which the Unseen reside."

Banshooo melts in amazement. "I made it then."

"You did."

"And I didn't dematerialize."

"Not yet."

"What?"

"It's complicated, but you need to know this. It was your aware-ness, your realization that allowed you to move through the realms without breaking apart. When your consciousness expands, you can go beyond where you were before, without breaking into pieces."

The shape has become more detailed, more defined. What at first seemed to be an angular outline of light and texture now has the appearance of a being, with a head, a body, and a full, grey beard. And two extraordinary eyes, deep and mesmerizing. Suddenly it dawns on Banshooo. "You cared for me when my mother died."

"We did."

"I saw her *parayama*."

"Yes. Your mother begged her *parayama* to protect you. She was such a nudnik, your mom."

"What?"

"Nah, just kidding. Actually, she was quite exceptional, a truly wonderful monkey. And we answered her plea."

"Everyone says that never happens."

"Everyone says a lot of things."

"Why did you save me?"

"Because it is written that a regular guy will 'give witness to that which is beyond the ordinary world.'"

"You read that book?"

"We wrote that book."

"About me?!"

"Well, it's about *some* regular guy. You're the one who made it here."

"You mean it's not my destiny?"

"It is now."

"I'm so confused."

The being steps away, gesturing for Banshooo to follow. They move through a smoky underbrush that swirls around them like the fog in his map. Soon, they stop walking, the fog clears, and Banshooo sees they've come to a fork in a road.

"I assume you're familiar with the concept of the Crossroads?"

"Like 'Two roads diverging in a yellow wood…'?"

The being smiles. "How nice. You're into the art of the verse."

"Not really. We had to learn it in school."

"Ah yes, the poetry anthology. Well, the road less taken is the least of it." He waves his hand and the divided pathway becomes three, five, seven, eleven, thirteen, seventeen, nineteen, twenty-three, twenty-nine paths and more until the whole thing turns into a swarm of wriggling branches multiplying out into space.

"In the Seen world there appear to be two roads. At the Unseen level…well, see for yourself." The dazzling array continues to proliferate into ever more branches, creating such a thick twisting swarm that Banshooo becomes dizzy watching it.

"What *is* that?"

"It's The Reality of Possibility. All the possible next steps you might take, combined with everything that isn't you, unfolding into a possible future." He looks at Banshooo with unconcealed satisfaction, "Pretty cool, huh?"

"It's making me nauseous."

"Yeah, well, Ooolandians aren't equipped to see this. Every once in a while some poor creature is born with the capacity, but they usually end up going crazy. It's kinda sad, really."

The being waves his hand and the overwhelming Reality of Possibility disappears and they are standing again at a simple crossroads.

"You see, Banshooo, everywhere in the cosmos there are retrievable expressions of data that are perceived by different beings in different ways. These perceptions influence reality as decisions are made and steps taken that, in their turn, move things along to other decisions and other steps taken and soon—voila! A prediction comes true." He pauses, his eyes twinkle. "Don't you love that expression? 'Comes true.' A thing is possible and then the thing '*comes true.*' There's a big clue about the whole time/space continuum hidden in that little phrase." He chuckles to himself. "Language is amazing, don't you think?"

"What are you talking about?"

The being arches his eyebrows and nods. "Good one."

"What?"

"Okaay… Nevermind. Let's start again. It was you who saw past the subterfuge of The Last Gate. You braved your fear and made it into The Mythic, and you persevered all the way to One More Mountain. Then, you took the big leap, following the map to what looked like certain doom." He tilts his head. "If you hadn't taken those steps, the prophecy would just be another empty bit of literary pretense. It was *you* who made the prophecy come true."

"But what if I'd decided not to go past The Last Gate or ride the myth to the mountain? What if I hadn't held on to the map? What if...?"

"What if doesn't really count once the 'what' has been 'iffed.' And, in this case, the what has been completely iffed. It's what *you* did that fulfilled the ancient prophecy and made it come true. Now, as they say on the Directory at the Galleria, **You Are Here.**"

The being intones, "You will never untangle the circumstances that have brought you to this moment. Arise, embrace your destiny."

Banshooo looks at him. "I'm...I'm already risen."

"Oh. Right. Still, it's an important point, don't you think?"

Banshooo's forehead is wrinkled in thought. "Is this like 'go with the flow?'"

"No. Don't go with the flow. Life is *not* a fountain. It's an interaction between you and all that is not you. It's a mutual thing. A fifty-fifty deal. You gotta do your part."

Banshooo stares at this apparition who is now completely revealed as a radiant being, wearing a simple white robe, leaning against a banyan tree that has appeared next to him. His arms are crossed, and one foot is tilted over the other at the ankle implying an ageless vitality despite his gray beard.

"Who *are* you?"

"I have many names, Banshooo, but you can call me Sid."

"*Sid?*"

"You remembered us, not in the everyday part of your memory, but in the heart part. In your deepest knowing, you were drawn to try and find us again."

"I dreamed of this."

"Yes, you did."

"Am I in a dream now?"

"No, my friend, you are not in a dream. You are in the Unseen realm, where the quanta dwell, at the very edge of knowledge, the very edge of possibility. It's the opposite of a dream. It's a place so real it makes everything else happen."

Sid raises his hand, opening his fingers to reveal an astounding panorama.

"Ooolandia is filled with worlds and beings, matter and energy, seen and unseen, born and dying. We are the elements and influences that create your realm. We generate warm breezes whispering across soft sands, lush groves of mango trees and frangipani, vast deserts, monumental forests, deep lakes and massive mountain ranges. We manifest rain, hail, snow, volcanoes, red hot lava, hurricanes, earthquakes, great storms spawning funnels of such force they devastate everything in their path."

Sid raises his hand again, and Banshooo sees a vision of terrifying power, tentacles lashing out, eyes bulging, teeth ripping with a fierce, devouring intensity.

"We have appeared as dragons and monsters, dralas and kami, angels and fairies, babbling water sprites and tree spirits dancing in the limbs and leaves. These days you see us as waves and particles, electrons, photons, quarks, muons, neutrinos, and patterns of elements and influences." Sid lowers his hand. The scene settles once again into a humming equilibrium. "We are there, whatever name you give us, whatever you perceive or don't perceive. No matter what. No anti-matter what. We are there."

"Where?"

"Everywhere. We create. We preserve. We destroy. We exist on many levels, in many realms, in many forms. The closer we are to you, the more we look like you, or like something you would recognize as a 'being' or a 'thing.' The farther away we are, the more abstract we become. In some realms we are so abstract, so un-Ooolandian, we aren't even one thing or another yet. We are a mist of possibilities."

"Like the crossroads?"

"Yes. And I'm here to tell you, Banshooo, there are some pretty dreadful possibilities looming at that junction. Ooolandians are bulldozing their way through something so intricate, so complex, they don't even realize how badly they're messing up. Unfortunately, they have not yet grasped the incredibly subtle interwoven, interacting, multi-level, multi-dimensional, multi-multitudenous-ness of the whole thing. It's breathtakingly vast and so mind-bogglingly complicated that they simply can't conceive of its entirety." He sighs deeply. "In a case of unprecedented arrogance, you guys are screwing with stuff you don't even know is there."

❨

In the Grand Oooland, rumors of drought and earthquakes in outlying regions are quickly obscured by the constant promotion of next-best-things paraded 24/7 on chatterdee networks throughout the realm. The most recent topic of gripping collective interest is the annual Topless Flaming Bicycle Jousting Tournament, which has become a highlight of the tourist summer season.

In the Surveillance Bay, Joe sits in front of his assigned screen along with Jonesy and all the other Central Services surveillance employees. The scanners are scanning, the mesmers are humming, and the Total Information Domination program is engaged to the max. Joe tries to focus, but he can't stop thinking about Banshooo disappearing from the monitors and about the whole idea of what can and cannot be seen. He can't shake the feeling that something else is going on, something that can't be recorded by the OOOCScams, something that won't be solved by building bigger and bigger and more and more.

The day drags on until, finally, Joe's shift ends. Heading home, he comes to the usual fork in the road, the same one he comes to every day. One road leads to his place; the other leads to Blooo Meadow. Today he decides to take the road to the Meadow. Maybe Banshooo has come back from beyond the boundaries and can tell him what's going on. But Banshooo isn't back. Instead, Joe finds Sukie neck-deep in data, her forehead scrunched up, her expression perplexed.

"Hey Sukie."

She looks up. "Hey Joe."

"Whatcha doing?"

"Oh, uh, just going over some notes, some lists, and uh, you know, things."

Joe looks around and whistles. "Wow, you guys brought all your stuff here."

Sukie winces. There's no hiding the fact that she's sitting in the midst of a vast pile of material. "You won't report us, will you?"

"No. No, I wouldn't do that. They were just going to shred it all anyway."

Sukie's shoulders relax. She likes Joe but still, he's a Central Services employee and you never know how that's going to go.

"I was just thinking Banshooo might be here."

"No, he's not here." The mouse goes back to her notes. "A map fell on him. Taboook went too."

Joe isn't sure how to respond to this statement. He decides to stick with the question he came with. "Well, I was just wondering because I saw them on the scanner and then I couldn't see them anymore. They went past The Last Gate. Why would they do that?"

Sukie continues making notes. "They're looking for The Threshold to the Unseen."

Joe nods slowly. "Oh." He wonders if he should know what that means. He decides to change the subject.

"So, what are you working on?"

Sukie continues calculating. "I'm double-checking the anemone anomaly."

"I love anemones."

"Well they may not be around for long."

"Why not?"

"They're drying up. There's ash in the bracts cluster, inside the corolla."

Joe just stares at her.

Sukie looks up. "You know where anemones have a velvety round thing in the middle and all around the round thing are those little spokes circling it like a kind of ruff?"

"Yeah."

"Well, the ruff around the round thing stopped happening. It just disappeared. Then the velvety thing turned to ash. It was kind of awful. Beautiful living anemones, opening up with ash all over their faces."

"I didn't know that."

"Yeah, well, the chatterdees don't publicize this stuff. But it matters."

"I know it's supposed to be, you know, all connected or something."

"Not just supposed to be, Joe. Everything actually interacts with everything else."

"Ecosystems, right? I've heard of that."

"Yeah. Aquifers drying up, anemones drying up. Totally connected." She furrows her brow. "We need to find the pattern that reveals that connection."

"Pattern?"

Sukie looks at Joe. She considers trying to explain case classification, vector spaces, integer values, and statistical algorithms. How can she describe the joy of seeing a well-designed graphic representation of data that reveals a heretofore invisible pattern of predictability? Time passes.

Joe tries again. "A pattern?"

"Here's the thing, Joe. Patterns are everywhere but they're often hard to see because they're either incredibly subtle and deep inside of something, or incredibly big and way outside of everything else. That's why our data is important. It can reveal patterns."

Joe nods. "And the pattern shows what's happening?"

"The proof is in the pattern, Joe. If these anomalies are connected all the way up to the blue moon, then it's really big. And if it's really big, it includes us, and if it includes us, then we're in danger of disappearing too."

"Shouldn't Central Services know about this?"

"They do. The managers said it sounded like we were talking about unforeseen consequences and since there was no longer a Department of Unforeseen Consequences, there was nowhere to send our reports. They gave them back to us." Sukie points to a stack of folders with CATCH-22⅔ stamped across them in big red type. "It was frustrating."

Joe is nodding. He's beginning to realize that the authorities don't pay attention to anything they don't want to pay attention to. He's also beginning to realize that this makes them untrustworthy. But he *had* trusted them, pretty much. Without even thinking about it, in some basic way, he had trusted them.

Sukie sighs. "The answer is deep in the data, really, really deep. What I need is a bank of mesmers like they have in the calculating division."

"Would that do it?"

"Yeah, it would. I mean, that's what the mesmers are good at. Taking lots of stuff and organizing it. Banshooo tried to get them to put our data in the machines. They didn't think it was worth it, but I'm telling you, the connection is hidden in our reports, deep within the little details we have noted from careful watching over time."

Joe tilts his head. "You know, they stored a bunch of brand new mesmers in the old Department of Nature office. Cutting edge, latest model, fast as anything."

"They did?"

"They're very shiny and they've got goggles."

"What do you mean, goggles?"

"This guy called them maximal mesmers. He kept talking about quantum this and quantum that. I can't remember exactly what he said but they can upload your brain. It's something about the mind's eye. I don't know. It's pretty complicated."

"Quantum mesmers …" Sukie's eyes are shining. "Maybe they could upload multi-dimensionally, and download too." Suddenly her whiskers droop. "But we can't even get into the place. We've been sacked."

Joe is thinking some more. He doesn't want to be sacked himself but, on the other hand, the mesmers are just sitting there, all new and fancy, in the D of N office. In a way, it's almost as if they were meant to be used for D of N business. If you didn't know the D of N had been eliminated, you'd assume that's what they were there for.

"Look, Sukie, we could sneak into Central Services. I could help you. We could load all this information into the mesmers and see if they could find the pattern."

"You'd do that?"

Joe takes a deep breath. "Yeah." He nods. "Yeah. I'll do it. I mean, I believe in you guys. You've paid attention, and I think it's true, what you're saying. And now, with this whole new blue moon project, it's kinda scary."

Sukie nods. "It could be the tipping point."

"What could tip? Where?"

"Everything, Joe, everywhere. It would be bad."

Joe pauses, then says, "Maybe if they see the connection, they'll realize they shouldn't go ahead."

"That would be the idea, but geez." Sukie looks around at the piles and piles of data. "How are we gonna get all this stuff back there without them knowing? It took four of us all night to move it here."

Joe nods. "Yeah, we need help, but then we'd have to tell others and you know how hard it is to keep anything secret around there and how quick you can get, you know, kicked out into the cold."

Sukie tilts her head. "Wait. What was that you said about goggles and the mind's eye?"

Joe tries to remember what the mesmer technician was telling him. "He said you put the goggles on and they connect you to the mesmers and what you've seen shows up on the screen. "

Sukie begins rocking slowly, back and forth. "Ambrose. Ambrose could do it."

Joe looks at the mouse. "Who's Ambrose?"

☾

Soon, the owl is standing in the middle of Banshooo's living room looking at everything and recording, in his mind's eye, the complete inventory of Banshooo's reports, Algernon's archive, and Sukie's lists. The sound of his humming drifts through the house.

While Ambrose hums, Sukie sits at the desk, working feverishly to design a pattern-recognition program to feed into the mesmers, a program that will reveal the unseen truth that she believes lies deep within their data. She calculates, thinks, mumbles to herself, and makes notes feverishly. "Maybe I should go with primes … or not … a quantum algorithm could reveal the patterns behind the numbers. That might be better … or…" She fills one sheet of paper after another.

Joe makes tea and listens to the sound of a mumbling mouse mingled with a humming owl. The two sounds meld into a kind of soft music and he is inexplicably filled with a new feeling, a feeling quite different from his usual state of vague anxiety. He stands in the doorway between the kitchen and the living room, holding clean cups and wondering what this feeling might be. It was a bit like exhaling, or would be if he had been holding his breath, which he hadn't been, he didn't think.

Slowly he realizes that he's feeling good, as if he's part of something, part of something for real not just in a slogan. Something small. Smaller than Central Services, smaller than the grand projects, smaller than the vast surveillance of everything everywhere. Small and important.

"Dammit!" Sukie suddenly grabs her notes, wads them into a ball, and throws them across the room. She sets her jaw. "This isn't going to work."

Joe starts out of his reverie. He walks to the desk and shyly sets a fresh cup of hot tea in front of Sukie. "Not going so good, huh?"

The mouse holds her big head in her paws and mutters, "It's too much."

Joe frowns. "But you're so smart."

Sukie raises her head and sighs. "Here's the deal, Joe. First the program has to detect the connections hidden in all our data. I think I can do that. It's a fractal kind of thing. And if these maximal mesmers are what I think they are, they'll be capable of detailing information at such a precise level, that connection will show up. It'll arise out of the total universe of information and it will be extant. But if we want others to see it, it'll have to be translated into something more than numbers, something beings can relate to, something that communicates in a way that can be *felt* … something that is clearly, unequivocally true and is seen to be true on its face." She shakes her head. "That's the hard part."

Joe thinks for a minute. "It's that Seen and Unseen thing, isn't it?

The mouse sighs again. "Pretty much, yeah."

"But, Sukie, you can't let the anemones turn to ash. Anemones are beautiful. Especially the magenta ones. I just love that color.

The pink ones are nice, and everybody likes the red ones but for me it's...

"Ma-gen-ta." Sukie interrupts.

"Yeah."

"Magenta!" Sukie's little ears perk up. "No spectral frequency and yet ... it is perceived!" She looks at Joe. "Perception that transcends the spectrum." She grabs a stack of clean paper. "That could be it! Joe, you're a genius." Her eyes are gleaming, her whiskers aquiver. She begins calculating furiously while muttering non-stop to herself again.

Joe steps back. "Okay, well ... good. Glad I could help." He turns to check on the owl. Ambrose is blinking a lot and the humming seems to be winding down. Joe moves closer and the owl takes a deep breath. He lifts his majestic head and looks at the humanoid.

"I've got it all. Let's do this thing."

Joe, Sukie, and a very puffy owl walk out of the little house and head toward the wooded area where the entrance to the clandestine tunnel lies conveniently available. Sukie chuckles. "Funny, eh? We dug this tunnel to load all the data out and now we're going to use it to take it all back in. Only this time it's in the owl. How cool is that?"

Ambrose totters a bit and mumbles, "Yeah, great."

They continue toward the wood but Joe has stopped, standing still, biting his lip and squinting. The mouse turns around.

"What's the matter, Joe?"

Joe swallows hard. "I'm not so good in small spaces."

"Define 'not so good.'"

"Can't do it. Can't even think about doing it. Can't even breathe right now cause I'm thinking about doing it." He starts rocking back and forth making whimpering sounds as he tries to block out the thought of the tunnel.

"Okay, okay, calm down. No tunnel. We'll figure out something else." Sukie frowns. "Problem is, there's surveillance everywhere around the whole Central Services complex."

Joe, extremely relieved at not having to go into the tunnel, perks up. "Well, yes and no."

"What do you mean?"

"There are gaps in the surveillance, pan-field dead zones where the cameras lose resolution and become basically blind. I know where they are. Follow me."

They head off. Ambrose tries to fly but can't even begin to get off the ground. "I'm too full of all I've seen." He laughs shakily, almost falling as they walk down the path. Sukie moves to steady the owl. "Are you going to be all right?"

"Just a little dizzy. I'll be okay. Let's go."

Joe leads Sukie and the wobbling owl along the outskirts of the Central Services complex. They creep through the gaps in the OOOCScam system until they are shuffling sideways along the outside wall of the monitor bay itself. Inside the building, Joe leaves the two of them huddling in a janitor's closet while he ambles in what he hopes is a nonchalant manner to the main switching station housing the internal surveillance system. There he disables the camera that monitors the hall leading to the D of N office.

The three of them proceed through the corridor. When they get to the office, they slide inside and close the door. Sukie flicks the wall switch and the overhead lights come on to reveal the gleaming new Maximal Mesmers sitting in a row on a long stainless-steel table.

Joe sees the poster covering the tunnel egress on the far wall. "*Shawshank?*"

"It's the mole's favorite film."

"That figures."

Sukie peers closely at the mesmers then steps over to what may or may not be a quantum printer. The large box has clear plastic sides and red seams. Sitting in the center of the box is a gray tray. She looks at Joe.

"For this to work, these mesmers have to translate quanta to materiality. I'm not sure that can even be done, let alone that I've created an algorithm to do it."

Joe shapes his face into what he hopes looks like fierce determination.

"We've got to try." He boots up the mesmers. A whining whirr fills the room. Sukie taps in keystroke after keystroke. After many long minutes she turns to face the owl. "Okay, now you."

On the table are a pair of immense goggles with big, round lenses sporting many facets, all popped out like the compound eyes of an insect, like a fly's eyes. She picks them up. They feel like a medieval device created to cause some grim manner of distress or outright mutilation. She looks at Ambrose. "You sure you're up for this?" The owl fluffs his feathers. "Strap them on me and be quick about it. We don't know how long this will take, and we don't want to be here when everyone comes back to work in the morning."

Joe keeps watch at the door while Sukie takes the black leather straps and wraps them around the owl's head, buckling them securely. She checks the cables running from the goggles to the mesmers. All appears secure. "Okay, go." She hits the key marked *Engage*.

Ambrose focuses in and instantly the screens begin to generate pictures, one after another. Sukie watches as figures from Banshooo's notebooks move faster and faster across the monitors until the screens become a flashing blur. She turns back to Ambrose, whose entire being is concentrated on transferring his vision into the digital realm.

"I think it's working, Ambrose. I think it is." The owl shudders and fluffs himself once more, leaning even further in toward the mesmers.

Sukie tries to activate the printer. It makes a loud whirring sound then clicks off. She tries again, turning the switch back on. The printer just sits there. She turns the switch off then on again. Nothing. She traces the cables and checks all the inputs. Everything is connected. Her eyes narrow as she growls at the machine.

"Manifest, you hunk of junk. Manifest!" She hauls off and pounds on the device as hard as she can.

Joe whispers, "Jeez, Sukie, take it easy. You'll wake the guard."

Abruptly, the printer comes to life with a grinding, gurgling sound. Ambrose continues to empty his mind's eye into the mesmers. After what seems like a long time, something begins to form itself in the drawer of the tray. It flashes and blinks, like a light reflected in a mirror. Sukie bites her lip, holding her breath. As the light in the tray grows brighter, the printer begins to cough and shimmy, trembling and shaking, making a whining sound that grows louder and louder until the whole thing suddenly erupts in a huge puff of smoke. It coughs once more and finally sputters to a dead stop, red plastic dripping onto the table.

Waving her paws to clear the smoke, Sukie looks into the tray. Nestled there is what appears to be a small pane of silvery transparent glass the size of a standard sheet of paper and about an eighth of an inch thick. She slides open the drawer and lifts the Image out of the tray. It's warm to the touch. She swallows hard, her eyes wide.

Joe calls over. "What does it look like?" Sukie stares, speechless, her eyes fill with tears. Joe crosses the room and peers over her shoulder. He gasps.

Before him is a vast and glistening network of interconnected threads, incredibly delicate and fine like a spider web covered with dew. Where the threads meet there is a flawless jewel, each jewel shining like a dewdrop in the morning sun. And every jewel contains the reflection of all the others, and in each of those reflections are the further reflections of all the other reflections, and it goes on and on, pulsing within itself, each reflection opening outward, forming and transforming in a never-ending dance of diversity.

He stares in wonder at the divinity of the existing world, a world that holds within its infinite complexity his own heart's breath.

He looks at Sukie. "Is this…?"

She nods. Neither of them can speak. They're almost afraid to move, as if the tiny room is too small to hold this knowledge.

Suddenly, they smell something burning. They turn to Ambrose and see a curl of smoke rising up from the owl's head.

"Holy moly! Get those things off of him!"

They pull Ambrose back from in front of the mesmer screen and Joe unbuckles the goggles. There is a ring of singed feathers around each eye. Sukie takes the owl's head in her paws. "Ambrose, Ambrose, are you all right?"

The owl seems stunned. He shakes his head and fluffs his wings. His voice is hoarse. "Did it work?"

"Yes, Ambrose, yes it worked! Look at this! Look! Isn't it breathtaking?"

The owl blinks. He shakes his head and blinks some more. Joe and Sukie look at each other and then back at the owl, who stares into the space in front of them.

"I can't see anything, Sukie. I think I'm blind."

In the sudden quiet, the whine of the mesmers fills the little room.

CHAPTER 14

"Do you see that?"

In the transparent shimmer of the Unseen realm, Sid points Banshooo to a pale arc of light glowing above them. The arc glistens with millions of green, blue, and yellow bioluminescent beings blinking in a rhythmical wave, in and out, like breath.

"Essence rises up from that which is not yet manifest, takes form and interacts with what is, enabling the ever-evolving change that existence demands. We see this principle in action when the fireflies fly up and the stars spill down. During such interactions, a profound connection is made."

Banshooo murmurs, "The Dipper Dance."

"I'll be the first to admit it was a good excuse for a party, but that wasn't what it was for. That moment signaled the shift in geospace that helped propel the season through its appointed course." He looks at the monkey.

"Do you have any idea what it takes to shift a season? How complicated it is? How much really hard work it takes to get from winter to spring? From spring to summer?"

Banshooo shakes his head, his eyes wide.

"Trust me, it's a big freakin' deal. The fireflies played a significant part in that operation but now, while you guys are drinking and dancing with your big artificial lights, the cosmos is looking for the rhythm of the live blinking—for the breath of light and dark. Problem is, you got the light on day and night. It's breathless. Everything speeds up, gets manic. There's no respite, no rhythm. It wreaks havoc in the supply chain. This, in turn, causes an additional build-up of breakdowns, each rupture merging into the next like a vortex of vanishing, lost firefly by lost firefly until one day ... bang, you got a bigger problem.

"Is that what happened to the blue moon?"

"That was part of it." Sid waves his hand and conjures Ooolandia's moons, the blue one, the crimson one, and the apricot-colored one. All three hang so close, it's as though Banshooo could touch them.

"The blue moon rules water. It moves vast oceans and ancient rivers pulsing through canyons of rock. It pools secret lagoons and nurtures aquifers great and small. And it plays a key role in that extremely clever process wherein water evaporates into the air, cools, condenses, becomes precip and falls back down to the Ooolandian earth. It's a wonderfully efficient cycle and the blue moon helps to regulate it, maintaining the rhythms of ebb and flow. But as the air got fouler and the water got dirtier, it became harder and harder to ebb and to flow. Frankly, the moon just got exhausted. It couldn't see any point in coming out of eclipse."

While Banshooo is trying to wrap his brain around the idea of a lunar existential crisis, Sid continues. "That blue moonlight soothed, cooled, and nurtured the Icefields where great masses of frozen water have gathered over unimaginable lengths of time to create mammoth glaciers. Without it, the weakened glaciers are losing their ability to hang together. As the ice melts and the water heats up, it's changing everything ... and not in a good way."

"What about the other two moons?"

"The crimson moon warms things up. This you don't want when you're already melting."

"And the apricot-colored moon?"

"Actually, that one is just for apricots."

"What?"

"It does a couple of other things but mainly, yes, it feeds those delicate blossoms and bathes the juicy, golden plums in midnight sweetness." He smacks his lips. "*Prunus armeniaca.* Yum."

"Apricots have their own moon?"

"They deserve it. But I digress... Where was I?"

"Uh...the crimson moon is all alone?"

"Right, and this isn't good because the crimson moon feeds the arctic volcanoes."

"Volcanoes in the ice?"

Sid's face grows solemn, his kind eyes darken.

"Listen up, kid, this is important. Within the secret depths of the Great Ooolandian Icefields lies a core of molten fire. This bastion of liquid magma surrounds and protects a subsonic pulse reverberating through the ether. This pulse is nothing less than the beating heart of energy made manifest. It is so essential to maintaining the balance of the physical world. It's guarded in a unique alliance of fire and ice, a Concord that has insured its safety for millions of years. But now, Ooolandians are about to break through this citadel. And when they do..." Sid's hands move in slow motion as he spreads his fingers in the universal symbol for *Kabloooey!*

Banshooo gulps. "But Ooolandians don't know anything about a Concord."

"It's worse than that, my friend. They don't believe such a thing could exist." Sid sighs. "They fail to recognize the sentience of the elements or to take into account that which they cannot see, that which they cannot fathom." He shakes his head. "It's insulting really. We work our teeny, tiny little butts off to keep it all in some semblance of sustainable balance, and what do we get? No respect. Which is a big mistake seeing as how we're essential to the whole manifestation." Sid pauses for a moment then leans forward, raising his eyebrows. "Ooolandians, however, are expendable."

Banshooo gulps again. Sid shrugs a little. "What can I say? It's not personal. It's business."

☾

Ambrose, his beautiful head lowered to his breast, is staring, with vacant eyes, toward the floor. "What does it look like, Sukie?"

"Oh, owl, it's breathtaking. All just blooms forth, everything unfolding out of everything else and from all that has gone before. It's dazzling. And then you see a pulsing, a kind of rhythm like breathing."

Joe steps in. "And it shows we're part of it, Ambrose. We're *in* it."

Sukie's voice is steady. "It's a revelation, Ambrose."

The owl is quiet for a moment, then he raises his head. He pulls his wings in tight to his tired body and closes his empty eyes. "All right, then. It was worth it."

Joe looks at this noble owl who has sacrificed his extraordinary sight in order to expose the blindness all around them. Then he looks at the golden reflection of the great web as it pulses on the page. He sets his jaw. "I'll take this to them. When they see it, it'll change everything."

Sukie is thinking. "Well, maybe..."

Ambrose turns suddenly. "Do you hear that?"

A clomping sound echoes through the hall as the night watchman approaches. The three of them look around frantically. There's nowhere to hide. The clomping comes closer. The door handle turns and the door begins to open. A second clomping sound comes near.

"Hey, Charlie. They want us back at the switching station, some kind of disconnect or something."

"Oh great. A nerd spills his energy drink over a motherboard and we get put on alert."

"You don't even know what a motherboard is."

"Yeah, I do. It's a board that's, you know, like the mother of the other... uh... boards..." The door is pulled shut and the clomping moves away down the hall.

Joe exhales. "We've got to get out of here."

Sukie takes up the Image that reveals the true nature of the natural world and looks around for a way to carry it safely. She sees a large manila Department of Nature envelope sitting on an empty shelf. She slips the Image inside. Joe lifts the owl in his arms and the three of them scurry down the back hall, out through heavy doors and up an old access road to the top of a hill high above the Central Services complex. A long gully runs behind scrub brush winding between a dirt path and the Biolab. They scoot down into the ditch and take a minute to catch their breath.

The massive concrete structures below cast eerie shadows across the terrain as the first faint light of the Ooolandian dawn comes into the eastern sky. Joe whispers, "I can't wait for Banshooo to see this. It's what he used to talk about."

Sukie looks at Joe holding the blind owl gently and securely in his arms. She decides not to say anything about the possibility that Banshooo could be scattered about the Unseen in the form of de-constructed body parts.

She holds the Image close. "Yes." She nods. "Yes, me too."

Joe frowns. "I wonder where he is."

☾

Banshooo has slumped into a puddle of despair. "Ooolandians won't go back. Life was too hard before all the material achieve-ments. No one wants to go back."

Sid shakes his head. "Going back is not the answer. Going side-ways would be good. Taking one freaking minute to consider al-ternatives would be nice." He bends over and lifts Banshooo up so they are standing directly in front of one another.

"Here's the recap, my friend. Ooolandians are not in control. They do not have dominion. They are not the custodians of nature. They are children within it. Even the oldest and wisest among you is but a babe held in the arms of the natural world. Understand that and it will change everything. You have the tools. You have the talent. You have what you need to redress the mess you've created. The problem is the story."

"You mean like what Ursula said, in The Mythic?"

"Exactly. Stories define what is possible. They create and rein-force beliefs. Beings act on what they believe. How they act makes things the way they are." He spreads his hands, palms upward. "You can see how it's all connected."

Banshooo nods slowly. "Yeah. Yeah, I do."

"Unfortunately, at this moment in time, Ooolandians have been hypnotized by the story of MORE, a nasty, imperious story, heavy-handed and cruel. Sucking out compassion and respect, it has become the only story there is. And let me tell you, there are few things as dangerous as the idea of a single story holding the narrative voice for all. Whether it's a monoculture or a master race, proto-paradigms ignore the basic universal requirement for health and survival—a thriving diversity, be it bio, agro, socio, ethnic, specie, racial, or religious.

"Even your sciences serve the story of MORE, moving you toward a technological singularity that will do nothing but accelerate the difficulties you now face." Sid's eyes narrow. "The world is not digital, Banshooo. It's fuzzy—really, *really* fuzzy.

"You guys have the potential to develop so much more than the gross mechanical detritus you're so enamored with." He sighs, as if lamenting an opportunity foregone. "So many new stories are longing to be told. Stories of relationship, of integration, of working *within* the natural world. This would be the opposite of going back. It would be going ahead to the newest thing there could possibly be; the next big step toward a living future. *You could come to understand how matter and consciousness interact.*"

"Uh...run that by me again."

"Key point right here. Matter and consciousness interact. Far from operating independently of one another, they work as complementary aspects of a unified reality; the Seen and the Unseen, creating one another." He watches Banshooo. "Think about it. It's how you got here. Awareness grows, perception unfolds, possibilities open up and pretty soon, everything that seemed so set, so... *real...* is seen differently." He leans down and whispers, "Experience moving through time."

"You knew Algernon!"

"He was a good guy." Sid puts his arm around the monkey's shoulders. "Come on, kiddo, you've got work to do. During a dark era such as this, when one story threatens to suck the life out of everything that doesn't serve it, the most important thing to do is to bring other stories to the fore. That's where you come in."

Banshooo stops in his tracks. "Me?"

"Yeah, you. What do you think you're here for? Your looks?"

"But how?"

Sid purses his lips. "Hmmm. How. Well, you have to find a way to break through the trance, keep The Concord from being broken, and save the world's water." He pats Banshooo on the back. "Have confidence, kid. You'll figure it out."

Banshooo gulps. "But aren't you supposed to give me something, some kind of tool or martial arts move or something?"

"You mean like a secret mantra or a way to tune into the Force?"

"Yeah, like that."

Sid thinks for a moment. "I could make you glow, give you an aura kind of thing. Would you like that?"

"That's not funny."

"I thought it was…a little bit."

Banshooo's head drops down to his chest. He's having doubts about the whole idea of destiny altogether and is wondering if it's too late to go back to that crossroads place and take a different tack. He may be whimpering.

"Ah, come on. Don't despair." Sid tilts his head. "Awareness can grow. It's a living thing, a *literal* force in the world, like magnetic waves or subatomic particles. It influences how things unfold. It changes what happens. You yourself are a good example. You studied, you learned, you watched, and you came to see the miracle of what is already there."

Sid waves his arm in a wide gesture of revelation and again Banshooo is surrounded by the vast and glistening network of delicate threads shining like jewels. Sid waves once more and the jeweled world becomes Blooo Meadow, and all the shapes and beings in the meadow radiate their essence, dancing before him. Melding in and out of the most astounding patterns and harmonies, they coalesce into dazzling designs and brilliant archetypes, reflecting the primal nature of all things. As he watches, they evolve through all the guises they have assumed from the beginning of time and display before him a great panorama of form and manifestation. They move kaleidoscopically into ever more stunning colors and emanations, creating a beauty and intensity that threatens to explode until suddenly softly settling into the most perfect equilibrium space can hold. A deep resonance encircles him as his heart echoes the pulse of existence and he perceives the precious reality of the many worlds, Seen and Unseen, born and dying.

Banshooo is filled with the most profound happiness. He looks at Sid, who smiles and says, "Now get the heck outta here."

"What?"

"You have to go back, kid. Look at yourself. Look at what's happening." Banshooo looks down and sees that his body is beginning to disappear. In the same way as the Unseen beings appeared to him, slowly manifesting and coming into focus, in that same way he is now slowly disappearing and slipping out of focus.

"Yikes!"

"You are still a being of the Seen World and you need to be in that world to survive. Take what you have learned and bring it into the Seen. Bring our plea back to Ooolandia. Tell them there is something else. Something larger and smaller, deeper and closer, forever and for now."

Banshooo doesn't want to go. He doesn't want to lose this wondrous feeling. He reaches out with his paws, but they are beginning to fade away. Sid leans toward him and whispers.

"Remember the crossroads. There are many possibilities, and some of them are really cool."

Sid too is fading from focus but Banshooo can still see his face, his remarkable eyes, can still see him wrinkle his brow as if he's trying to remember something. And he does.

"Oh, yes. One more thing. Some will see, some won't. But it must be shown."

Banshooo cries out. "Wait. What? What must be shown?"

But Sid is gone, leaving only a wisp of mist and, oddly enough, the lingering scent of Old Spice aftershave.

Banshooo stares at the spot where Sid was standing. He feels sad, as if he'd lost a friend. And at that moment Taboook is there, bouncing maniacally up and down in front of him.

"We're in the meadow! We're in the meadow!" Taboook shouts gleefully. "We floated right back home."

"Taboook! You're here."

"Of course I'm here. We're both here."

"I mean before, while I was gone."

"What do you mean while you were gone?"

"You didn't lose sight of me? You didn't tumble on by yourself?"

"No, buddy, I didn't. We both kept on floating down and down as if it would never end, like this entire journey to a place that probably wasn't even there to begin with. And we survived! Can you believe it? Whew! Wow! Good! Let's eat!"

"Wait, Taboook. What are you saying?"

Taboook stops, stares at Banshooo, and speaks slowly. "We floated down that weird wormhole together. You, me, and that freakin' map."

A whistling sound erupts from above and the map swooshes down and bounces off Taboook's head, landing at Banshooo's feet. Taboook swears and rubs his head. Banshooo picks up the dirty, torn parchment, dusts it off, and gently unfurls what's left of the map. It toots plaintively, as if from far away, a wheezing echo, wilting at the ends.

A few wiggling lines appear on the frayed page, then sputter into branches, stumbling in thin, gasping threads to create a writhing swarm. Banshooo recognizes the Reality of Possibility and as he does, the lines shrink themselves down to a single point. Now they struggle to shape what look like letters, pale and sketchy. Banshooo stares intently, waiting for the words to come clear. When they do, he reads: *Goodbye and Good Luck.* Then the letters churn themselves into an eddy, spinning like a circle of wheels within wheels, whirling around and away, as if spiraling down a wormhole. Or a drain. He couldn't be sure. With that, the map wheezes its last, goes blank, and expires in his paws.

Banshooo smiles, rolling up the empty parchment and tucking it under his arm. "Come on, Boook. We have work to do."

The one-off watches him as they head up the blooostone path toward the front door. "Hey bro, you look kinda glowy, like you're all glowing or something. 'Sup with that?"

PART V

"We must insist on a recognition of the mystery, the miracle, and the dignity of things, from frogs to forests, simply because they **are**."

—Curtis White

CHAPTER 15

Joe makes his way through the labyrinthine halls that house OOOCS managerial headquarters. He feels so good that even the dolorous atmosphere of this bureaucratic maze seems filled with possibility. He has taken a stand and been proven right. He has the proof of his rightness in his hands and he's eager to share it. He feels as if he's bringing everyone a gift, a gift that will make them happy. He is, himself, very happy.

Humming along in this euphoric state, he turns a corner and bangs into Jonesy, his fellow surveillance monitor. The collision sends Jonesy's briefcase sliding across the floor. Joe picks up the shining new Halliburton and hands it to the big badger.

"Hey Jonesy, I'm glad I ran into you."

"Oh, hi." Jonesy nods quickly and looks around in what Joe would normally have noticed is a nervous manner except that Joe is so happy, it doesn't register.

"Wait till you see what I've got. It's so great."

Jonesy glances up toward the ceiling and then back to Joe. "Oh yeah?"

"I have proof of the most astounding thing. It turns out Banshooo and Sukie were right all along."

"Banshooo?" Again, Jonesy looks around before he says, in a loud voice, "Banshooo is fired, everybody knows that."

"They'll welcome him back with open arms when they see this." He holds out the big envelope he's carrying.

Jonesy steps back. "What's that?"

"The proof. The proof is in the pattern, Jonesy. I've got it right here and it's beautiful. Wait till you see." He starts to take the Image out of the envelope.

"Whoa!" Jonesy backs away. "I don't want to see anything. Banshooo is prohibited. No one is supposed to fraternize with him."

"Fraternize?"

"That's what they said. Don't fraternize. It sounds like you've been fraternizing, and I don't want any part of it. I just got promoted, Joe. I'm working in the Total Information Domination Command now." He looks around again and then leans in to whisper, "Me and Gareth are the only two fur-bearers to advance that high."

"Gareth? The sloth?"

"Yeah. The sloth. Me and the sloth. It's a big deal and I'm not going to wreck it. I'm not going to lose this job."

"You won't lose anything. This is a game changer. When they see this they'll reinstate the Department of Nature for sure."

"They already did."

"What?"

They have a new Department of Nature. They call it the Department of Environmental something or other. They've got a new office and everything."

"Where? Where's the office?"

"I don't know, somewhere. I gotta go, Joe. You better be careful. You're gonna get fired for sure."

Jonesy moves quickly down the hallway. Joe shakes his head. "He'll see. They'll all see. It'll be great. It'll be the way it's supposed to be."

After many detours, false starts, and inquiries addressed to uniformly nervous Central Services personnel, Joe stands in front of a door marked: **Department of Environmental Appreciation and Development.** Inside he finds a standard-issue reception area. Lining the walls are poster-sized pictures of what were once Ooolandia's many beautiful natural landscapes and scenic panoramas. The receptionist, a furry black squirrel, tilts her head in a friendly manner.

"May I help you?

Joe smiles in return. "I'd like to see the head of the department right away. I have astounding information that will change absolutely everything."

She fluffs her tail. "How nice. If you'll just wait one moment?" Joe nods as she proceeds to relay this message to the director, who responds immediately. "Send him in."

Joe is ushered into a large office where a bearish humanoid wearing expensive designer glasses sits behind a highly polished desk. Joe looks hard at this guy. He seems familiar. Then Joe remembers. When the Blue Moon Project began, the head of OOOCScam brought this fellow into the surveillance bay and introduced him to all the workers as one of the VIOs promoting the great effort. The entire department was ordered to demonstrate the OOOCScam system and to show him how quickly the drilling was progressing. There was nodding and back-slapping and expressions of approval all around.

Joe frowns. "What are you doing here?"

The director removes his glasses. "Excuse me?"

"I thought you were part of the New Blue Moon Project."

"I did have the honor of consulting on that unparalleled undertaking, yes."

"And now you're here, where you're supposed to evaluate the whole thing and regulate it and make sure it's safe?"

"Who better to know what's what? And speaking of 'what'—what is this astounding information that will change absolutely everything?"

Joe hesitates. He didn't like this guy before, when he was giving speeches about the supremacy of MORE, and he can't understand how it would be that he would head an agency dedicated to protecting anything. Seeing Joe's hesitation, the director stands up, walks around the desk, and puts a big paw-like hand on his shoulder.

"We're all working together, Joe."

"We are?"

"Of course we are. Now, what is this astounding information that will change absolutely everything? Is it in here?" The director takes hold of the envelope and Joe lets go. It seems silly to get into some kind of tussle and besides, the whole idea is to show the Image to everyone, even the most duplicitous of OOOCS management. In fact, these are the beings who most need to see it.

The director pulls the Image from the envelope. He holds it in front of his big belly as Joe watches with anticipation. He's eager to see this fellow stunned by beauty, to see him melt with awe at the power of it all.

The director frowns, looks up, and shrugs. "I don't get it. What's the deal here?"

"What do you mean? Don't you see the web? The glowing wonder of it?"

"There's nothing here but some lines and circles. Nothing's glowing. Nothing's doing anything." He sticks the Image back into the envelope and shoves it into Joe's chest. "I'm a busy man. I don't have time for practical jokes or whatever it is you're up to. Get out of here." He pushes Joe out of his office and slams the door behind him.

"But wait... I..." Joe stares at the door. After a moment he opens the mouth of the envelope and peers inside. The golden glow reflects off the glue on the envelope's flap. It's there, the jewel-like splendor of the great web shining beautifully in the proof of the pattern. He mutters to himself. "How could he not see this?"

The squirrel looks up. "I beg your pardon?" Joe walks over to the reception desk. He pulls the Image from the envelope and holds it up in front of her.

"What do you see?" he asks.

"Is this a riddle?" She bites her lip shyly. "I'm not good at riddles."

"It's not a riddle. I just want to know what you see."

"Well..." She puts on a pair of reading glasses, fluffs her tail reflexively, and leans in toward the page. "I see..." she peers closer then looks up at Joe with a slight shrug, "...some lines?"

"Just lines?"

"Well," she looks again, "they're connected to dots, like little circles or something?"

"That's all you see? Just lines and dots?"

"Yes, lines and dots. Is that the wrong answer?"

Joe is bewildered. "Uh... well, uh..."

The squirrel blinks her big black eyes and fluffs her tail again. "Is there anything else I can help you with?"

Joe shakes his head slowly. "No, no thank you. I'll be leaving now." He walks out into the hallway, where he stands perplexed. He looks at the Image one more time. It's just as strong as ever. What's going on here? How can they not see this? Walking down the hall, he sees a door marked: **Regulatory Inspection Program**.

He opens it. The office is empty. He turns back into the hall. A janitor is pushing a broom down the corridor. Joe stops him. "Do you happen to know when the regulatory staff will be back?" The janitor shakes his head. "Ain't no regulatory staff. Budget got cut. They're waiting for some kind of stimulated economy to trickle down from the Blue Moon Project or some b.s. like that."

"But it'll be too late."

The janitor shrugs as he moves on down the hallway. "I don't know, man. I'm just glad I still have a job."

Joe stands alone in the narrow corridor. What's going on here? Why can't they see? He looks around at the drab walls, up at the long span of light fixtures running along the ceiling. He sniffs the stale air. Maybe it's something in this building, in the ventilation system. He walks out into the adjacent quad, thinking some more. Or ... maybe it's because of their job, maybe their job keeps them from seeing something different, something that isn't part of their normal daily experience, something that isn't what they already know. Could it be that he can see the Image because his own job is about watching? That must be it. He's used to looking at things. He needs to go where what they do all day is look at things.

Eagerly, he makes his way to the Surveillance Bay where he stands in front of his boss, the OOOCScam Supervisor, a big capybara with beady eyes—eyes that are now staring at Joe with suspicion.

"A web that connects all living things? This sounds like the kind of woo-woo stuff Banshooo used to go on about. I told you not to hang around with those guys. You better be careful, Joe. If you keep this up, you'll wind up on the outside."

"But look! There *is* a web. And it's remarkable!" Joe holds the Image in front of the supervisor who glances at it and frowns.

"You're losing it, dude." He turns and begins to walk away. Joe follows, holding the page before him.

"I don't believe you can't see this. You must see it. You must!"

The super turns and looks Joe right in the eye. "You're a nice guy, Joe, and I hate to do this, but clearly you're hallucinating. You can't work surveillance if you're hallucinating. I'm afraid you're fired."

"What?"

"Sorry, them's the rules. No dreamers. No hallucinators. You're outta here." He turns and walks away leaving a security guard to escort Joe out of the bay.

Dismayed, Joe makes his way to the Employee Complaints Department. He sees a receptionist sitting at a large desk made of some type of synthetic material. He walks up to the desk and clears his throat,

"Excuse me. I'm here to show you something very important."

The bright and shining figure behind the desk smiles. "Do you have a complaint?"

Joe holds up the envelope. "It's really more like a discovery. I have a discovery. A very important discovery."

The figure smiles. "I do not recognize your response. Please say yes or no."

Joe tries again. "Let me explain. I need to see someone about the proof … the proof in the pattern."

"I do not recognize your response. Please say yes or no."

"What do you mean?"

The figure smiles again. "Let's start over. Do you have a complaint? Please say yes or no."

"I'm trying to tell you, it's not a complaint, exactly. It's something that the administration needs to see. It's very important."

"I'm sorry. I do not recognize your response. Do you have a complaint? Please say yes or no."

"Geez. Okay, Yes, I have a complaint."

"You said yes, is that correct?"

Joe sighs. "Yes."

The figure smiles again. "Fine. Which of the following categories best describes the nature of your complaint? Hardware, Software, or Billing?"

"What?"

"I do not recognize your response. Let's start again. Do you have a complaint?"

Joe looks closely at the figure behind the desk. He had assumed it was a one-off, since he'd never seen anything that looked like that exactly, but now he isn't sure. He notices it's still smiling. He peers in closer, putting his face directly in front of its face. It doesn't move. He sticks his tongue out and blows a raspberry. Nothing changes. Joe pokes it in the head with his finger. Nothing. He walks around to the back of the unit and sees that, in fact, the receptionist is part of the desk. It's all one solid apparatus, a desk, a talking robo, and a big synthetic smile. He walks back in front of the device.

"No offense, but do you think I could talk to a real Ooolandian? I'm not particular. Just something ... you know ... alive?"

"I'm sorry. I do not understand your response."

Joe turns away in frustration and is heading toward the stairs when he hears his name being called. A friendly middle-management marmot bustles up to him, smiling broadly and holding out his paw. "Joe! We understand you're having some kind of problem." He takes Joe's elbow and walks him toward the executive offices.

"Let's go see the CEO. He's the one who can clear all this up. Come with me."

The next thing he knows, Joe is sitting in a huge chair in an opulent office. The bright, luxurious space is appointed with large oil paintings of Very Important Ooolandians and framed photographs of the CEO with other dignitaries, celebrating the many achievements of MORE. Chandeliers hang from the vaulted ceiling. Richly patterned rugs silence every footfall. Silver appurtenances sit atop highly polished furniture.

Sitting across from a massive desk, behind which are tastefully carved mahogany panels, he's still trying to get his bearings when one of the panels opens soundlessly and the CEO breezes in, tall, handsome, exuding authority. He strides over to where Joe is sitting and offers his hand.

"So! Joe, is it?"

Joe nods.

"What seems to be the problem, my friend?"

Joe is suddenly aware of the fact that although he is of the same species as this being, there could be no greater example of the wide variety of subcategories within the standard biological taxonomy. Joe's personal classification pales in comparison to this paragon of hominid characteristics. His smile makes Joe blink. Getting no answer, the CEO tries again.

"Joe? Hello? What is the problem?"

Joe is thinking as fast as he can. So far, showing the Image to officials has gotten him thrown out and fired. Not what he was expecting. But this is the head guy, the guy who makes the big decisions, the guy with the grin that can eat anything. If Joe can see it, surely such an important being will be able to see it. He takes a deep breath and holds up the envelope.

"This. This is the problem."

The CEO looks at the envelope. "The Department of Nature is the problem?"

Joe turns the envelope around and looks at the label. "Oh, that's just ... uh ... I found this, uh, just lying around. Scrap, you know."

The CEO nods genially. "I see."

Joe starts again. "No, it's about what's in this envelope. It's about the Image. No one seems to understand how important it is, what it shows, what it means."

The CEO reaches out his hand. "Okay, let's have a look."

Joe takes a deep breath and hands him the envelope. The CEO walks to his desk and sits down. He lifts the Image out of the envelope and places it on his desk. He narrows his eyes, studying carefully. After a long moment, he leans back, his elbows propped against the arms of his chair, his hands forming a tent, fingertips together in front of his chin, tapping lightly, the very picture of thoughtful consideration. He looks at Joe and smiles.

"This is very important, Joe, very important indeed."

"You can see it?"

"Of course I can see it. It's very important. Very important indeed."

"Yes! Great! I'm so glad you can see it. Whew." Joe slumps down in his chair with relief. "I thought no one was going to help."

"Help?"

"Help to save it. I mean, us." Pleading creeps into his voice. "You can see, right? You can see how connected we are, how it holds all of us."

"Yes, yes of course, all of us." The CEO leans back in his chair. "Tell me, Joe, how did you come to obtain this ... uh ... document."

"It comes from Banshooo's data, all the records and reports and details and descriptions he's collected over all these years." Eager to give credit to his friend, Joe continues. "It's incredible really, what he's done. And to think he was fired. I mean, it should be the other way around. Everyone owes him a debt of gratitude."

"So where is this Banshooo now?"

"I wish I knew. I was watching him on the surveillance monitors and he just disappeared."

The CEO gets up from his chair and walks around the gigantic desk to where Joe is sitting. He puts a hand on his shoulder.

"It's quite something you've done here, Joe, quite something. How exactly *did* you do this, anyway?"

Joe is suddenly aware of a tone in the CEO's voice that reminds him of the fact that he broke into OOOCS headquarters, disconnected the surveillance and used Central Services property for his own purposes, all of which he knows carries stiff penalties. On the other hand, he has just saved the day, or the night, or maybe both, and shouldn't he be excused for whatever minor transgressions were performed in the course of rescuing the entire natural world, not to mention producing an actual image of the extraordinary web of being that underlies everything? He looks at the CEO whose steel-gray eyes are staring a hole through him.

"Well." Joe swallows uncomfortably as he tries to guess whether he's in a good situation or real trouble. "Well, it's complicated."

"I'm an intelligent guy, Joe. I think I could understand."

"Yes, yes, of course, I didn't mean…" Joe isn't used to dissembling. The hand on his shoulder tightens a bit. Joe coughs. "Well, we, uh, that is, Sukie and me and the owl, we took all the data back to the office cause Sukie said it's about patterns, 'the proof is in the pattern,' she said, and then, well, then we, uh..."

Joe is lost in that place where what has happened and what might be about to happen aren't in the sort of sync you assumed they would be. He's not used to lying and wouldn't be good at it even if he were. As he hems and haws, the CEO tightens his hold until Joe looks up, grimacing, trying to slide out from under his grip.

"You're ... uh, hurting me there on my shoulder..."

The CEO removes his hand abruptly. "Oh. I'm sorry, Joe." He walks back around his desk, picks up the Image and slides it into the center drawer, closing and locking it in one swift motion. He looks up and smiles again, his face assembling itself into a perfect picture of reassurance.

"You must be exhausted, my friend."

Joe shrinks down into the depths of the chair. "Well, now you mention it, I am pretty tired. We were, uh, I mean, I ... was up all night and to tell the truth, I was tired already cause I haven't been sleeping so well what with everybody being fired and all and I don't even know where ... uh, where some of my friends are or what they... well, what they're doing and..."

"Yes, yes indeed, you do look tired. Why don't you go home, fella, and leave this to me?"

Joe stands up. The CEO puts his arm around Joe's shoulder and walks him to the door. "You get some rest now. We've got the problem in hand. No need to worry anymore."

Joe looks back over his shoulder at the big desk. "Maybe I should take the Image with me, you know, for safe keeping."

"I'll hold on to it, Joe. It'll be safe with me. You can stop worrying now. Go home and get some sleep." He pats Joe on the back in a comforting gesture, flashing one last dazzling smile. "Everything will be taken care of. You can be sure of that."

As the big door closes behind him, Joe isn't sure of anything. His mind is fried and he is, truth to tell, utterly exhausted. This whole thing has been a big stretch for him. He finds his way back down the many winding hallways of Central Services and walks out into the cool night air. He's thinking about the big fat pillow on his bed at home when he sees a cadre of Security Police approaching. The officers are dressed in thick black gear from head to toe, and helmets mask their faces. Slowly, deliberately, they encircle Joe, like a squad of automated machines. A voice declares, "You are under arrest."

Joe can't tell where the voice is coming from. He looks around the ring of armored figures, trying to see who is speaking, tripping over himself as he turns from one encased form to another.

"Arrest? What for?"

The disembodied voice answers. "For the unauthorized use of OOOCS property." One of the black-clad figures raises a gloved hand holding the empty Department of Nature envelope that the CEO had dropped in the trash.

CHAPTER 16

"D o you have it?"

Mabooose stares at the CEO who hands him the Image. He places it on his desk and studies it intently. Standing to his side is the Colonel, looking like a cardboard cutout on a recruitment poster for OOOCS Security Services.

The CEO puts his hands in his pockets and shrugs. "I did as you asked. I pretended to see something and agreed that it was very important. But I don't get it. What's the big deal? It's just a bunch of lines and circles."

The Colonel says, "It's a code of some kind, isn't it?"

Without looking up, Mabooose mutters, "You could say that."

In the silence that follows, the CEO looks around the room. The light from the single window mingles with the sickly fluorescent glare in the undecorated space. He's always wondered why the most powerful individual in the entire OOOCS hierarchy wouldn't want a more impressive office but then, you never knew with one-offs. They looked different and they were different and Mabooose was the most different of all. He clears his throat and says, in what he hopes sounds like an interested tone of voice, "So. I guess this is pretty critical, huh?"

Mabooose looks at the suit standing before him, so handsome in the casual presumption of entitlement. Groomed to project a confident authority, a model toward which others might aspire, the CEO conducts the power of celebrity like copper wire conducts electricity. The perfect, pliant figurehead creating the appearance of leadership. Mass media creating the appearance of an ever-expanding affluence toward which all might strive. MOREism creating the appearance of providing that possibility. Chatterdees spreading so much nonsense no one could even begin to distinguish between fact and fiction. It's quite a perfect system really. No one questions "the way things are." No one asks if there might be another way to live. The only thing that could change this perfect system would be a widespread awareness of what is revealed in the Image he now holds in his possession,—proof of the true nature of reality, the real world beyond the world of appearances created by MORE.

He answers the CEO. "It's nothing for you to worry about." He looks at the Colonel. "Are there other copies of this thing?"

"No, sir."

"And a surveillance worker had it?"

"Yes, sir."

"How did he get it?"

"Evidently he and some of his friends managed to access the quantum mesmers. We're still looking into it. They're all connected to this Banshooo character. We don't know where he is but the surveillance worker is under arrest."

"Good. Keep him in solitary confinement. Make sure he talks to no one. That's crucial. He is to talk to no one, no one is to talk to him. Do you understand?"

"Yes, sir."

"Find Banshooo's original data and destroy it. All of it. And put surveillance cams on Blooo Meadow. I want to know the moment that monkey returns. Do you understand? The *moment* he returns."

"Yes, sir!"

The Colonel turns smartly on his heels and heads for the door. When he gets there, he stands and waits for the CEO who shrugs and follows him out of the office.

Alone now, Mabooose continues to study the picture in front of him. He is so still he stops breathing, every fiber of his pale being focused on the golden beauty reflecting off of his white visage. He thinks about the power of images. He thinks about how this would be life-changing for anyone with the capacity to see.

After a long moment, he slides open the desk drawer, carefully places the Image inside, and locks the drawer. He sits as still as stone.

❨

The Colonel marches a security unit down the long hall leading to the rear wing of the Central Services building. He passes the janitorial closets and heads directly into the Department of Nature office. The room is a tight fit, and only three of the heavily armed guards can follow their leader into the room. The others stand watch in the hall.

The Colonel looks around the dusty space, eyeing the mesmers sitting on a long table in the otherwise empty office. He picks up the goggles lying next to the monitors. The rubber around the eyepieces seems to be burnt. Obviously OOOCS has been far too sanguine about the end of activism.

Yes, the general population has become quite passive under the mass surveillance program, but this has lulled the authorities into a false sense of security. There's always going to be someone somewhere who questions the way things are. As he never grew tired of saying, it was a mistake to leave anything unguarded.

He sees the poster on the far wall: "Dig We Must, For a Greater Ooolandia." It seems to mock him. He swears in anger, grabbing a discarded paperweight and hurling it against the wall. It smashes through the poster and bounces into the tunnel hidden behind.

"What?!"

He marches up to the wall and peers through the torn paper, pulling it apart furiously. So this is how they did it. He turns to the nearest guard. "Fire into that hole!" The black-clad figure drops the visor on his helmet, automatically activating the gas mask and respiratory filter. His comrades do the same. He raises the wide-barreled

153

gun to his waist, inserts a canister into the circular chamber, and points into the tunnel. He fires.

"Again!" the Colonel barks.

The second figure raises his gun and repeats the procedure, firing into the tunnel.

"Again!"

The Colonel continues shouting "Again!" until the floor is covered with empty canisters. Finally, the cadre marches out of the office, locking and sealing the door permanently.

A sickening vapor saturates the tunnel. Soon it leaks into all the nearby burrows and setts created by the myriad Ooolandian species whose nature inclines them toward the warm and musky feel of loam and soil. The smell of dead bodies pervades the area for days.

❨

Back in Blooo Meadow, Banshooo and Taboook stand in the open doorway of Algernon's little house. Furniture is upended and debris litters the floor. Pillows and cushions have been cut open and gutted, shelves ransacked. The place has been trashed, and every single book, folder, journal, report, monograph, manuscript, map, list, notebook, catalogue, and composition has disappeared. All of Banshooo's years of work, all of Algernon's archive, all of Sukie's calculations—gone.

Taboook is shaking his head. "I don't get it. No one cares about your work. Why would anyone bother to steal it?"

Banshooo stares at the mess with a steely expression. "Someone cares. Someone knows it matters."

Suddenly a loud squealing erupts from the air. "No, no, to the left, to the left. Look out! Look out! Look out!" They turn to see Ambrose dropping down from the sky, swinging dangerously close to just about everything with Sukie hanging precariously from his talons. As the owl swoops down toward the ground, Sukie lets go of his claws and lands on her head, her little body rolling like a wheel until she comes to a stop in front of Banshooo and Taboook. Ambrose touches down unsteadily then gathers himself, shaking his

PATRICIA J. ANDERSON

head and folding his wings in to his sides. Sukie straightens up and spits out a mouthful of grass and dirt. She turns to Ambrose.

"Okay, we gotta work out the whole letting-go-of-the-mouse thing, but otherwise, I think we've got it."

The owl blows a big puff of a sigh. "Sure."

Banshooo and Taboook stare at the two of them. Sukie's coat is rumpled, her whiskers tangled up and her glasses held together with duct tape. Ambrose is wearing a helmet-like beanie strapped onto his head with elastic bands. Wires, transducers, and antennae sprout from the contraption like the creation of a drunken haberdasher. This bizarre headgear is so conspicuous it takes a moment before they look into Ambrose's face and realize his eyes are empty, each one circled by a ring of burnt feathers.

Banshooo is the first to speak. "Ambrose, what happened to you?"

Sukie answers. "He scanned all our data with his envisioning vision, and then Joe helped us sneak into Central Services. We fed his eyes into the new quantum mesmers and it worked, Shooo, it worked! We got this amazing multi-dimensional image of the connection underlying everything!" Sukie stops. "But it fried his eyes. He can't see a thing."

Everyone stares at the owl. No one knows what to say. Finally, Ambrose breaks the sad silence.

"Hey! I'm not *dead*. Evidently I'm no longer a symbol of great dignity, but I'm not dead. And this thing on my head allows me to get around. I'm sure, in time, it'll become less … awkward."

Taboook puts his arm around the owl. "You look … futuristic. It's kinda cool."

"Do you think so?"

"Oh definitely." He turns to Sukie. "What the heck is it anyway?"

"It's an ultrasound generator in a beanie. It sends out sound waves and converts the feedback to a frequency within his audible range, a kind of customized echolocator, like with dolphins and whales. It's like audio eyes." She smiles proudly. "Neat, huh?"

Suddenly they hear velvet harmonies floating out of Ambrose's head.

♫ *"Baby, I need your lovin' … Got to have all your lovin'…"* ♫

155

Taboook frowns. "Is that the Four Tops?"

"Yeah, well, sometimes it picks up an oldies station." Sukie's smile has turned sheepish. "It's a working model, okay?"

Banshooo speaks quietly. "You're very brave, Ambrose."

The owl furls his wings slightly and murmurs, "I'm just glad it worked."

"And it did, Shooo." Sukie's eyes are bright. "Now there's a picture, an Image of the connection that underlies the natural world. Everyone can see how complex it is, and how marvelous, how powerful."

"I know," Banshooo says. "I was there. I was inside it."

Everyone looks at Banshooo. Sukie whistles slowly. Ambrose makes a low hooting sound. Taboook looks puzzled.

Banshooo continues. "I know what's happening to the moon, the fireflies, all of it. And I know why. I was there, Sukie. I was in The Unseen."

Taboook is frowning. "What are you talking about?"

"Okay. Well. You know when we fell into the crevasse?"

"Yahaaah." Taboook is waiting. Sukie and Ambrose are waiting too.

"I was somewhere else."

"No, you weren't. You were with me. We fell. Together."

"Well, maybe, but I was also somewhere else."

"Where else?"

"I was in the Unseen realm. I...I slipped through The Threshold."

"You slipped? On what?"

"On my own awareness."

Sukie is thinking hard. "Wow. This could be a many worlds kind of thing, or maybe a cyclic multiverse, or a quilted multiverse. Definitely some kind of multiverse-type situation."

Taboook is beating the side of his head with his foot.

Sukie's still thinking. "Or maybe every possible configuration of reality has happened at some point in time and one of them was identical to the one you were in and you fell into it?"

Taboook growls. "What he fell into was the wormhole, just like me!"

Sukie's whiskers stand straight up. "A wormhole! You traveled in space!"

"In a way." Banshooo looks at his friends and at that very moment, the sun comes out from behind a cloud and alights upon them all. He smiles. "It's about consciousness, Sukie. The Threshold is the threshold of perception, the gateway beyond our assumptions. You step through what you thought you knew and into another place. That which was unseen to you becomes … perceived."

Sukie's eyes are bright. "Perception. Of course. Time, Space, and Perception."

Ambrose murmurs in wonder. "The alchemist was right. They're all linked together."

Banshooo places his paw on the owl's feathered shoulder. "They are, my dear friend, they really are."

Sukie smiles broadly. "You've done it, Shooo. You've seen it with your own eyes." Banshooo smiles back. "And you've made manifest an Image to prove it to all. They have to believe us now."

Taboook heads for the kitchen. "Ahhright! We did it! Hooray! Let's party!"

Suddenly, a singular buzzing sails through the open door. It flits around the room, darting up to Taboook, then to Sukie then to Ambrose and finally settling in front of Banshooo's face.

"Okay, Pussyfoot, you and your crew gotta get outta here."

Banshooo sighs. "Come on, Durga, I've asked you not to call me that."

"Yahright. Now listen up. OOOCSecurity is on its way here right now. They're going to arrest you." The dragonfly rockets around the four of them so quickly, they lose sight of her until she stops again, hovering in front of Taboook.

"You too, Bozo. In fact, all of you. I don't know what you did, but it must have been big cause they've issued an all-mammal-alert. Blooo Meadow is under surveillance, but something here is creating a lot of interference and messing with their reception." She whirrs over to Ambrose, hovering above the beanie. "Okay, it's gotta be this." She stops in front of Ambrose's face. "What *is* that thing on your head?"

♫ *"Baby I need your lovin'… Got to have all your lovin…"* ♫

In the secret nerve center of the Total Information Domination Program where the chrome panels, the high-tech mesmer stations, huge screens and complex switching mechanisms gather, organize, store, and distribute countless coordinated data banks, Jonesy is trying to explain to his superior the very unusual thing that has happened.

"Well sir, Banshooo and Taboook just appeared out of the air."

"What do you mean, 'out of the air?'"

"One minute the meadow was empty, the next minute they were just...*there*. Like they *materialized* or something."

"What are you talking about? Check your gear."

"Running diagnostics now, sir."

The scanners blink and hum. Gareth, Jonesy's fellow fur-bearing techie, watches anxiously. "The cameras are working, sir. And there's more." The transmission is suddenly interrupted by a flash of static and the monitor goes all fuzzy. Jonesy turns and looks up at his supervisor. "One minute there was a clear signal and the next minute it was gone. And for a second, I thought I heard ..."

"Heard what, Jonesy?"

"I thought I heard ... singing, sir."

"Singing?"

"Yes, sir."

The supervisor looks askance. The badger shrugs. "What can I say? That's what I heard."

Jonesy is trying to do his job, but he feels bad. Really bad. As a once proud member of the Ooolandian Central Services Surveillance System, he has tried to be loyal but has paid a high price. His mates and babies have been gassed in a security operation that many believe was overkill; a vindictive move against Banshooo and the old Department of Nature resulting in an unnecessary loss of life in a wide network of inter-species burrows that housed many innocent beings. He has tried to move on but his heart's not in it. He's beginning to question whether he can continue being part of such a system.

He confided his misgivings to Gareth, his closest ally in the nerve center, but the sloth offered little sympathy. Gareth was proud of being one of the only non-Erect-Bipedal-Primates hired at this level and felt strongly that, since the two of them were pioneers in the fight for equality with the bare-skinned, Jonesy should suck it up. He hopes they're on the cutting edge of a movement on behalf of furred beings everywhere, and as such, he accepts that certain sacrifices must be made. After all, Gareth has, himself, made significant adjustments for the cause.*

---

*On the outside, the Ooolandian Sloth looks like just another mammal but inside, snuggled quietly within its hairy fleece, lives an eccentric species known as the Sloth Moth. For the most part, these tiny creatures snooze quietly, hidden deep inside the host coat. However, should the host become nervous or excited, they spread their wings and flutter. As it happens, their wings are a surprising neon pink and they tend to spark and fitz when frightened, like a loose electrical outlet. Any sloth who hopes to work for the OOOCS hierarchy knows to keep his biome quiet at all times. Gareth takes a daily dose of anti-anxiety medication in order to be sure no sudden surprise awakens the moths within.

CHAPTER 17

Meanwhile, back up on One More Mountain, Raoul is losing patience. As soon as the raccoon replaces one prized tchotchke tumbling off its shelf, another falls. His rare Staffordshire sheep has a big chip in its nose. Yomolakhi is going to pay for this. He walks out of his cave to find the beast staring at the ground with a mixture of indignation and fear. A fierce shock ripples under his massive feet. He howls plaintively.

"Well. This isn't you, is it?"

Yomolakhi shakes his head decisively. Raoul looks around. There is no sign of his erstwhile guests. "Did you eat the monkey?"

"I haven't eaten *anything*!" The beast whimpers.

"You sound like the one-off."

"All I got was a piece of his ear."

Another severe shock rocks the terrain. Raoul looks up at the overhang on top of the cave entrance directly above their heads. It cracks ominously. With the next shuddering wave, it begins to fragment. Suddenly they both realize it's not going to hold. They scramble up to the ridge above and watch, stunned, as the astounding sound of fracturing granite echoes over them. The entire cliff face collapses on to Raoul's cave, completely blocking the entrance and spewing dust and rock across the path below them.

As the shock waves recede, Raoul sighs. "Oh, man, there goes my stuff."

"And my broom."

"It's not your broom."

Yomo looks at Raoul. "What's happening?"

Raoul sighs. "I think this could be what is sometimes referred to as 'the beginning of the end.'"

"The end of what?"

"The end of sanctuary, my friend. The end of sanctuary." The ground trembles. Raoul is thinking hard. "What happened to the monkey and his cohort?"

"He wouldn't let go of this papery thing that made a sound like some kind of horn or something. It pulled both of them over the edge into a big crevice. They totally disappeared."

Raoul's eyes widen. "The map found a wormhole."

Yomolakhi stares at Raoul. He knows Raoul is waiting for him to say, "What?" and when he does, the raccoon will talk real fast and, in the end, Yomo will be left more confused than when he asked the question in the first place. He's thinking to himself: "This time I won't ask. If I don't ask, there won't be explaining. If there's no explaining, there'll be less confusion. If there's less confusion, I won't get a headache."

This tactic results in a long pause. Raoul waves a paw in front of Yomo's face. "Hullo? Anybody home?"

Yomolakhi turns away, but another violent shudder opens a fissure directly under his big body. Splaying his four legs apart like a sawhorse, he looks down, his entire attention focused on an effort to avoid falling into the breach. Raoul tumbles sideways, knocked off-balance by the violently shaking terrain. He scrambles to stand up, pulling himself away from the expanding gap.

"Okay, this is bad. We're in some kind of paradigm shift. The whole mountain could go. We gotta get out of here." He grabs Yomo's long mane and swings himself up onto the beast's broad shoulders with a shout.

"Go to where the monkey jumped."

Yomolakhi hesitates. Raoul leans over and speaks into Yomo's ear, quietly and matter-of-factly. "Believe me, buddy, it's our only chance." Yet another aftershock hits. The beast gathers himself and heads out to the tundra flatlands. Soon, they are staring down into the yawning maw of the crevasse. Raoul sets his jaw.

"We need to jump."

"No."

The raccoon tries to sound encouraging. "It'll be fine. Don't worry, I've read about this … or, rather, about the possibility of this."

"Oh great."

"We just jump. Just jump right in."

"But what if there's no bottom?"

"That's the whole idea."

They stand on the very edge of the fissure. Raoul begins to count. "Okay. One—Two—Wait." He holds up a paw. "There's one more thing."

Yomo looks at him warily.

"Once we're in there, you have to empty your mind. I mean *completely*. It's like you have to stop thinking." He tilts his head up. "This shouldn't be that hard for you."

"Huh?"

"That's good. Stay with that."

"Huh?"

"Exactly. Surrender understanding. Clear your mind so that a completely new possibility can pop into your head, a totally different thought from anything you've ever thought before. Like I said, this shouldn't be that hard for you."

Yomo groans. "I don't feel so good."

As another violent quake rips through the fractured terrain, Raoul shouts out.

"One—Two—Three!" He jumps.

The great beast hesitates, trembling.

☾

Carrying Ambrose as a makeshift electronic jamming device, Banshooo, Taboook, and Sukie sneak to the far north edge of Blooo Meadow until they reach Algernon's bamboo grove. There they huddle together amongst the blue-green stalks, looking out on the periphery where scruffy ground cover grows down the hill that serves as a buffer between Blooo Meadow and the beginnings of Ooolandian sprawl. Beyond that are the outskirts of urban Ooolandia and, in the distance, the gleaming skyscrapers of the Grand Oooland. Dotted throughout are the ubiquitous Cubes and Cams, broadcasting, recording, gathering and emitting the data that creates Ooolandian reality.

Banshooo turns to Sukie. "Where is the Image?"

"Well…" The mouse bites her lip. "We thought … that is, Joe wanted…" Everyone looks at Sukie, who sighs. "We thought if it could be seen, it would change everything, so Joe took it to OOOCS. We haven't heard from him since."

Banshooo hears Sid's voice. "*Some will see, some won't. But it must be shown.*" He looks out at the vista miles below them where the vast Central Services compound looms, brightly lit and formidable, like a massive prison. He repeats Sukie's words. "…if it could be seen."

Suddenly a siren sounds from somewhere behind them. Taboook looks around. "We gotta keep moving." The little group scoots and scuttles down the rise and lands in a large tract of empty acreage housing a huge construction site where a new ooomall is being built. It's twilight and the bulldozers and earth-moving equipment sit empty and still, surrounded by mounds of gravel and piles of steel girders waiting to be erected into yet another marketplace of MORE. They crouch amidst the industrial bestiary, staying well away from the brightly lit outskirts of the metropolis.

Banshooo frowns. "We need a place to hide."

Sukie clears her throat. "Yeah, and right away." She points to Ambrose's head. "It won't take very long for this to go from being a shield to being a big fat target."

"It already has."

They turn in surprise to see a figure standing behind them wearing classic ninja gear replete with black hood, mask, and jumpsuit. This would have been a formidable vision were it not for two large, floppy blue ears sticking from the top of the hood. The figure speaks.

"My name is Naruto. I belong to a secret group of ninja hackers. We couldn't help but notice some unusual interference in the system which I now see must emanate from the owl's...uh...hat." He looks around at the surprised faces. "Some kind of ultrasound echolocator?"

Sukie pipes up. "It is."

"Who made it?"

"I did."

"Nice."

"Thank you."

"Problem is, OOOCS has found you too, not as quickly as we did, but they have figured it out."

Sukie gulps. The ninja bunny makes a reassuring sound. "Don't worry. We're creating additional random interference system-wide so they can't pinpoint the owl as yet. You're still safe. For a while anyway."

Banshooo smiles widely. "Well." He bows to the hooded figure. "How very helpful. Do you fellows do this sort of thing on a regular basis or...?" The bunny bows deeply in return, then stands up ramrod straight. "We fight for justice. The day of the samurai is over. It is the time of the ninja. There is no honor in the era of **MORE**. OOOCS is corrupt. It's also very big. Confront it head-on and you'll be crushed. Covert methods are appropriate to a dark time. Besides," he jumps suddenly into the air and whips his hands through a whirl of movement, then lands in an agile crouch and slowly straightens himself, arms akimbo, "it's incredibly cool, don't you think?"

"Oh, incredibly." The four nod enthusiastically.

"Really."

"Awesome."

The bunny continues. "You'll have to be quick, whatever you do. Central Services will come up with a workaround soon enough. It's never-ending. They go then we go then they go then we go then they go then..." He continues this litany as he bounds away, skipping up over the pile of stacked girders, springing off a bulldozer, flying from one surface to another through the construction site and disappearing into the night.

After a long silence, Taboook speaks. "Well, that was certainly unexpected."

Suddenly the ground shakes with a sharp jolt, knocking them off of their various feet, claws, and paws. Taboook frowns. "Okay, since when do we get earthquakes in this part of the world?"

Banshooo sounds grim. "It's the Concord. The drilling is weakening the Concord, and it's going to get worse. If they actually go through with the moon launch, it could break the alliance altogether."

Taboook looks at the mouse. "Do you know what he's talking about?"

Sukie shakes her head. "Not really."

Banshooo steps forward. "Come on, guys, I think I know where we can hide."

☾

On the hill above Central Services, the silvery Biolab gleams in the sun. Inside, the staff devotes itself to the unquestioned pursuit of science and its application to any and every possible function. Electron microscopes are flanked by banks of monitors; shelves of beakers, flasks, and test tubes rise behind polished steel tables while mesmers hum day and night, encoding chains of genetic material.

In a restricted area on the top floor, Dr. D. Doootch stands staring down at a large petri dish where broken-winged, worm-like creatures wriggle blindly under a glass cover. He looks up, takes a deep breath, and moves across the room to a window, gazing out at the Central Services compound below. He takes no note of the scene outside, conscious only of his own mental landscape, the complex workings of the intricate world inside his head. It fills the entirety of his awareness, a simulated reality continually generating itself, like a set of mathematical questions whose answers, once calculated, lead to the next set of questions, the answers to which lead to the next set, *ad infinitum*.

Doootch is usually quite comfortable within this cerebral generator, but lately he has questioned whether he might not be running an outdated program. Disputed renderings have crept in. A static-like interference has been keeping him awake at night. He knows it has to do with the fact that re-engineering living beings is proving to be a greater challenge than he first assumed. It's not that he can't do it; the problem is they don't look so good. He knows Mabooose is right: the aesthetics are critical. Squealing, limping, twisted creatures cannot be presented to the public if he hopes to advance his reputation. The public wants cute. He hates having to devote even a moment of his uniquely valuable time to making something cute. It's beneath him. He had wanted to create a new mammal, something that hadn't been seen before, something special, a designer species he could put his name to. It wasn't working out.

Doootch pulls a tissue from his pocket, removes his glasses and wipes them methodically, his thumb circling the lenses slowly as his mind circles a new possibility. Maybe he should go back to the basics. He's been wanting to fool around with Crispy-10, a recently developed technique that allows for quick and easy genome editing. He could be editing embryos, creating beings that look familiar on the outside but are genetically reprogrammed inside. That way, no one knows you've done it until you switch on the gene.

He finishes cleaning his glasses and replaces them on his nose, carefully settling the tips over his ears and adjusting the bridge. He tosses the tissue in a nearby waste basket and calls out to an assistant who scurries up and waits expectantly. Doootch turns and walks decisively down the hall. The assistant follows.

"Empty the cages. We're going to start over."

"Very good, sir."

Doootch stops and looks at the assistant's lab coat which is spattered with blood. He purses his thin lips, shaking his head. "And no more of your hyena friends in the live labs, understand? Use the crematorium. That's what it's for."

"Yes, sir. Understood, sir."

❨

Behind the Biolab sits a long, low, windowless building with three short black smokestacks sticking up from the roof. The entire structure is hidden behind a wall of ivy growing over a chain-link fence. A path of packed dirt leads from the back of the glass lab, up a long incline directly to a gate in the fence. Four OOOCS employees, dressed in dark overalls and thick, heavy gloves, maneuver a large metal cart along this path, stopping at the fence where one of them pulls a set of keys from his pocket and proceeds to open two separate locks chained around the gate. He holds the gate open while the other three push the cart through. Breathing hard, one worker complains to another,

"You'd think with all their fancy high-tech hardware they'd have a better way to do this."

"I thought the hyenas were a good idea," one of his colleagues answers.

"The hyenas made a mess."

Grunting from the effort required to get the cart through the gate, the third member of the crew mutters, "There is no other way to do this."

Inside the fenced-off area, the perimeter is devoid of growth. They stop at a wide door set in the front of the building while another collection of keys is deployed, then they push the cart through the door which closes automatically behind them. After a while, smoke begins to pour from the stacks, leaving an acrid smell in the still air.

☾

Joe stands forlorn inside a six by eight foot cell with three grey walls and a seriously secure door made of bars, bolts, and several large locks. He's confused, surprised, and painfully aware of the fact that he's stuck in a very small space. The walls are close and seem to be getting closer. He's humming to himself in a desperate attempt not to think about it when suddenly, and without even the slightest warning, a raccoon plummets out of the air and lands right in front of him. The creature picks himself up, checks his appendages, fluffs out his whiskers, and looks around.

"Dammit! Back in the real world. That's disappointing."

Joe stares, shocked and speechless. The raccoon walks over to the cell door and presses on the bars, taking a moment to consider the situation. Finally, he turns to Joe affecting a wide, toothy grin.

"Hi there. I don't suppose you've seen a very large, hairy beast anywhere around here, have you? It'd be hard to miss him. He's orange. Really big feet."

Joe continues to be unable to form words.

"It would be recently, very recently. I'm not talking yesterday or anything. It would be as recent as, well, as me … landing here … just now."

Nothing.

"Okay. I guess I'm on my own. What have we got here?" He looks around the cell and then back at Joe. "Where am I, and who are you?"

Joe swallows hard and squeaks, "I'm … I'm Joe."

"Joe. So. Joe. You don't happen to know a monkey named Banshooo, do you?"

Joe is now so additionally startled. Words jump out of his mouth of their own accord.

"Banshooo? I know Banshooo. Do you?"

"I do. And what I'm wondering right now is, where is he?"

"Oh man, I wish I knew. He went past the Last Gate and then I was talking to Sukie and then we got the owl to help and we made the Image and it was so incredibly beautiful and also really powerful and you see how small we are and what might happen and I took it to Management cause we thought it would change everything but they fired me and then they arrested me. Why would they do that? I don't understand. They put me in this cell and it's really tight in here and I don't like tight spaces, and I'm completely and totally alone, and no one will tell me what's going on and the guard says I'm not supposed to talk to anyone, not even him, but I have so many questions and I'm getting kinda scared I mean you would be too if you…"

Raoul raises his paw to stop the avalanche of words. "Okay, Joe, thanks for that. Now, where exactly is this guard?"

"I don't know. He comes, he goes, he looks in, then he just leaves me here." Joe makes a little whimpering sound. "It's hard being alone, you know? I thought it would be hard and it *is* hard. I brought them the Image and I thought they'd all be amazed when they saw the incredible nature of nature, but they can't even see it." He takes a breath then asks plaintively, "Why can't they see it?"

Raoul looks about the cell carefully, assessing the problems inherent in this new situation. He answers absently. "There's a lot of closed minds out there, Joe. Most beings can't see anything beyond their own nose." Staring at the video camera lodged in the corner of the ceiling, he proceeds to jump up and down, waving his arms back and forth. "Hello, hello. Is anybody there?"

Joe gulps. "Wait! Maybe you shouldn't…"

Raoul stops jumping and steps over to the cell door, tilting his head and listening. All is quiet. He turns to Joe. "Just as I thought. The guard's asleep. All the tech in the world can't override the mammalian inclination to snooze."

"It's a good thing he's not a robo. They never sleep. Over at OOOCS, some of them actually *are* robos. Real robos."

"That's unfortunate."

Joe is nodding in agreement. "And you can't even talk to them unless you use certain words … the words *they* choose. You can't say what you want to say."

"Yeah, there's no room for your individuality."

"Exactly! It's so one-sided."

"Yes indeed." The raccoon is studying the lock on the cell door. "Conversation needs to be fluid, otherwise it's stagnant, dead, not to mention incredibly boring. You gotta be able to flow with it." He turns to Joe with a cunning smile. "I'm quite good at talking, if I do say so myself which, I might point out, is what makes one good at it. Saying so oneself, I mean. Add that to the fluidity thing and talking can get you a long way, my friend. Just watch." Raoul turns and shouts. "Yo! Guard! Wake up, fella, you got a situation here."

Joe gasps. "No!"

"Don't worry. I'll take care of him while you make your getaway."

"My what?"

"Trust me. I've had experience with this sort of thing. It's all about distraction, redirecting attention. That's the key to the success of any nefarious operation, my friend. The Ooolandian authorities use it all the time."

Joe gulps. "I don't…wait…uh…"

Raoul takes Joe by the arm and leads him to the back corner of the cell away from the door. "Stand here." He turns to face the guard who has responded to this summons with sleepy surprise.

"Huh? What? How did you get in there?"

"Well that's a very interesting story, my man, very interesting indeed. Would you like to learn more?"

"What?"

"It's quite fascinating really. It's physics."

The guard frowns. "I don't care how physical it is, you're not supposed to be here."

Raoul pauses for a moment to consider the wide range of intellectual acuity found in the various realms, but then he hears Joe trying to muffle a case of nervous hiccups and moves ahead with some dispatch.

"Yes! Absolutely! I'm *not* supposed to be here. After all, this is *solitary* confinement, right?"

"Right."

"And 'solitary' means one guy. Right?"

"Right."

"So it would seem we've lost the solitary component of the whole confinement principle. I mean, do the math, one and one ain't one!"

The bear is beginning to utter a low, angry growl.

Raoul backtracks. "Okay, let's consider this from your point of view. My guess is, it wouldn't be so good for you if someone saw we weren't in solitary anymore."

The guard is remembering his orders. Absolutely no one is allowed to speak to Joe. He is to be kept in super-lonely solitary confinement with no visitors allowed.

Raoul continues. "This is going to be hard to explain to your superiors. To start with, it's so confusing."

The guard bobs his big head up and down nervously.

"And really, it's just bad luck, this happening on your watch. Why should you get the blame? It's not your fault."

The guard continues to nod in agreement.

"After all, you can hardly be held responsible for an act of quantum physics that even Einstein was unsure about."

The guard blinks haplessly. Raoul puts his paws to his cheeks and furrows his brow. "Hmmm. Now let me think. What can we do? How can we fix this?" Suddenly he smiles broadly and gasps. "I've got it! All you gotta do is get me out of here! That'll make a big difference, right off the bat. If I'm not in here, it's solitary again."

The guard frowns. Raoul continues.

"Think about it. Once I'm outside this cell, you have nothing to worry about." The bear hesitates. Raoul smiles easily, spreading his paws palm up. "It'll be as if this never happened." Slowly, the bear takes the keys from his belt. Raoul keeps talking as the key slips into the lock. "Excellent, you have just taken the first step toward solving all your problems." The bear opens the cell door just enough for the raccoon to slip sideways into the hall.

"Well done!" Raoul looks up with a big smile as he casually slides the door behind him. The guard watches the raccoon's face intently, waiting for further instructions. Raoul takes the guard's arm and steers him toward the hallway. "Now. I'm sure, if we work together on this, between the two of us, we can make everything right again." He points to the baton hanging from the bear's belt. "Hey. Nice club. I'll bet you look great on parade with all your gear and polish. One wants to make a good impression, don't you think? Appearances are so important."

Raoul tugs on the club, pulling the guard forward in an encouraging manner. "You know, this reminds me of an incident from my own past..." and proceeds to lead the guard down the hallway while relating a fascinating story about his days playing bass with a six-piece pre-ska band who couldn't get a gig until they changed their look to a meta street kind of thing, thereby gaining a certain cult status. Of course it didn't hurt that they became a must-see at the Many Worlds Music Festival after the legendary concert where the band's vocalist, a blond Ooolooon, was eaten whole, right there onstage, by the keyboard player, a wolf who felt she was grandstanding during his solos. But not to worry, they found another blond Ooolooon looking for her big break and replaced the wolf with a double-jointed basset hound who, as it turned out, was a much better fit for the kind of sound they were going for at the time.

"Like I said, it's all about appearances, my friend, all about appearances…" and they disappear down the hall.

Joe pushes tentatively on the door of the cell. It opens. He stands there, uncertain at first then regrouping enough to slither along the hallway until he comes to a window left unlocked in the assumption that no one would ever get this far anyhow. As he climbs over the transom, he hears Raoul asking the guard, "You didn't happen to see anything else land around here, did you? Anything really big?"

CHAPTER 18

Taboook, Sukie, and Ambrose follow close behind Banshooo, creeping out of the bamboo grove and into the depths of Careless Wood. Suddenly, the monkey stops short. The others bump up against him.

"What's the matter?"

Banshooo squints ahead. "It's the alchemist's place ... everything's trimmed and pruned and mowed and ... wait ... there's gnomes."

Ambrose squawks. "Gnomes?"

"And the house has been painted, some kind of earth tone, I think."

"Maybe Morie died and someone else lives here now."

A figure strolls across the new cedar deck wearing designer clothes, its grey hair pulled back in a ponytail and a pair of expensive sunglasses resting on top of its head.

"I think you may be right."

Then the figure trips and stumbles across the porch, landing on its bottom at the edge of the stairs. "No. That's him."

The alchemist stands up and dusts off his posh pants. He squints out at them as they make their motley way up the beautifully manicured path to his house.

"Hello? Who's that?"

"Hey, Morie, I guess the energy drink business is doing well, huh?"

The alchemist looks closely at Banshooo. "My word. What a surprise. How unexpected, how completely unexpected."

Taboook, who is carrying Ambrose, grunts and sets the owl down beside the stairs. He extends a big mitt toward the alchemist.

"How do you do? We haven't been introduced, but I was wondering if you had anything to eat inside this exceptionally lovely dwelling. We have come a long way, including, apparently, from Unseen worlds, which my buddy here will tell you about while we're eating." He twists his big mouth into what he hopes is a hospitable grin. "Whadaya say?"

Morienus steps back, pauses a moment, and then nods. "Well. Certainly. Of course, of course, do come in. Yes, yes, do come in."

The one-off picks up the owl and marches up the stairs. Sukie and Banshooo follow. Inside, what had been dark, dusty and filled with ancient equipment in various stages of disrepair is now light, airy and filled with fashionably matching color schemes.

"Wow. You've really cleaned the place up."

"Yes, yes, well." He looks around as if surprised himself. "It was the weasels."

"Excuse me?"

"It's a makeover firm. They give you a whole new look, new clothes, new abode, nest or burrow, as the case may be. Their motto is: 'Weasel Your Way into the Big Time'"

Ambrose mutters, "Really?"

"Oh yes, and they hired a cleaning company, a bunch of domestic cats, very neat, very tidy … well, you can see how nice everything looks." His guests smile appreciatively as they are invited to sit in matching chairs around a cherry wood table with a unique centerpiece made of edible flowers.

The alchemist distributes china cups and saucers, puts a kettle on the gleaming stove, and chooses from a series of tea tins, all labeled and ordered alphabetically. "Please, yes, do make yourselves comfortable." He pulls a variety of gourmet items from the cupboard and places them about the table.

"Great!" Taboook digs into the generous spread. Morie passes around a plate of fruit-filled macarooons. "The weasels helped me establish my brand. Evidently you have to have a brand, Banshooo. That's how it's done."

"That's how what's done?"

The kettle whistles loudly, and Morie invites Taboook to do the honors. While the one-off pours tea, the alchemist looks at Ambrose. "What happened to you?"

Sukie answers. "Ambrose lost his sight helping us create a multi-dimensional Image, an Image that reveals the true nature of reality."

"Excuse me?"

Banshooo leans across the table. "And I've been there, Morie, I've seen it for myself. It's about perception, just as you said. Time and space are entangled with perception. It's all connected to our awareness, our own consciousness. When I realized that, I saw the Unseen."

The alchemist leans back. "You *saw* it?"

"I did."

"I can't believe this."

Taboook dunks a biscotti in his tea. "I think it's probably true, man."

"Why do you say that?"

Taboook thinks for a moment. "Well, Banshooo doesn't lie. And there was the glowy thing."

"What glowy thing?"

"When we first landed back in the meadow, he was all glowy."

"He's not glowy now."

Taboook shrugs. "Evidently it wears off."

Banshooo pushes away from the table and stands up. "We don't have time for this. The launch of the new moon will pierce the Concord of Fire and Ice and that will destroy us all."

Morienus frowns. "How do you know about the Concord of Fire and Ice?"

"I learned of it in the Unseen. We need to move quickly. Everything is rushing toward a tipping point."

The alchemist snorts. "Everything is always rushing toward some kind of crisis or another, Banshooo. It never quite comes."

"It's different now. It's a matter of scale. We're messing up everywhere, not just one or two things here and there. It's *everywhere*. Now we've lost the blue moon, and soon we'll lose the water. We have to change."

Morie shakes his head. "No one wants to go back to the old ways."

"It's not about the old ways. It's about the newest way of all. It's about the fact that matter and consciousness influence one another. With a greater awareness we could learn to engage with the natural world, engage with what's already there instead of trying to override it."

Morie shakes his well-groomed head. "OOOCS doesn't like what is already there. They want to be in control. They believe they *are* in control."

"What if there was something that could provide a direct experience of the nature of reality?"

Sukie narrows her eyes. "You mean like the Image."

"Exactly." Banshooo looks at his friends. "What if we could broadcast the Image on the Cubes? What if everyone could see it at the same time? Not only here, but in the Icefields, too. There are Cubes and Cams in the Icefields, right?"

"There are Cubes and Cams everywhere now."

"If we could broadcast the Image where everyone could see, it would change awareness. They might stop the launch. It might save the Concord."

Morie scoffs. "Why do you think anyone would even know what it was?"

Banshooo sets his jaw. "I have it on good authority. Some will see, some won't. But it must be shown."

Sukie clears her throat. "Look, Shooo, I get where you're going with this, but there are quite a few obstacles in the way of such a plan, starting with the fact that we don't know where the Image is, or where Joe is for that matter."

The alchemist sighs so heavily his beard puffs. "Give it up, Banshooo. No one will pay attention. Trust me. You're not going to make any difference."

"But it was in the ancient book, it was a prophecy. You read it to me."

"The prophecy says you fail, Banshooo."

A loud silence falls leaving the sound of Taboook's chewing to fill the suddenly quiet space. The one-off looks around sheepishly and swallows with a noisy gulp. Banshooo frowns.

"You didn't tell me that before."

The alchemist walks to the bookshelf. He lifts out the ancient leather-bound book with the illegible title. He thumbs through to the last page and reads aloud.

"'And then the iron bird will fly and the voices of the Seen will fill the land with hubris and hate. The hope that lies within the ever-unfolding future shall be lost to fear. And the Daughter of the Wind shall turn to ash while wraiths of ill will and fair divert themselves in battle.'"

The words send a chill through the white light of the modish décor. Everyone is looking at Banshooo who narrows his eyes, thinks for a moment and then, to everyone's surprise, smiles.

"That's not the future, Morienus. That's now. You calculated it yourself. This is an ancient prophecy about what is happening now. And it's true. We're lost in fear and diverted in battle. But the future, the *actual* future is open, open and waiting for our next step."

He looks at the faces watching him. "Believe me, guys, there exists a vast number of choices. I've seen it. I've see the Reality of Possibility. We stand on the edge of it right here, right now. It unfolds as it is perceived. And the next step we take, all the possible next steps we take, *that* is what creates the future, *that* is what makes a prophecy come true. It's us, standing on the threshold of our next step, on the threshold of our awareness."

Everyone is quiet for a moment, then Ambrose nods slowly, his antennae waggling back and forth. "You're right, Banshooo. It's the way change happens. I've seen it, in the mind's eye, when an experience changes awareness."

Sukie's eyes widen behind her glasses. "Of course. Our consciousness influences the outcome. It's quantum indeterminacy. It's Schrödinger's Cat. And we haven't opened the box yet. We don't know the cat's fate!"

Taboook pumps his arms in the air. "Ahright! Let's save the cat!" The owl's hat bursts forth in song.

♫ *"Dancin' in the moonlight, everybody feeling warm and bright, it's such a fine and natural sight, everybody dancin' in the moonlight..."* ♫

Suddenly a tremendous crash sounds through the house as a dozen heavily armed and booted troops knock the door down and march into the kitchen, scattering designer objects onto the rosewood floor. They quickly surround the table rousting Banshooo, Sukie, Taboook, and Ambrose. As the fugitives are collared and cuffed, the alchemist stands aside sheepishly.

"I'm sorry, Banshooo. Really, I am."

PART VI

"*We are at the crucial moment in the commission of a crime. Our hand is on the knife, the knife is at the victim's throat. We are trained to kill. We are trained to turn the earth to account, to use it, market it, make money off it. To take it for granted. Logically, we will never be able to reverse this part of our culture in enough time to stop the knife in our hand. But that is the task at hand—to cease this act of violence.*"

—Charles Bowden

CHAPTER 19

Mammoth structures cover the glacial terrain of the Icefields. In the face of subfreezing temperatures, unstable geology and arduous conditions, Ooolandian determination has produced a sprawling edifice so audacious it must be admired by all.

In the dead center of this astounding achievement sits a towering rocket, held in a scaffolded framework like a giant phallic-shaped deity, momentarily tamed in a cage of steel, impatient to be unleashed. Attached to the rocket is a container housing the synthetic moon. When the payload reaches its assigned vector in space, the container will be shot forth, the moon inflated and sent into orbit. The rocket and container will fall away and crash back down out of the sky, scattering noxious debris someplace very far away from the Grand Oooland.

To achieve this end, a vast staff of engineers, technicians, and workers have been led by a gruff but lovable wolverine, the grizzled veteran of many bold constructions, though none as complex and challenging as this one.

Now, he sits in Mission Control, at the helm of the console commanding every aspect of the launch. Large screens reflect views of the entire site, and before him stretches an array of mesmers monitoring hardware, software, status report updates, and timeline indicators. Lights flash and blink on panels of switches, toggles, clocks, communicators, and flight control modules.

In the center of it all are two big square buttons, one green, labeled Go, and one red, labeled Abort. The final decision will fall to him. He is ready, secure in his role and proud to have reached the penultimate stage of preparation, eager to guide the project to what he is sure will be a successful fruition.

Meanwhile, unknown to this paragon of the can-do ethos, the drilling process has penetrated subglacial lakes of primordial water that has gone undisturbed for eons. Microscopic plankton, paleolithic paramecium, and other microbial entities have escaped from the ancient ice, spreading into the atmosphere, singing an ominous song.

deepest bonds
pierced in peril
the unfolding is slow
and then
it isn't

☾

Having escaped detection, Joe and Raoul lie low in the gully on top of the hill between Central Services and the Biolab. Joe is thinking about how good he felt when he was hiding here with Sukie and Ambrose just a few hours ago, so full of hope. What a naïve idiot he was. He swallows hard and looks at the raccoon with hopeful eyes.

"What do we do next?"

Raoul is peeking out through the thick shrubbery. "There is no 'we,' white man. I'm just a lone hitchhiker on the road to nowhere who needs a place to bunk for a while."

"But I've got to get the Image back. I was wrong to take it to OOOCS and now I've got to get it back."

"Good luck with that, fella. I've got to find Banshooo. He owes me some hospitality." Raoul raises his nose above the underbrush and squints about near-sightedly. They are adjacent to the promontory along the side of the silvery glass building. From here they can see the dark, squat, windowless structure, its smokestacks rising from the rear.

Joe frowns. "What is that?"

"You don't want to know."

A siren blares as a contingent of police pour out of the OOOCS compound and surround the security building from which Joe and Raoul have just fled.

Raoul chuckles. "Looks like someone checked up on that doofus bear."

"I've got to go down there."

"What are you, nuts?"

"I've got to get the Image back."

"So is this thing valuable or what?"

"It reveals the underlying nature of nature, and when you see it, when you actually *see* it, it'll change you. It changed me. I could never go back to work for OOOCS after…" He stops.

Raoul cocks his head sideways. "Gee, Joe, that would probably explain why they don't want it shown around."

"Oh man, I really screwed up." He begins crawling out of the ditch, awkwardly scooting forward on his belly. Raoul grabs him by the ankles and holds him there. "You don't handle pressure well, do you, Joe?"

"But what else can I do?" He looks at Raoul with desperate eyes, his ordinary humanoid face filled with extraordinary dismay. He is dangerously close to tearing up.

"Oh god, don't blubber." Raoul raises up on his elbows, letting out a big sigh. "Okay, okay, so where is this precious Image?"

"The CEO has it. He put it in the desk in his big office where he controls everything."

"He doesn't control everything, Joe. He's more what you'd call a figurehead, a front man, an actor on the great stage of MORE."

"How do you know?"

"I used to work for OOOCS myself."

"Raoul! Is that you?" Something fast and flitting drops down in front of them.

"Durga! Hey! How's it flying? Yikes!"

A screaming comes across the sky and slams into the dragonfly. Raoul and Joe watch in horror, expecting to see bits of her delicate body crushed and falling to the ground. A second later they realize she is high above them, having zoomed straight up at the last millisecond before contact. Now the drone is whirring back and forth above them as if looking for something. Durga drops down in front of it, wiggling her terminal appendage in its face. It turns to chase her as she whizzes away toward the dark, squat, windowless structure. She rises again high in the air. The drone chases her up higher and higher until she turns in a flash and nose-dives straight down, the drone following on her tail. Just before she smashes into the belching smokestack, she executes a perfect one-hundred-eighty-degree turn, sailing free as the drone plummets straight into the smokestack. They hear a screeching, clacking sound as its metal rotors and plastic body break apart. An industrial smell wafts up as pieces of synthetic material burn fitfully along with the other cremated entities meeting their final fate that day.

"Wow! Sensational moves, girl!" Raoul would high five Durga if a raccoon could do that with a dragonfly. She shrugs all four wings.

"It's a matter of speed, distance, direction, and the angle of approach—they have to calculate it all. I'm a nanosecond quicker cause with me, it just comes naturally. That gives me a slight advantage, just a couple of breaths, but it's enough." She pauses. "And it helps that they're stupid. I don't want to think what will happen when they perfect the damned things." Her huge compound eyes focus on Joe. "Who's this?"

"Ah. Allow me. Durga, Joe, Joe, Durga."

Joe stares in awe. "Glad to meet you. I must say that was really impressive."

"Yahokay." She flits over to Raoul. "So, big guy, what are you doing back in the USSR?"

"One More Mountain is falling apart. Literally. I'm looking for somewhere to hang, thought I'd check out the monkey's place."

"Forget that. The Meadow's been clear-cut, brush-hogged, and drilled, and the monkey's been busted, along with his crew. It's getting tight around here."

At that moment, a fierce buzzing cuts through the air like a chain saw. Durga shouts above the din. "I can keep them occupied for now but they're going to get a fix on you sooner or later. "Stay clear of the...!" Her warning is lost as she cuts straight up and away, executing a breathtaking acrobatic maneuver, looping, rolling and spinning off at top speed. Drone and dragonfly disappear into the sky.

Joe stares after them, his mouth agape. Raoul jabs him in the ribs. "Okay, Joe, looks like you and I are in the same boat now."

❨

Sukie, Taboook, and Ambrose stand before a security detail threatening them with Ooozies, a fearful weapon that stings something fierce while instilling a wave of self-doubt so intense it renders beings incapable of trusting their own common sense. If aimed at the heart, victims die from a total loss of confidence both in themselves and the world around them.

The squad marches them into the Detention Center and down a long corridor between a stark white windowless wall on one side and a series of cells on the other. The cells house drooping and hapless beings of various species, beings so thoroughly dispirited they barely look up as the new contingent marches by. Glaring overhead lights cast shadows across the floor and wall, shadows that mirror the cell bars, creating the feeling that the very air itself has been imprisoned in a noir-ish black and white world.

Taboook tries to sound defiant. "Where's Banshooo?"

"Don't know. Don't care." The guard pushes him forward until they reach what at first appears to be an empty cell. As they are ushered in, they see someone else is already there. A small, cylindrical being is trembling in the corner.

"Ralphie?" Taboook hurries over to the mole who lies stunned and shivering, his hope Ooozied away along with patches of burnt fur leaving bare red marks across his little body. He looks up and whimpers. "All is lost. All is lost."

A guard grabs Taboook by the arm and pushes him against the

wall of the cell along with Sukie and Ambrose. The officers stand back and study their captives. One of them moves close to Ambrose and begins poking at his helmet, pulling on the wires and antennae.

"What the heck is this?"

Another growls. "Whatever it is, it's a violation of the Electronic Protection Act. Confiscate it."

"No, wait." Sukie steps in front of the guard. "He needs that to see."

The officer shoves Sukie to the side and tears the helmet from Ambrose's head, yanking some feathers off in the process. The owl hoots in pain. The guard ignores him, staring at the cobbled device in his grasp. "Boy, this is weird." His cohort pokes at the drooping antennae. "Take it to Surveillance. It'll help make the case against these guys."

Another officer has patted down Taboook and found a small gold packet wrapped in a red satin ribbon. "Ah ha! What's this then?" He slides off the ribbon and opens it.

"Oooh, nice. A little treat, eh? Thank you, we will enjoy it."

The guards chuckle as they file out, pulling the cell door closed with a resounding clank. As they disappear down the hallway, Sukie looks at Taboook questioningly. Taboook shrugs. "The alchemist invited us to help ourselves, so I did."

"What is it?"

"Chocolate-covered something."

"You don't know what it is, but you took it anyway?"

"Maybe you didn't hear me. It's covered in choc-o-late."

Sukie slumps against the wall next to the owl. Ambrose sighs and lowers his head to his breast. Taboook shuffles over to Ralphie. He picks him up and slides down to the cold floor, cradling the mole in his arms, polydactyl forepaws and all. Ralphie closes his tiny eyes against the harsh fluorescent glare.

❮

Banshooo is standing in front of a desk in a somber, grey office. His paws are bound behind him. Nearby, an armed guard and an extraordinarily buff mammal wearing a colonel's uniform await further orders. Seated at the desk is a pale, affectless one-off. An opaque light seems to diffuse any focus. Banshooo senses that the opposite is true, that here in this small drab space, there is a frighteningly focused purpose.

After making it clear to Banshooo that his life is not worth any trouble he might give them, the one-off dismisses the guard and the colonel, then leans back in a posture of total ease, as if about to engage in a mildly entertaining discussion of little significance but some slight interest.

"So, you're the monkey who thinks we should change the way things are."

"The way things are is leading to disaster."

"And you know this…how?"

"I've seen the true nature of reality."

"Reality." The one-off snorts. "What's real is what we say is real."

The tie around Banshooo's paws is cutting into his flesh. "Where are my friends?"

"Don't worry, you'll be joining them soon enough." He narrows his eyes. "It must be difficult, saving the world and still finding time for friends."

"It's all connected."

Mabooose raises his chin and looks at Banshooo with what appears to be genuine interest. "How so?"

"The love we have for one another is an expression of the same energy that fuels the physical world. Respect and compassion are not abstractions. They are forces in the world. Actual forces that exert real influence."

Mabooose nods thoughtfully. "I think you're right." He leans back. "Disdain and hatred are also forces, forces that are much easier to provoke than kindness and consideration. Why is that, do you think?"

Banshooo mutters. "It's the wolf you feed."

"I've heard that. It appears to be true."

Suddenly a screen on the table across the room begins flashing as an electronically generated voice declares: "We interrupt your regular programming to bring you this special bulletin. We are now T minus three hours and counting toward the launch of Ooolandia's latest and greatest technological achievement. Stay tuned to your Cubes as the countdown proceeds in the upper right-hand corner of your screens." A bright red square appears with yellow numbers flashing on and off. "We now return to our regular programming."

Banshooo sets his jaw.

"You have to stop this launch. It will break the alliance of fire and ice that maintains the balance of the natural world."

"Alliance? What alliance? What are you talking about?"

"There is a Concord, held deep within the earth. Breaking it will lead to Ooolandia's destruction."

Mabooose snorts. "An alliance between the elements? You're delusional."

"What's delusional is thinking you can retrofit the natural world. You don't understand it, so how can you presume to re-engineer it?"

Mabooose stands up and moves around the desk, coming closer to Banshooo. He folds his bony arms.

"Face the truth, monkey. The fact is, in spite of all the blather about beauty and greenness, no one really wants to deal with nature. It's too hot or too cold or generally uncomfortable in one way or another. It bites, it scratches, it gives you hives and rashes, it stings, it's dirty, and it doesn't care if you get lost and hungry. So we build secure buildings that keep nature at bay, that keep everything under control." He smiles. "The Ooolandian populace wants things to be under control. They count on us for that." His eyes shine with a pitiless zeal. "And now we will create a better 'nature.' That's what Ooolandians want—nature that doesn't cause problems. A moon that doesn't disappear."

"The moon disappeared for a reason. It's a message to be heeded. We need to pay attention to what that means, to understand the causes that have led to the consequences we're facing."

"You sound like your friend, Morienus, before he faced '*reality*.'" He shrugs his shoulders slightly. "Personally, I don't have any faith in alchemy, but his familiarity with arcane chemical formulas has proven quite helpful indeed."

"What are you talking about?"

Mabooose raises his eyebrows. "Oh, you don't know? He helped us develop the solution that melted the molecules that were obstructing the moon project. And now he's provided us with a formula that will erase the clouds. It will keep the synthetic moon from degrading in weather."

"Why would he do that?"

"Well, it seems his fabled energy drink had some unfortunate side effects. When imbibed, it had a tendency to cause the mammalian heart to explode. A large class action suit was initiated. It would have ruined him. We changed the law, so he was, effectively, free from prosecution. In turn, he helped us with a few of our little problems." Mabooose tilts his head. "Extraordinary, really, that such a discredited science should still be effective in this day and age. You surmised as much, monkey. What you don't seem to realize is that such effectiveness will never be allowed to be utilized outside of our control." He moves back behind his desk. "Like that precious Image of yours."

Banshooo stares steadily at Mabooose. "I don't know what you're talking about."

The one-off pulls the Image from the drawer and places it on the desk between them.

"So you've never seen this?"

Banshooo watches the glowing object alive before him. He smiles, filled with gratitude for Sukie, Ambrose, and Joe; for their determination and for the magnificence of the Unseen. He looks up at the being across from him, suddenly realizing what is happening.

"You can see it. You can see it and still, you are not changed."

Mabooose sneers at Banshooo. "You think seeing something shiny will change beings? Will change what they want? I'm telling you, nothing will make them willing to do without all that our science and technology has provided."

"It's not about doing without. It's about working *within*. It's about developing science and technology in sync with the natural world, *with* it instead of against it. If everyone could see it in its essence, see their place in it…"

Mabooose interrupts, making a sound half way between a laugh and a snort. "Don't be a naïve chump. What ordinary beings understand is More, getting More, and having More." He crosses from behind the desk and steps in front of Banshooo. His breath is unpleasant.

"How did you create this Image? Who else is involved? How many of you are there?"

"I can honestly say I've never seen this before in my life."

"I don't believe you."

Banshooo shrugs. "I'm telling the truth."

Mabooose glares at Banshooo and then speaks slowly and evenly, marking each word with an ominous significance. "You have no idea who you're dealing with. You have no idea how big we are."

"I know that no matter how big you think you are, the natural world is bigger and will have the last word."

"The natural world? The natural world?!" He points toward the window. "You see that building up on the hill? Right now, in that lab, we're designing new sequences of DNA from scratch, growing organisms that do what we want them to do, producing synthetic crops, synthetic insects, and self-replicating beings from proto-cells that we create ourselves. Soon there will be no difference between what's 'natural' and what's 'synthetic.'" Mabooose looks directly into Banshooo's eyes.

"We are *replacing* your natural world, monkey, even as you and I stand here today. And when we launch the new blue moon, it will prove, once and for all, that *we* are the controllers."

Banshooo holds the cold gaze.

"You're running out of water and a synthetic moon will not bring it back. When the water's gone, that will be the end of all your grand plans."

Now Mabooose laughs out loud. "We'll create water! We'll modify our genetic structure so we don't need water! We'll generate a technological world that bypasses biology altogether!"

Banshooo's eyes reflect the sadness of a great unacknowledged truth. "It's fear, isn't it? Fear of death. Fear of the impermanence inherent in biology."

Mabooose growls low. "The impermanence inherent in biology is out of date." He picks up the Image and walks briskly to the safe, opens it, places the Image inside and slams it closed. He turns and glares at Banshooo.

"In the service of MORE, our technology will eliminate impermanence and all the other troublesome features of the natural world." His eyes burn like laser beams. "And there's nothing you or anyone else can do to stop it."

CHAPTER 20

From their gully hideout, Joe and Raoul watch a grim parade as a row of dark boxcar-like carts files up the hill to the top of the ridge behind the Biolab. The gate in the chain-link fence and the door of the crematorium both stand open as crews of orderlies in overalls and heavy gloves maneuver one cart after another up the hill and through the gate. The two escapees can hear them grumbling to each other.

"What's with the heavy rotation today?"

"They're clearing out the live labs."

"All of them?"

"All of them."

"Why now?"

"I don't know. I just do what I'm told. Push."

Howls and whimpers rise in volume as the carts roll by.

Peeking up from the edge of the gully, Joe whispers to Raoul, "What are they doing?"

"They call it D&I." Raoul purses his lips in disgust. "One more euphemism for one more crime."

"I don't understand."

"Disposal and Incineration, Joe." Raoul looks at the naïve humanoid huddled next to him. "It's where they take the beings they experiment on. When they're done with them they bring them up here, gas them, then burn their bodies."

"Oh." Joe's eyes are wide with dismay. "I never thought."

"Yeah, well, most don't."

Another thought most never have moves from Raoul's brain to a gleam in his eye. He raises his head up out of the gully. "Maybe it's time for a little liberation action."

Joe grabs the raccoon's forepaw. "Wait. What are you doing?"

Raoul leans down and whispers instructions to Joe, who responds by looking much the same as he did when the raccoon first landed in his cell. Raoul pats him on the back. "Trust me. I'm a master of the diversionary tactic." He heads up the promontory and saunters over to the gate in the chain-link fence where two workers, a gruff gorilla and a humanoid, are taking a moment to catch their breath. Raoul effects a sympathetic nod.

"Ah yes, it's a hard life for the rank and file. You guys must be exhausted. They gotcha working double shifts here or what?"

The two mammals turn in surprise. The gorilla frowns. "What's it to you?"

"Well, I'll tell ya, friend, it's a lot to me. And here's why. We working stiffs have to stick together, otherwise we're nameless fodder. The boss can do whatever he wants with us if we're alone. But if we—and by 'we' I mean you," he points to the big primate, "and me," he points to himself— "if we stick together, side by side, shoulder to shoulder, we got power, we got influence, we got leverage. So you see, what you do means a lot to me, understand?"

The two look at each other. The humanoid mumbles, "I do feel pretty powerless most of the time, I've got to admit…" The gorilla shrugs. "But that's just the way it is."

Raoul raises his clawed paw, pointing enthusiastically upward.

"Ah, but my friend! That's *not* just the way it is. That's the way they want you to *think* it is, but, in fact, it's just the opposite. We're the most powerful piece in the whole system, in the whole world of MORE. We're the engine, the key, the very force that keeps it all going. All of MORE has been built with our time and energy. We're not powerless. We're the source of all power." He leans in.

"But only if we organize. Only if we all come together and unite. Then we can use our muscle to help ourselves instead of serving the bosses."

The two orderlies are now listening intently. From his hiding place, Joe watches as other members of the disposal crew join the circle growing around the raccoon. Some are nodding in agreement, and another asks a question. Raoul responds animatedly. He has their full attention.

Joe creeps up to one of the carts sitting some distance from the confab at the gate. It's about eight feet tall and six feet wide, on metal wheels. The door is fixed with a large iron bolt. He looks toward Raoul and sees that he's drawing the crew's attention away from the carts, gesturing and pointing at the crematorium. Joe takes hold of the bolt, lifts it up, and pulls. The door slides open. Something inside snarls at him. He jumps back as it lurches forward. It stops and stands framed in the opened door, startled at the sudden light. Part rhino, part dog, with thick armor-like skin covering the top half its body leaving a mottled belly shivering and naked. It's bloodshot eyes catch sight of Joe, and it opens a massive mouth baring fanged teeth and foaming red gums, growling fiercely. It leaps out and heads toward Joe, who drops to the ground and crawls frantically under the cart. Another version of the same creature flies out of the dark box and runs past him down the hill.

Raoul's union meeting falls apart as the gorilla turns in surprise at the sudden ruckus below. Joe recovers himself and, moving quickly, loosens the bolt on the next cart, casting the door wide. Lurching through the opening is a twisted leopard-like beast with bleached white boney knobs protruding along its spine. Its weakened haunches cause it to stumble and fall to the ground. Joe is crouched down alongside the cart. The feline creature lies writhing on the ground beside him. He looks into its tortured eyes. The pain he sees there is beyond physical. He is looking into the ocean of suffering left in the absence of empathy.

Raoul materializes next to Joe. "Come on, man, get a grip." Joe stands up, takes a deep breath, and follows the raccoon to the next cart and the next, trying not to look at the deformed and frantic beings scattering everywhere. As the carts empty, a mass of mutant panic explodes across the terrain. The lab crews rush about in a desperate attempt to corral the crazed experiments, but it's too late. Snarling pig-dogs, hairless beaver-rats, and fearsome antlered grizzlies growl, howl, bay, and scream. Sirens erupt. Chaos is achieved.

☾

Banshooo tries to keep pace between two very large beings encased in military gear and carrying Ooozies. They have marched him out of Mabooose's office and down a long, empty hallway into the southeast section of the compound leading to the Detention Center. He stumbles and the officer behind jabs him in the back. "Keep going, buster."

Moving along the concrete path crossing the quad, they hear what sounds like distant howling. They stop abruptly and listen as the eerie wail grows louder. A large shape appears suddenly, running down the hill directly toward them. As it gets closer they see a weasel-like creature the size of a bear with the head of a pit bull, it's mouth stretched open baring huge yellow teeth flecked with spittle. It jumps onto the guard behind Banshooo and before he can react, it tears his throat open. Blood spews everywhere. The second officer fires, narrowly missing Banshooo who stands back in confusion. The beast rolls over howling, its legs flailing in the air. The guard shoots again and again until, finally, it lies still in a dead heap. Soon another mutant is charging toward them and then another. As the guard fires wildly, Banshooo staggers, trying to maintain his balance. Out of the corner of his eye he sees what looks like a particularly ugly mutant with the head and claws of a raccoon spliced onto humanoid legs. It's heading straight for him. He starts to turn away, but the raccoon-half grabs him by his shoulder while the human-half runs right into him. Tumbling to the ground, they roll over in a ball coming to a stop hard against a chain-link fence bordering the wall of the compound. They get up unsteadily, spitting grass and dust. The raccoon recovers first.

"Well. If it isn't the monkey."

Banshooo shakes his head and blinks. "You? What are you doing here?"

"Saving your ass, my friend." Sirens ring out as the sound of charging boots and heavy gunfire erupts from above the hill. Raoul grabs Banshooo by the arm and pushes him toward Joe, who is sliding under the fence and scrambling toward the compound wall. He disappears around a sharp corner. They follow him into an alcove-like space under a high parapet. The three of them duck down, hidden from the chaos above. As they catch their collective breath, Banshooo squints at the raccoon.

"How'd you...?"

Joe burbles excitedly. "He dropped out of the air right in front of me and then he got me out of jail and then we made this whole thing happen. Amazing, huh?"

Banshooo hesitates. "I...guess..."

Raoul peers over the concrete wall surrounding them. A cordon of OOOCS troops have formed a line along the quad, kicking and shooting at packs of crippled creatures, pushing the mutant outbreak away from the compound and trying to corral the rampage before it enters the sleek and fashionable suburbs of the Grand Oooland. As the cacophony of howling and gunfire begins to fade from earshot, the raccoon turns back with a grin.

"I think that went well, don't you?"

Joe nods enthusiastically Banshooo just stares. Raoul takes a deep breath and looks around.

"Okay. So where are we?"

"It's a pan-field dead zone. Surveillance techs come here to grab a smoke."

Raoul points toward a steel door in a service entrance nearby. "What about that?"

"It's an old exit behind the monitor bay. No one ever uses it."

At that moment, the door swings open. They freeze. A badger emerges and freezes in his turn.

"Jonesy!"

"Joe!"

They stand staring at one another. Joe recovers first. "Okay, okay, don't run away. I'm not going to try to show you anything."

Jonesy lowers his big striped head. "I should have looked. I should have helped you. I'm sorry, man. I didn't realize..." his voice trails off.

"What's happened, Jonesy?"

He looks up with tears in his eyes. "They killed my family, Joe, all of them."

"Oh."

Raoul clears his throat. "Uh, sorry for your loss and all but ... who are you exactly?"

Joe puts his arm around the badger. "He's my friend. We worked surveillance together. He was the first fur-bearer ever promoted to the TIDC."

Raoul takes a step back. "Whoa."

Jonesy shakes his head. "Don't worry. I won't turn you in. I'm not going back. What they do is just ... wrong."

Raoul squints at the badger warily, pointing to the silver Halliburton cuffed to his wrist. "What's in there?"

"It's nothing. Just a couple of memos and schematics. You're supposed to keep it with you at all times. At first, I thought it was cool, now it just seems ... heavy."

Banshooo is thinking. He looks at Jonesy. "The TIDC controls transmissions on the Cubes, right?"

"Right."

"And the moon launch is set to be broadcast on the Cubes, right?"

"Right. They've scheduled a big chatterdee event at the Great Hall. Every screen in Ooolandia will be zeroed in."

Banshooo looks hard at the badger. "If I can get the Image to you, could you get it into the system?"

"What Image?"

Joe bites his lip. "But they took it, Shooo. I don't know where it is."

"I do."

"What?"

"A one-off named Mabooose has it."

Raoul's eyes widen. "You saw Mabooose?"

Joe frowns. "Who's Mabooose?"

"He's the *eminence gris* behind the whole shebang."

Banshooo looks at Raoul. "How do you know this?"

Joe nudges the raccoon, proud to promote his new accomplice. "He used to work for OOOCS too."

Banshooo's eyes widen as it dawns on him. "*You're* the guy who leaked the truth about the Cubes."

"I do have that honor."

Banshooo looks at him quizzically. "Aren't you worried you'll be caught?"

"Eh, you know how it is. To the unfurred, all raccoons look alike." He glances toward Joe. "No offense."

"None taken."

"The point is, sadly enough, my heroic feat didn't make any difference. Most Ooolandians have their paws full just keeping a nest together. They don't have time to even think about how it could be different, let alone make it so. OOOCS has successfully created the illusion that MORE is all there is. They don't want anyone to believe there might be an alternative."

Joe is bereft. "How could I have thought they would see?"

Banshooo's voice is resolute. "Mabooose sees. I saw him see. He knows how powerful it is. That's why he hasn't destroyed it. He wants to find a way to use that power for his own ends."

Suddenly, a black streak drops straight down from the eave above and lands squarely in front of Raoul. It bows low, its blue ears flopping forward. "*Konnichiwa*, Raoul-san."

Raoul bows back. "Naruto-san. My man." They execute a six-step high five ending with an old-school *Fresh Prince* fist bump.

The masked figure points to the havoc on the hill. "Did you do this?"

"I did."

"Ah, chaos. The ninja's ally."

He turns to Banshooo. "So. The alchemist gave you up."

Banshooo nods. "My friends have been arrested. I need to help them."

"Don't worry about them. Seems some kind of edible was confiscated off your buddy, Taboook. The guards consumed the evidence and became convinced they were the custodians of Kubla Khan's pleasure-dome. They decreed it only fitting that all prisoners be released."

"Shroooms? Boook had shroooms?"

"Evidently they were covered in chocolate."

Raoul laughs. "Good for the freak."

Naruto nods. "Yeah, but the bad news is, Central Services has beefed up all their firewalls for this launch thing. We can't get back into the system."

Banshooo turns to Jonesy.

"Tell me, how will the launch broadcast work?"

"Well, in the hall the CEO will press a button. That will signal the crews in the Icefields to start the countdown."

Raoul looks at Banshooo. "What are you thinking?"

"I've got to get back in that office."

Joe's eyes narrow. "Wait. Is it on the top floor of the main building, way in back of the rear wing?"

"Yeah."

"There are surveillance gaps back there." He nods slowly. "Now I know why."

"Okay, good. That means you can steer us past the cams." He turns to Raoul. "And you, well, let's just say you know how to uh, appropriate items that aren't readily uh, available to…"

Raoul interrupts the monkey. "If this is you trying to convince someone to join in a suicide mission, you're not very good at it."

Joe frowns. "But how do we know Mabooose won't be there?"

The black-clad ninja bunny stands erect. "Have no fear. I'm on it." He shoots up the wall and balances nimbly on the edge of the parapet.

"I am Naruto. I will be victorious or my name doesn't mean 'Shining Golden Warrior of Virtue.'" With that, he disappears from sight.

Banshooo whispers to Raoul, "I'm pretty sure *naruto* means steamed fishcake."

The raccoon nods. "I know. Don't say anything."

Jonesy drops his head. "We are so screwed."

CHAPTER 21

In the center of the Grand Oooland, a large park surrounds a great Hall. The flawless green expanse stretches for acres, lined with trees and bushes manicured to maintain an impressive setting for the hall itself, the architectural jewel in the center of the crown of global Moreism. Ornately carved Corinthian columns support the roof over the main chamber. Archways of sculpted marble define a colonnade running the length of the hall. Inspirational mottos are carved in porticos over heroic sculptures, creating an air of historical inevitability. Walking into this space is walking into the full power of the story of More made visible, fixed and ingrained, like a weight in the air, like the marble it's made of.

In outlying areas, farmland burns in drought while islands are inundated with rising waters, but here in the Grand Oooland, all glows and glitters in the opulence of MORE. Twilight reflects off the glass towers and teeming energy of the city as a procession of powerful VIO's parades through the park and into the hall, gathering to witness the launch of the new moon.

The President and Chairman of the Board lead the procession, followed by the CEO. Next comes the Head of Public Promotions, the Head of the Department of Great Big Projects, and the Head of Systems Operations. Inside, the stage is set to accommodate the

plethora of VIOs and celebrities. An extensive collection of chatterdees eagerly line the aisles in anticipation of quotable chirps ex-
tolling this once-in-a-lifetime event. Giant screens cover the walls,
broadcasting live shots of the launch site. An air of pageantry prevails as Ooolandia prepares to bask in the light of its totally automated, totally guaranteed, totally owned and operated blue moon.

In the wings, two bodyguards stand sentinel on either side of a
pale figure whose features are hidden in the shadowy background.

☾

Inside the Central Services compound, Joe creeps along with Raoul
and Banshooo to a plain, unmarked door at the end of a long,
empty hallway.

"Are you sure this is it? It looks like a janitor's closet."

"This is it."

"Are you sure he's not in there?"

Raoul nods. "I'm sure. Naruto may be a little lame, linguistical-
ly speaking, but if he says Mabooose has gone to the Hall, then
Mabooose has gone to the Hall."

Raoul tries the door and it opens. They slip inside and close it
behind them. Joe looks around in surprise.

"Well, this certainly isn't very fancy for the guy who runs everything. I mean, you should see the CEO's office. It's huge. It's got
all kinds of swanky furniture and curtains and silver things and a
gigantic desk and…"

Raoul interrupts him, pointing up at the ceiling where surveillance cams would be. "The proof of this guy's importance is what
isn't here."

Banshooo walks over to the framed photo of OOOCS headquarters and pushes it to the side, revealing the safe. Raoul pulls a
chair over to the wall, climbs onto it and assesses the situation.

"Hmmm. Not the easiest boost in the world, but not the hardest
either."

He interlaces the digits on his two front paws and stretches his
arms in front of him, then shakes out his sharp, nonretractable

claws like a pianist preparing to play a particularly complicated scherzo. Finally he leans in, his ear close to the big combination dial in the center of the safe. Slowly he turns the dial, his brow furrowed in concentration. Joe watches, his fear palpable. Could his own gullibility have destroyed the last best chance to make things better? Ever?

Raoul turns back toward Joe. "Hey, buddy, you're shivering so loud, it's breaking my concentration. Chill, okay?"

Joe tries taking deep breaths. Raoul turns back to the safe. Banshooo watches the monitors. The yellow numbers count down one hour to blastoff.

Raoul works the dial, listens, then turns it again. After what seems like a long time, he smiles. "Got it." He pulls down on the lever and the safe swings open.

Sitting on top of a pile of documents, the Image gives off a light that makes him blink. Carefully he lifts it out of the safe and stares into it, whistling softly. "Holee muthaa."

Joe turns to Banshooo. "So why can he see it and the managers can't?"

Banshooo sighs. "A lot of OOOCS employees have been trained not to see beyond their immediate role in the MORE order. They've learned to ignore any other story." He straightens his shoulders, his voice determined. "Trust me. Some will see, and that will make a difference. That will make a change."

A long pause deepens as a flutter of hope fills the somber room. Raoul jumps off the chair and grins. "Okay! Let's do this thing!"

They open the door and stick their heads out. The hallway is empty. As they step out into the corridor, Joe cannot contain his excitement. "We got it! We got it back!"

Raoul looks at him with a jaundiced eye. "That's great, Joe, but the critical part of any caper is getting away with it."

As he says this, steel-toed boots marching in lockstep reverberate through the hallway and before they can react, the three fugitives are looking at a firing squad, planted directly in front of them, a virtual wall of black helmets, face visors, and full riot gear. A voice declares, "Stand where you are!"

They stop frozen in place. At the sound of rifles being raised, Joe whispers to Raoul. "Okay, what's our next move?"

"No more moves, this is it."

"Stop kidding around. What do we do?"

"I'm wide open. Whaddaya got in mind?"

"How do I know? You're the expert, think of something."

The lead officer stands to one side, his arm raised. He shouts. "READY!" Five rifles are cocked. "AIM!"

Banshooo steps in front of Joe and Raoul. He holds the Image up and moves it slowly side to side, directly in the squad's line of sight. They lower their guns. The officer growls. "Put that down and step back."

Banshooo doesn't move. There is a long pause then the officer shrugs. "Okay, don't put it down." He raises his arm again.

"READY!"

The squad lifts their guns once more. Joe swallows hard. Raoul squeezes his eyes shut.

"AIM!"

Banshooo is thinking it must be the visors. The visored ones seem to see only what they are ordered to see.

As the officer is about to exclaim the word "Fire," a gigantic orange entity plummets out of the air and crashes directly onto the firing squad. Pieces of Kevlar sail through the air, guns and gear thud off the walls, a cloud of corporeal dust billows up, filling the hallway.

When the dust settles, the scene is grim. Joe watches in disbelief as the orange thing struggles to right itself, its huge feet crushing the remaining life out of two uniforms still wriggling in agony.

Raoul is jubilant. "Yomo! You made it! You finally made it!"

The creature raises its head from the grotesque heap and looks around with a dazed expression, blinking and breathing heavily. Joe backs away from this fearsome mammal of indeterminate species attempting to disentangle itself from what is now nothing more than a pile of guns, gear, broken bones, and the twisted bodies of dead military-type personnel who were, until a moment ago, just following orders. Finally, the beast focuses on Raoul.

"You said this would be easy. It was not easy."

Raoul grins. "But you made it! You're here. And I must say your timing couldn't be better, old buddy. Couldn't be better."

Yomolahki shakes his head fiercely. "I'm hungry. I'm very, very hungry."

Banshooo is trying to protect the Image. Joe is plastered flat against the wall, looking frantically up and down the hallway, unsure about whether to run over or around the pile of dead police.

Yomo is eyeing Banshooo. "He bit my foot."

Joe looks at Banshooo in disbelief. "Why would you do that?"

Raoul steps in front of the beast, pointing a sharp claw directly at his nose.

"Yomo! You just landed in a new realm. Turn the page, man. Let bygones be bygones. No need to prey on friends when you have such a delicious buffet lying right at your feet." He points to the heap of mangled officers. "Check it out." He picks up the uniformed leg of what was apparently some type of gibbon. "Look, I'll bet this guy is very tasty. Yum!"

The beast hesitates. Raoul insists. "Come on, try one. Take *one bite*. If you don't like it, you don't have to eat it." Yomo begins rummaging through the bodies, sniffing here and there. Joe, still spread-eagle against the wall, shoots a panicky glance at Raoul who shakes his head back and forth and mouths the words, "Don't worry."

After more sniffing and snuffling and poking through the pile, Yomo takes a mouthful, chews, swallows, and nods slowly. "Hmmm. Not bad. Crunchy on the outside, creamy on the inside."

As Yomolahki begins to eat in earnest, Banshooo tiptoes along the hallway, past the pile. He turns back waiting for Joe who hesitates, still in shock. "Come on, Joe. Take this." He proffers the Image. "Get it to Jonesy. I'm going to the Great Hall to try and stop the launch."

☾

Jonesy and his Halliburton are pacing nervously back and forth beneath the compound wall. This is taking too long. What's he doing anyway? Is he nuts? It's impossible to fight OOOCS. And this is such an insane idea, why did he say he'd help? He admires Joe's determination, he really does, but this? This is crazy. He's going to bail.

The badger has his paw on the door when Joe comes barreling up. "I've got it, I've got it. Hang on Jonesy. It's right here."

As he rushes up, the badger steps back, shaking his head. "I don't know, Joe. This is a pretty wild scheme and it probably won't work and I'll get jailed or shot dead. I'm really thinking maybe I shouldn't…"

Joe is holding the Image in two hands. He raises it to eye level in front of Jonesy's face. Jonesy stops talking. His mouth falls open, his eyes reflect the tender glow, his entire face grows full of awe. Moments pass.

Joe removes the Image from Jonesy's view. "Don't you think everyone deserves a chance to see this? Don't you think, if they did, it might change things for the better?" Jonesy smiles and slowly nods his head. He opens the Halliburton. Joe places the Image inside, next to a picture of Jonesy's firstborn son.

The two of them lock hand to paw, hugging each other closely. Then the badger closes the case. Just as he turns to go, the door opens and a low-grade surveillance technician steps out for a smoke.

"Hey Jonesy, what's up? I thought you high mucky-mucks had your own cafeteria and rec rooms and massage therapy and all that. Whatcha doing down here with us plebs?"

Jonesy recovers quickly. "Very funny, Frank. I do, however, have to get back to work." He steps through the door and is gone.

The technician stares at Joe. "Say, aren't you that guy who was fired for hallucinations?"

"You must have me confused with someone else." Joe scoots through the door and disappears. Frank's eyes narrow. That was definitely the whack job.

☾

Yomolahki has sated himself and is taking a nice long snooze. Raoul has pulled one of the tasers out of the pile of the half-eaten firing squad and is trying to figure out if it still works. Lost in concentration it takes a moment before he notices the whirring translucent form hovering around the leftovers. She zooms along the contours of the big furry expanse that is Yomolahki, stopping for a moment in front of his face until his snoring exhalation blows her back toward Raoul.

"What the heck happened here?"

"It's a long story, my dear." He pulls the uniform off of the trooper nearest him and tries it on. "What does this look like?"

"A raccoon in military drag."

He adds the boots and the helmet. "How about this?"

She studies him for a moment. "Short. You look short."

He pulls on an additional pair of boots, adding a few inches. "How about this?"

Durga shakes her head. "What are we doing here, fella?"

He stops, looks into her huge compound eyes, and sighs.

"Well, girl, I seem to have gotten roped into an effort to effect a radical advance in the evolution of consciousness."

She thinks for a minute then nods. "Okay. I'm in. Whaddaya need?"

❧

In the Detention Center, the night shift has discovered their colleagues slumped against the opened doors of empty cells, unable to move their legs and complaining to one another about their teeth. Sirens blare and police units fan out across the compound and beyond.

Sukie, Taboook, Ambrose, and Ralphie have taken cover in the same gully behind the Biolab where Joe and Raoul hid just hours before. Most of the evidence of the mutant melee is gone. Carts and carcasses have been cleared away but the ground is still pit-marked with hooves, feet, boots, and claw marks of all kinds. Here and there a smear of blood glistens on the genetically modified grass.

Scrunched down in the ditch, the foursome is trying to figure their next move. They are not the most confident group ever stuck in a hole. Taboook's fur is matted and dirty, his right ear bitten and torn. The mouse, while trying to put a good face on it, is smudged with exhaustion, her glasses are cracked, and her whiskers bent. Ambrose is stooped over like an elderly hominid, his lifeless eyes cast down. Ralphie lies limp in Taboook's arms. The one-off places him gently onto the ground. The mole looks up, his tiny eyes glimmer.

"I'm done for, Boook."

"Hey, don't talk like that, little fella. We'll get out of here. Somehow."

"I'm … I'm sorry I called you a freak."

"Forget it. I shouldn't have made fun of your paws. They're amazing, they really are."

Ralph doesn't answer. His body is quiet now and his eyes are closed. As they watch, his head drops down onto his velvety breast. A long, slow breath leaves him. Moments pass but another doesn't come.

"Oh maaan." Taboook sighs deeply.

Ambrose raises his head. "Is what I think just happened what happened?"

Sukie speaks quietly. "I'm afraid so."

The owl shivers, his feathers streaked with dust. "You should leave me here. I'll just slow you down."

Sukie sets her jaw. "Okay, first of all, we don't know where we're going so how can you slow us down? Second of all, we're not leaving you anywhere, and third of all…"

Suddenly, a whirring sound interrupts overhead. A surveillance drone hovers above them. Sukie looks at Taboook but before they can react, another whirring swoops in and buzzes around the drone like a twirling lasso. The drone darts one way and then another and then rises straight up and stops, hovering again. The lasso follows, encircling the drone furiously, faster and faster until the machine appears to lose its bearings and crashes straight down onto the dirt road behind the gully, leaving bits of tritanium, pyerite, and mexallon scattered across the hill.

Sukie squints upward and sees two big bright eyes floating above them. "Durga!"

Taboook's mouth is hanging open. "How'd you do that?"

"Turns out, if you confuse their stupid little gyroscopic system, they crash themselves." She flicks her translucent wings and sets herself directly in front of the gully.

"Okay, everybody out of there. Groom yourselves and try to look presentable. You're being taken to the Great Hall."

Nobody moves.

Durga buzzes her wings determinedly. "Seriously, guys, we got this."

Hesitating, they look at each other. After a minute, Sukie crawls out of the gully and peers around nervously. A police unit is waiting at the bottom of the hill. Joe stands within their midst.

"What the heck...?"

"Trust me, it's okay."

Taboook picks up Ambrose and growls. "We trusted the alchemist and look where it got us."

"Did I just save your asses or did I not?"

One of the officers has marched up the hill. He raises his visor. Two piercing black eyes stare out above a whiskered snout.

Taboook gawks. "How...?"

Raoul gestures toward the police. "I told them we've been dispatched to escort you guys to the hall."

"You're kidding."

"They believed me when I told them you're scientists." He squints at the disheveled pair. "Eccentric scientists."

"What about Ambrose?"

"He's a genetic experiment you're working on, okay? Can we get a move-on now?"

Taboook turns back toward the gully. "What about Ralphie?"

They all look down at the mole, his soft round body held in Death's great stillness.

Raoul sighs, then sets his jaw. "It'll be all right. Nature will take care of Ralphie." He drops the visor on his helmet and pushes Taboook forward. "Go!"

In the Total Information Domination Command, technicians prepare for the live transmission of the launch. As lift-off approaches, the ambient energy in the room rises like a digital spike in virtual blood pressure. Dedicated split screens are filled with mesmer-generated overlays, delineating the countdown. Simulated routines are rehearsed. The staff is focused and on the alert. Jonesy continues to play his part while nervously eyeing the Halliburton stashed under his desk. Gareth ups his daily dose of Xanax.

CHAPTER 22

T he streets of The Grand Oooland are filled with the feathered, the furred, the scaled, the shelled, the shorn, and the
nearly naked. Mammals, hominids, humanoids and the
occasional one-off all gather to see history being made. Masses
of Ooolandians group themselves around the Cubes watching as
their CEO leans into the microphone and speaks with a friendly
intimacy.

"I think we can all agree that life can be hard and nature unfor-
giving." The crowd nods and murmurs in assent. "Tonight, I'm
happy to be able to announce that we're on the verge of making
our own nature, my friends, and we're going to make it better, more
comfortable and more convenient." He continues with a rising enthusiasm. "It's the nature of the future, providing jobs, energy, security, and MORE!"

All join in applause. A festive atmosphere prevails. Hiding in the
crowd, Banshooo has joined the stream of citizenry. A phalanx of
guards stands in close formation around the entrance to the Hall.
He looks at their helmets and thinks about how the firing squad
couldn't see the Image, their visors shielding their eyes from anything that isn't a designated target. A wave of despair overwhelms
him. Maybe no one will see. Then he hears Sid's voice: "...*it must be
shown.*"

Shrill police whistles blow as crowds are directed into side streets to make room for new arrivals. Banshooo finds himself shuffled into an alleyway near a side entrance to the hall. Standing in front of this door is a single guard in police gear and helmet. As Banshooo considers the impossibility of getting past this figure and through the door, a shadow passes across the building's marble facade. He looks up. A large flock of migratories are flying overhead. He thinks of the godwit who fell out of the storm, of how they fly thousands of miles through all kinds of weather using the pulse from deep inside the earth for guidance.

Directly behind him a muscular mongoose snarls. "Dirty migratories. Why don't they stay where they are?" Another voice pipes up. "Hey man, what's your problem? Some of my best friends are migratories." The mongoose turns and spits. "Oh yeah? Well maybe you should migrate outta here with 'em." A scuffle breaks out as the two push and shove one another. A gibbon and a humanoid join in the fight and soon they are surrounded by others, yelling and cursing. The guard steps into the crowd, raising his Ooozie and shouting.

"Okay, okay, everybody calm down."

As the crowd moves backward, Banshooo sneaks forward, around and behind the guard whose attention is taken up with the fight. He creeps up to the door. Suddenly a shot is fired. Screams ring out. The guard yells, "Everybody freeze!" More police materialize. Unnoticed in the noise and commotion, Banshooo pulls on the door. It opens. He scoots through. The door shuts behind him and the sound of the fracas outside is replaced with the sound of keen anticipation filling the auditorium.

$$ \mathbb{C} $$

In the Icefields, at Mission Control, final protocols are moving the countdown toward the launch. The wolverine keeps a sharp eye on all systems indicators and communicators. Everything is running smoothly and on schedule.

$$ \mathbb{C} $$

In the Total Information Domination Center, Jonesy is growing ever more nervous. Time is running out, and he hasn't been able to find a way to insert the Image into the broadcast stream. An unexpected visit from the Colonel has added to his anxiety level. The steely being with the bulging biceps stands in front of the room. Complaining about a flurry of surveillance breakdowns and prison escapes, he lectures the technicians on the importance of the launch coming off without a hitch. His voice is hard.

"This is a great day for Ooolandia. I expect each one of you to do your job perfectly. We don't want any more screw-ups."

His eyes settle on Gareth and Jonesy. He turns to the supervisor and demands in a loud voice, "What are they doing here?"

The supervisor lowers his head. "Don't worry. They're competent."

"Well I don't like it. When this is over, replace them with erect bipedal primates." He aims one last threatening glare at the TIDC staff then turns on his heel and strides out the door. The supervisor clears his throat. "Okay, everybody, let's get back to work."

The sloth sits stunned. After all his hard work, after he excelled at every test, after devoting himself totally to OOOCS, now he's going to be fired? A wave of intense anger moves through him. The erstwhile slumbering moths inside his fur are awakened by the tremor within their host body. As Gareth's resentment grows, they begin to spark and sputter, an autonomic response to injustice. Spitting out of the hairy depths, loosed and livid, they turn him into a sloth-shaped fury of flashes, crackling like a gigantic loose electrical outlet.

Everyone turns in shock and surprise. The technicians near him jump away. Someone picks up a chair and throws it at him. Gareth flails about wildly, banging into a console then sliding across the floor. Jonesy cries out, "Wait!" but he's ignored as several staffers chase Gareth around the room shouting. "Get him! Get him!"

Startled, Jonesy realizes this is his chance. He can't help Gareth and he must act now, for the greater good. He opens the briefcase and lifts out the Image. Stepping away from the furor, he sidles over to the transmitting area and edges up alongside the quanta-to-material converters. Hastily he works to calculate frame rate conversion and the simulcast schedule. He opens the gem.lock file. He scans the Image into the mesmers. Turning back, he sees Gareth has been knocked out. The floor is littered with moth bodies, stomped, swatted, and squashed to death. He returns to his station having no clue as to whether he got this right or has just sent the Image to the recycle bin.

The unconscious sloth is rolled aside and covered with a tarp. Everyone tries to recover themselves, moving back into their assigned places and anxiously returning to the task at hand.

"Jeez, how weird was that?"

"This is why we need to make migratories illegal."

"I don't think Gareth's a migratory."

"Whatever, he's not one of us. "

They all work quickly to do their part to achieve the live transmission of Ooolandian supremacy. Jonesy feels sick.

☾

Inside the Great Hall, Banshooo finds himself standing amongst a pack of blinking, cheeping chatterdees too distracted to notice him. On the huge screens, the launch site seems to tremble with anticipation. On the stage, a big black button sits conspicuously on top of the podium. The CEO smiles his perfect smile, gestures toward the podium, and speaks.

"In a few moments, I will press this button to initiate the countdown to Ooolandia's future. But before I do, let me introduce a few of those who have helped us reach this glorious moment in our history."

The Very Important Ooolandians are introduced, including Morienus who is lauded for

"helping us complete the extraordinary accomplishment that you are to witness today. And soon," the CEO bows slightly in the direction of the alchemist, who stands basking in the spotlight, "he will make our lives cloudless. It will be our next great achievement." The applause in the hall is enjoined by applause throughout

Ooolandia as the general population happily anticipates another brilliant triumph for the magnificent ideology of MORE.

Banshooo sees one of the chatterdees nudging another, making a joke about the alchemist's looks. A wave of blinks, winks, and chirping follows. As the flurry continues, one of the birds fails to notice that he's dropped his all-access pass to the floor. Banshooo crouches down behind the line of chatterdees. He has his paw on the pass when another bird looks over and sees him. Banshooo prepares to dissemble, but a new wave of blinking grabs the chatterdee's attention and he's distracted again. Banshooo snatches up the credentials and walks down the main aisle. Seeing the pass, ushers nod, allowing him to move forward. He makes his way toward the podium.

☾

At that same moment, surrounded by their police escort, Sukie and Joe trot double-time up the main steps of the hall and into the auditorium. Taboook follows, carrying Ambrose. As they enter, chatterdees turn and cheep amongst themselves, wondering if these late arrivals are important enough to notice. After a closer look, they decide they're not and turn their attention back to the screens.

Taboook, still holding Ambrose, looks around. "So what are we doing here, exactly?"

Joe whispers, "Helping Banshooo delay the launch, to give Jonesy time to get the Image up on the Cubes."

"Who's Jonesy?"

The owl utters a low groan.

Taboook raises his paws. "Hey! No one told me the plan."

Raoul mutters under his breath. "There is no plan. We're acting out of sheer desperation." Sukie jumps up and down, trying to see above the crowd. "Banshooo must be here somewhere." She edges her way down the aisle, reaching the middle of the hall when an usher steps up and asks for her pass. Sukie tries to sound confident. "Oh, I'm sorry. It must be back with my…" She turns to see a new group of officers heading for Raoul's little squad. One of them points to Joe and she hears him say, "That's no scientist. That's the hallucinator."

Raoul finds himself staring at the business end of an Ooozie. A harsh voice utters a low growl. "Hand over the humanoid." Another officer arrives. He points to Taboook and Ambrose and utters one word. "Escapees." Security personnel gather around all of them. A big kingfisher jabs a gun in Taboook's back. "Let's do this quietly, one-off. We don't want to interrupt the ceremony now, do we?"

On stage, the CEO steps to the podium. In the audience, a murmuring begins. It grows louder. Someone in front shouts.

"Hey! What's that monkey doing?"

Everyone looks toward the stage where the CEO, oblivious to all but his place in history, stretches his arms wide and raises his voice.

"And now, I give you a moon we can count on,"

Banshooo scrambles onto the stage.

"…a moon we can control,"

Banshooo runs toward the podium.

"… a moon we can be proud of forever!"

The CEO brings his arm down toward the big black button.

Banshooo yells "Stop!" and leaps at him.

They fall to the floor.

The audience gasps.

Security personnel run down the aisles.

Sukie, Joe, and Raoul try to get to the stage but are held back by the guards. Ambrose rises out of Taboook's arms and sails upward, drawing fire. A shot rings out. The owl is hit, crashing down onto the stage. The audience screams.

Enraged, Mabooose rushes out from the wings and slams both bony hands down onto the button. In the Icefields, the signal propels Mission Control into action. The countdown begins. The screens flash. The engines rumble.

T-minus 10—9—8—

The launch structure starts to vibrate.

7—6

The roar of the engines reaches a peak.

5—4

The rocket trembles.

3—2

In the Total Information Domination Command, Jonesy hits "SEND."

Suddenly the screens flicker off, back on, then off again. A groan rises up from the crowd in the hall, echoed in the streets of the Grand Oooland and everywhere.

A long moment passes.

Then, slowly growing out of the darkness, a vast and glistening network of interconnected threads appears, incredibly delicate and fine, like a spiderweb covered with dew, and in the places where the threads meet there is a flawless jewel, each jewel shining like dew-drops in the morning sun. And every jewel contains the reflection of all the others, and in each of those reflections are the further reflections of all the other reflections and it goes on and on, pulsing within itself, each reflection opening outward, forming and trans-forming in a never-ending dance, creating order out of chaos.

A perfect silence descends on all of Ooolandia. In the Great Hall, in the streets and squares, in the malls and marketplaces, all eyes are consumed. Before them shines the divine diversity of the true nature of reality, the hallowed world that holds within it the breath of every living thing.

In the Total Information Domination Command, the staff sits motionless, immersed in awe, saturated in the shimmering rev-elation. No one moves to delete the transmission or sever the connection.

In the Icefields, the launch crew is mesmerized. The wolverine stares at the Image. His big, flat paw hovers over the two square buttons in the center of the console in front of him, one green, one red.

☾

In OOOCS headquarters, the Colonel is filled with fury. He marches his visored squad into the TIDC where, on his command, they raise their guns and fire a continuous barrage of bullets, killing everyone and sending glass, chromium, aluminum, plastic, cadmium, lead, and zinc exploding throughout the room. Jonesy falls to the floor. His last thought is of his family held in the cradle of the natural world. The screens go dark all over Ooolandia.

❨

The Great Hall is filled with a kind of stopping. Beings stare at the darkened screens, some with tears streaming down their faces, some filled with joy, some shining with a new kind of hope, some in profound confusion. The chatterdees have fallen silent. The visored troops await orders. Everything has simply stopped. A space has opened, a gap in time, a moment holding the possibility of a new awareness.

Then suddenly the stopping stops. A terrible shock hits the hall. Banshooo enfolds Ambrose in his arms. "Hold on, Ambrose, hold on." The owl's beautiful white breast is covered in blood. He murmurs, "I would like to have seen it." His majestic head falls back in death. Banshooo cries out, "No!"

Another shock hits, knocking Banshooo over. A low rumble snakes through everything as the floor beneath him rolls in surges of sickening instability. He tries to rise as pieces of broken marble begin to fall on the stage. The sculpted head of a once great Ooolandian leader crashes inches from his own. He staggers up and sees Morienus paralyzed in fear while ceiling plaster rains down all around him. Their eyes meet just before a huge Corinthian column lands directly on the alchemist's head, killing him instantly.

The tremors intensify. A terrifying force seems ready to rip Ooolandia into pieces. Pillars splinter and break, smashing onto the seats and tearing through the big screens. VIOs and audience alike scatter in all directions, screaming and running for their lives. Banshooo looks out into the hall.

"Taboook! Sukie! Where are you?"

Clouds of dust obscure everything. Banshooo scrambles off the stage and pushes forward. He finds Taboook trying to dig Sukie out from under a pile of chairs. The two of them pull the mouse onto her feet. She's covered in plaster, spitting and coughing and looking for her glasses. They hear Joe yell, "Look out!" as a chunk of marble statuary crashes onto Raoul's head. It bounces off the helmet and onto the floor. The raccoon points to his head and grins, giving a thumbs-up before falling face down in a dead faint.

"Let's get out of here!" Banshooo and Taboook each take one of Sukie's paws, swinging her between them. Joe grabs Raoul's boot and pulls him along behind. Dodging falling debris, they run from the suffocating building.

The air outside is ghostly. Billowing clouds roil the heavens taking on an eerie yellow glow. Rains pound The Grand Oooland, and wind tears through the sky. Trees around the hall are bent to the ground, their leaves scattered like confetti. All across the great lawn, beings hesitate in fright as one seismic jolt after another threatens to crack the earth open.

Banshooo looks around in despair. The alchemist was right. They have failed. The Concord has been broken. A tree limb flies through the air and hits him square on the head. He falls, unconscious.

☾

In the Central Services compound, the quaking has awakened Yomolahki from his nap. The beast is wondering if there's anywhere left that doesn't shake. He's trying to figure out how to go about finding Raoul when he hears footsteps in the hallway. The footsteps grow louder, turn the corner in front of him, and then come to a sudden stop. Yomolahki can't believe it. Here is one of those exotic delicacies his mama used to bring to cheer him up when he was just a little Yomo. He's going to have a nosh now. He'll find Raoul later.

As Mabooose is tossed into the mouth of something very big and orange, the affectless visage of his cold white face shatters in horror.

☾

In the sub-sub-sub-sub-sub-basement of the Biolab, Dr. D. Doootch congratulates himself for having had the foresight to establish a working lab deep underground, on the outside chance that some deluded beings might not realize that what he was doing was for the good of all. Granted, he had not foreseen the current apocalypse, but hey, whatever serves. Now, with a small team of like-minded associates whose recent work in bioinformatics has been very promising, a proto-cell may be within reach. It's not too much to assume that he could create artificial life from scratch. Wet Artificial Life Forms, a new race of beings, a mono race. All the muss, fuss, and bother of that which grows on its own will be replaced by that which can be controlled. He's almost glad it's come to this. He'll be left alone to design life as it was meant to be.

☾

Throughout The Grand Oooland, the quaking continues. Towers sway, wind wails. No one is chattering, chirping, or blinking, no one is in control of anything, and the visored ones are running for their lives along with everyone else. All of Ooolandia shudders and cries out.

Then … suddenly … the quaking stops. In a moment as stunning as when it began, it stops. Abruptly and inexplicably … it all simply stops.

The rain tapers off and the winds diminish. The sound of destruction dies away, and a new soft sound fills the air, like tender breathing. Like a sigh.

Beings of all species gaze about in wonder and confusion. They pull themselves out of the debris and stand trembling, filled with a whole new level of surprise. Tentatively, they begin to wander through the landscape, trying to get their bearings. No collection of sentient beings has ever experienced so many exceptional events within so short a period of time. They are now an entire population limp with the astounding realization that they know nothing.

A siren calls out an all clear. From the center of his consciousness Banshooo hears it growing louder by the second, an enormous wave making a high-pitched whine like a scream. It washes over him, and he is drenched in sound. Then everything becomes extraordinarily quiet.

Sid's face appears.

"Good going, kid. Turns out, the wolverine in the Icefields could see. He stopped the launch at the last second." His brown eyes twinkle. "It was touch and go for awhile there, but The Concord held. Congrats to your whole crew."

"Sid! Wait, Sid!"

"Who the heck is Sid?" Taboook pushes his long nose into Banshooo's face. "You having another one of those visions of yours?"

The monkey stands up shakily and looks around. The earth is unwavering. The sky has cleared. The rain and wind have stopped completely, leaving the panorama of damaged structures and torn foliage oddly, and most unexpectedly, clean. Wreckage lies quiet and still, as if purposefully set in place by some strange event innocent of disaster. A glass shard hangs from a broken frame, catching the last glimmer of light as the sun sets and the night begins.

Taboook takes Banshooo by the shoulders, gently rocking him back and forth in a gesture of relief. Behind Taboook is a big black nose attached to a mound of long brown hair making a snorting sound that might be chuckling but how would you know. Next to the beast is Naomi, her slender fingers wrapped around a bejeweled goblet of gold. She hands the goblet to Banshooo, who whispers, "Ambrosia?"

She smiles. "Water."

As the precious fluid courses through him, his mind clears.

He sees Sukie, whose eyes are twinkling behind her scratched up glasses.

He sees Joe, his guileless smile as wide as a wombat.

He sees Raoul who has shed his disguise, grooming his whiskers and fluffing his fur in anticipation of upcoming chatterdee interviews.

Durga whirls around his head. "Some saw, Banshooo, they really did."

He sees Naruto standing proudly in front of a team of ninja hacker bunnies. Next to them is the staff from the Department of Unforeseen Consequences, a little hungover but glad to be back.

And next to them a motley group shuffles about uncertainly. Joe tilts his head.

"So, who are you guys?"

"We're Some Others."

"Some who?"

"Some Others who were fired because we thought it was a bad idea to eliminate the Department of Nature."

"Oh." Joe nods. "Good. Good to see ya."

Yomolakhi comes lumbering up and plops down next to the bibballooon, holding his belly and looking dyspeptic. Taboook ducks behind Raoul trying to hide himself. "Oh no. After all this, I'm not going out as dinner."

Raoul smiles. "Don't worry, he ate something that really disagreed with him. He's gone vegan."

A wolf howls and a ray of light from a distant constellation lands at Banshooo's feet. In it he sees The Threshold of Perception, the very edge of awareness. He realizes that every little fragment of understanding, every smidgen of comprehension, every integer of discernment, and every compassionate act expands the threshold and increases the potential for wisdom. He sees that his own awareness, and the awareness of every living thing, will play a part in creating what will come, changing the world in a million imperceptible ways until, one day, it is perceived.

A blue crescent appears in the sky then expands steadily, growing fuller and rounder, gleaming brighter and more vivid until it shines in full lunar array. The true blue moon has revealed itself once more, an incandescent backdrop for a gilded flock of migratories moving as one rippling wave in graceful murmuration; a song of consciousness made visible, unfurling across the heavens.

Banshooo looks at the precious beings gathered around him, standing together amidst the wreckage. He takes a deep breath.

"Okay, guys. Let's try again."

Taboook looks at him sideways. "We're gonna eat first though, right?" His lone ear flops about as he trots after them. "No, seriously, Shooo. We need chips."

FIN

Author's Note

David Bohm was one of the most distinguished theoretical physicists of our time. He developed the concept of the Implicate Order, based on the idea that beyond the visible, tangible world there lies a deeper, implicate order of undivided wholeness. It was his hope that one day we would come to recognize the essential interrelatedness of all things and would join together to build a more holistic and harmonious world.

ACKNOWLEGEMENTS

I am grateful for the indispensable advice I received from early readers Hudson Bielecki, Maggie Iapoce, Constance Kieltyka, and Ellen Shifrin. I'm beyond grateful to Marlene Adelstein and Susan Krawitz for their patience, encouragement and astute editorial skills, and to Barbara Bash for reminding me that the heart is as important as the mind; to the wonderful yogini Mary Farel and the participants of the weekly Yoga Café Seminar and Roundtable (you know who you are.) And to Hudson Talbott for all the years and all the knowing; to my hanai sister, Gail Ludwig, and the entire Bielecki Zoo (2 legged, 4 legged, and winged as well.) Couldn't manage without you.

Many thanks to Ellie Sipila and Kirsten Marion and the whole herd at CDP.

And to the most wonderful animal of them all, Gregory Scott Shifrin, for his support and belief and steady energy.

If I have forgotten someone (and I undoubtedly have as so many folks were helpful in this process) please forgive me.

The description of the great web of being is taken from Alan Watts' depiction of Indra's Net, and "Indra's Pearls: The Vision of Felix Klein" by Mumford, Series, and Wright, (from the *Avatamsaka Sutra* – a Buddhist text from the late 3rd or 4th century CE.)

And the phrase "Crunchy on the outside, creamy on the inside" is a riff on a Gary Larsen cartoon featuring two polar bears reaching into an igloo as one says to the other: "Oh hey, I just love these things. Crunchy on the outside and a chewy center."

ABOUT THE AUTHOR

Patricia J Anderson's essays and short stories have appeared in numerous periodicals including *The Sun, Tricycle, Chronogram, Ars Medica, Glamour Magazine* and *Rewire Me.com*. Her books include *All of Us*, a critically acclaimed investigation of cultural attitudes and beliefs, and *Affairs In Order*, named best reference book of the year by Library Journal. She is the recipient of The Communicator Award for online excellence and has produced exhibition, kiosk and website copy for such institutions as the American Museum of Natural History and the Capital Museum. She lives with her family in New York's Hudson Valley.